T0032373

THE INCONVENIENT
HEIRESS

What Reviewers Say About Jane Walsh's Work

Her Duchess to Desire

"One of Walsh's strongest points is her ability to build a strong, positive queer community in a time period that is known to have sometimes been hostile to them. ...I love an Ice Queen heroine who melts in the hands of the right person, and Anne is a great personification of that."—*Courtney Reads Romance*

Her Countess to Cherish

"This book was a nice surprise to me in its portrayal of gender fluidity, along with a delightful romance between two sympathetic characters. If you love queer historical romance, you should absolutely check this out."—*Courtney Reads Romance*

Her Lady to Love

"If you are looking for a sweet, cozy romance with grounded leads, this is for you. The author's dedication to the little cultural details do help flesh out the setting so much more. I also loved how buttery smooth everything tied together. Nothing seemed to be out of place, and the romance had some stakes. ...Highly recommended."
—Colleen Corgel, Librarian, Queens Public Library

"Walsh debuts with a charming if flawed Regency romance. ...Though Honora's shift from shy curiosity to boldly stated interest feels a bit abrupt, her relationship with Jacquie is sweet, sensual, and believable. Subplots about a group of bluestockings and a society of LGBTQ Londoners add depth..."—*Publishers Weekly*

"What a delightful queer Regency era romance. ...*Her Lady to Love* was a beautiful addition to the romance genre, and a much appreciated queer involvement. I'll definitely be looking into more of Walsh's works!"—Dylan Miller, Librarian (Baltimore County Public Library)

"...it's the perfect novel to read over the holidays if you love gorgeous writing, beautiful settings, and literal bodice ripping! I had such a brilliant time with this book. Walsh's novel has such an excellent sense of the time period she's writing in and her specificity and interest in the historical aspects of her plot really allow the characters to shine. The inclusion of details, specifically related to women's behaviour or dress, made for a vivid and exciting setting. This novel reminded me a lot of something like Vanity Fair (1847) (but with lesbians!) because of its gorgeous setting and intriguing plot."—*The Lesbrary*

Visit us at www.boldstrokesbooks.com

By the Author

Her Lady to Love

Her Countess to Cherish

Her Duchess to Desire

The Inconvenient Heiress

THE INCONVENIENT HEIRESS

by

Jane Walsh

2022

THE INCONVENIENT HEIRESS

© 2022 BY JANE WALSH. ALL RIGHTS RESERVED.

ISBN 13: 978-1-63679-173-9

THIS TRADE PAPERBACK ORIGINAL IS PUBLISHED BY
BOLD STROKES BOOKS, INC.
P.O. BOX 249
VALLEY FALLS, NY 12185

FIRST EDITION: AUGUST 2022

THIS IS A WORK OF FICTION. NAMES, CHARACTERS, PLACES, AND INCIDENTS ARE THE PRODUCT OF THE AUTHOR'S IMAGINATION OR ARE USED FICTITIOUSLY. ANY RESEMBLANCE TO ACTUAL PERSONS, LIVING OR DEAD, BUSINESS ESTABLISHMENTS, EVENTS, OR LOCALES IS ENTIRELY COINCIDENTAL.

THIS BOOK, OR PARTS THEREOF, MAY NOT BE REPRODUCED IN ANY FORM WITHOUT PERMISSION.

CREDITS
EDITOR: CINDY CRESAP
PRODUCTION DESIGN: SUSAN RAMUNDO
COVER DESIGN BY TAMMY SEIDICK

Acknowledgments

Thank you to the team at Bold Strokes Books for the amazing work that they do. Thanks especially to my editor, Cindy, for all her feedback, guidance, and encouragement.

Thank you to my parents, for the seaside summers where our toes were in the sand and our noses were firmly buried in a book. I cherish many happy memories of the bungalows, late night Scrabble, the sound of the ocean and Fleetwood Mac, and bottomless pitchers of Sangria. Thank you for making it magical.

This book is about best friends, so it's a good time for me to thank my very best friend D for thousands of hours of chatting through the decades. From landlines to cell phones, in person and online, you've enriched my life forever with your friendship.

I couldn't do any of this without Mag's support and endless patience. Your enthusiasm for my work encourages me to aim higher and go further than I could have dreamed on my own. You've turned my writing studio into a flower garden with every hand-picked rose, and I couldn't be more grateful for your love.

Dedication

For Mag—forever my summertime girl
with the awesome tattoos

CHAPTER ONE

Inverley, 1813

Caroline Reeve hadn't been born with a head for figures. She felt the pain of it every time she sat down with the household ledger and tried to justify a joint of beef for dinner instead of another night of pigeon pie.

She thumbed open the thick book, her temples aching when she saw last week's tally of what she owed to the grocer. It was difficult to economize in a family of six, and finding new ways to squeeze their savings was an endless task. What little money Papa had left them seemed to slip through her grasp faster than a fistful of sand.

She blew out a sigh and picked up her pen with the gravity of a judge. It was never any use to run away from the facts. Will had spilled ink all over his Sunday trousers, doubtlessly during an argument with George. Now she needed to find enough coin for new ink *and* new clothes or she could never show her face in front of the vicar again. Reverend Thomson was good enough to tutor her brothers without charging for the lessons, and she couldn't bear to have them showing up to church full of stains after all his help.

Giggles and the clicking of shoes announced the presence of her two sisters before they bounced into the room. Betsy was tall and slender with a mass of brown curls framing her cheeks, and Susan was short with dark blond hair that she was fond of arranging into intricate braids. The pair of them were inclined to model their looks after naughty milkmaids, hiking their skirts as high as they could manage without appearing completely brazen, and tugging low the linen fichus tucked into their bodices.

"Caro, darling Caro! We are going out," Betsy announced, tying her straw bonnet beneath her chin with a bright purple ribbon that Caroline couldn't recall paying for. She hoped it hadn't been begged from a suitor. Her pride was hanging by a shred among the shopkeepers, and she couldn't bear it if they thought her sisters shameless on top of it all.

Susan peered over her shoulder and wrinkled her nose. "Figures *again*, Caro? Do you not ever do anything fun anymore?"

Caroline tugged one of her braids. "Not unless we wish to live on scraps of butter spread on crumbs of bread."

Susan sighed and moved away. "You worry too much. Everything's all right these days. The Reeve family is doing fine."

Because I take care of it all. But Caroline bit back the words. "Heading to the shore, are you?"

"To *town*, of course. Town is ever so much more interesting than the boring old sea."

Betsy fluffed her curls and she and Susan dissolved into giggles again.

Once visitors started to arrive from London for the summer, their attitude would change, and Caroline would hear nothing from dawn to dusk but rapturous praise for the endless diversions of the seaside.

"Stay out of trouble," she told them. "And be home in time for dinner."

They groused and rolled their eyes, then clattered their way to the front door.

Caroline looked down at the ledger again and bit her lip. Surely the household account could spare something for the girls? They were full of mischief, but still carefree enough to wish for nothing more than to spend their last ha'penny on lemon drops or a new lace trim for their skirts. Harmless enough pleasures.

Her heart clutched as she remembered Betsy's pale face and thin cheeks, her forehead burning up with fever, and she made up her mind. If she could bargain parsnips from a neighbor in exchange for doing their laundry, then she could lessen their bill from the grocer.

"Wait!"

Caroline went to the door and pressed a farthing into each of their palms. Her temples ached anew as her ears filled with shrieks of sisterly gratitude, and she found herself smothered in kisses.

"You are the best of sisters, Caro! Never doubt it!"

"Mind you don't spend it unwisely."

"Caro Lamb would be more understanding of our situation," Betsy called out as they left.

"Well, Caro Lamb isn't your sister. Caro Reeve is, and she says to *behave like a lady*!"

The door slammed shut before she finished admonishing them, but it was nothing that they hadn't heard from her before.

Betsy was the second eldest Reeve at twenty-three, and Susan was but a scant fourteen months behind her. Either of them ought to be helping more with the accounts and the household chores. But it didn't matter how old her siblings were. Caroline would always be the eldest, and she couldn't bring herself to burden her family with the responsibilities that were her duty to shoulder as best she could.

After all, she had made a promise.

She slumped over the ledger and tried not to be envious of a trip to town that she didn't even want. She wasn't young enough to be distracted from her problems by ribbons, and she had never been interested in making eyes at the local lads. If only her sisters weren't determined to make up for her own lack of interest by making sure they were twice as outrageous as any of the other young ladies in Inverley.

She strained her ears for sounds of her other siblings. It was reassuring to hear nothing but low-pitched chatter from the back garden, which meant that their maid-of-all-work, Maisie, was still outside with George and Will. They would be occupied for a while yet. Jacob was God knew where, but should be working. She wished it wasn't such an uncertain hope. The shopkeeper he worked for had dropped hints in her ears more than once that he could always find another lad if Jacob wasn't interested in coming in every day.

A half hour and a page of scrawled numbers later, Caroline pushed the ledger away. It was midafternoon on Wednesday, after all, which was her favorite time of the week.

In fact…she rose to her toes and peered out the kitchen window to be rewarded with the sight of Arabella Seton ducking into her brother's house next door.

Right on time.

"I'm afraid the tea isn't fresh," Caroline called out when she heard the front door creak open, though she wasn't worried that Arabella would turn up her nose. It was all too common for her to be offered twice or thrice steeped tea in the Reeve household.

Arabella wandered into the kitchen. She wasn't a woman who rushed, moving at the slow pace of life in Inverley, as if not only her head but her whole body was in the clouds far above. She was a dreamer, as optimistic as could be, and Caroline's very best friend.

She was short and soft and comfortably plump all over, without an angle to be found on her anywhere—and Caroline had looked. Her spectacles perched on her snub nose; her round cheeks, the color and shape of a ripe peach, flushed at the slightest attention, provocation, or surprise; and her elbows and wrists had little dimples in them where the bend was, instead of sharp bone. Even her honey brown curls were short and full, bouncing around her face under her bonnet.

Caroline preferred to think of her as adorable, or sweet, both of which she was in spades. After all, Arabella wouldn't be interested. And Caroline had sworn off the idea of any kind of dalliance with anyone who lived in Inverley, sticking to uncomplicated affairs with visitors' companions or fellow spinsters who were in town for a few days at most. It helped prevent her from thinking of Arabella's other assets, which distracted her eye far too often for comfort.

Her lush bosom, peeking above the neckline of her muslin evening dresses or nestled snugly under her cambric day dresses.

Her full bottom, which often pressed close to her own on benches and picnic blankets.

Her curved lips, overlarge and meant for kissing.

Caroline poured the tea with a little more force than necessary.

"I brought you a book from the library," Arabella announced, the same as she did every Wednesday.

She set her reticule on the table and fished out a slender novel from its depths, spilling a trail of ginger comfits along with it. She thrust the book at Caroline, accepted a cup of tea in return, and sat down in a rickety wooden chair that she knew from long experience exactly how to balance against the table at the right angle to stabilize it.

"It's the very newest Inverley has to offer. Scarcely two months behind London this time." She beamed and pushed her wire-framed spectacles up the bridge of her nose.

She really was adorable.

"Thanks, Bell. I appreciate you going to the trouble."

Caroline didn't have time for novels, or money for a subscription to the lending library. But she couldn't help squeezing in moments of reading here and there among the chaos that was the Reeve household, and Arabella knew it.

"It was no trouble at all." Arabella sipped her tea and rebalanced the chair. "I picked up a new book on painting techniques for myself."

Arabella sold watercolor landscapes to the visitors that swarmed the seaside each summer. Inverley made for pretty pictures, with its dramatic cliffs and walks, its shimmering sea and sandy shores, and its quaint village life that charmed Londoners out of coin every year. Caroline frowned. Most of the coins Arabella earned ended up in her brother's pocket.

"Is Matthew going to stay out of it, then?" she asked, scowling down at the book.

"I might talk to him." Her pretty face was full of the clouds that her head was usually immersed in, and Caroline hated the doubts that chased away Arabella's good humor.

"You do that," she said. "And if he doesn't listen to you, then I'll come over and set him to rights."

Arabella laughed, her face clearing. "I know you would. But I wouldn't ask it of you. You have too many family troubles of your own to handle mine as well."

Caroline had to acknowledge the truth of it. She always had her hands full of Reeve problems.

Shelley, one of Arabella's cats, leapt through the kitchen window and meowed a welcome at them. He was big, orange, and thick-witted, and an overall nuisance in Caroline's mind—but the rest of the Reeves doted on him.

"He's here for a visit," Arabella crooned. "What a clever kitty."

Shelley meowed again and pushed himself against Caroline's ankles. She tried to nudge him away, but he leaned against her and started purring. "He's just worried it's market day and he's missing out on fish." He had been successful only once in his pilfering, but Caroline had held a dim view of him since.

Arabella scooped him up together with her reticule. "Well, I should be going. Shall we walk together to the Martins' dinner party tomorrow evening?"

"I should like nothing better. Betsy and Susan promised to stay home and watch the young ones, and I have been looking forward to a free evening for ages."

She loved her brothers and sisters and felt a fierce responsibility for their health and happiness, no more so than if they had been her own children. She had borne the responsibility of them since she had been eighteen. Nine years ago now.

She had no regrets.

Sometimes though, in a quiet moment before falling asleep, Caroline wished for more. More opportunity for frivolity and leisure. More money. More family to help her shoulder the responsibility, but alas they had no aunts or uncles or cousins.

It was one reason she was so grateful for Arabella, and why she would never act on her attraction to her. It wasn't worth risking the friendship of the most important person in her life outside her family.

She pushed those thoughts aside, like her admiration for Arabella's curves. Neither had a place in her life. She was dedicated to her family, and everything else was a distraction she could no more afford than the joint of beef for dinner.

❖

If Inverley was small by country village standards, it was positively tiny compared to London. Arabella had heard the comparisons more times than she could count from visitors. They claimed to be shocked to hear that anyone could live in such constraints all year round, with the sea air forever making one's hair a quiz, and no more than five and twenty families well-bred enough to make up a card table in the evening! They made no bones about hiding such amazement while they riffled through her paintings.

It was thoroughly irritating.

But Arabella needed their money, so every summer she smiled and laughed alongside them, though sometimes she felt like pouring her dirty paint water over their sneering faces and fashionable skirts.

From the window in the attic room that she worked in, she could see the water. It was calm today, but she heard the waves lapping against the sand. The constant sound of the ocean could be heard from most everywhere in Inverley, as the town was settled shallowly by the long shoreline.

Arabella stroked her paintbrush against the pad of paint, mazarine blue saturating the damp bristles. She pressed the side of the brush against the thick textured paper and watched as color flooded the seascape. She blotted the paint with a handkerchief to lift color away from the whitecaps cresting the waves, then continued to add splashes and layers of paint. Green where the sun hit the water's surface, violet where the bluffs cast shadows and turned the water murky and mysterious.

It was easy to picture it in her mind's eye. After all, she produced the same paintings every year. The same views. The same colors. The clientele changed each summer, but they all wanted the same thing. A tiny slice of holiday to tuck into their valise and then hang up in their parlor at home to remind them of the happiness of time away from their everyday.

Creating that slice of holiday was *her* everyday, and it didn't exactly fill her with the same joy as it did the eye of the beholder.

She shook her head clear. She was grateful for her life.

All but one of her twenty-seven years had been spent in Inverley. Countless hours had been racked up roaming the shore, collecting shells and pretty pebbles, and walking with friends. Losing herself in thoughts and dreams and fancies with the crash of the waves for company.

She flung the window open to the warm June air and the scent of the sea, and Shelley leapt to the windowsill with his orange tail twitching. Her other cat, Byron, was a dark grey shadow napping on a stack of canvas cloths that she draped over finished paintings to protect them from the elements.

Footsteps sounded in the stairwell, and Matthew propped a shoulder against the door of the whitewashed room that abutted the servants' quarters. He crossed his arms over his barrel chest. "That's a pretty one, Arabella. Should fetch a pretty penny, too."

Her brother was a cheerful and uncomplicated man with an unshakable faith in his own decisions, and for the most part, Arabella liked living with him and his wife, Rachel. She paid her share of expenses through her painting sales, and she and Rachel handled most of the household duties together, with a pair of maids and a manservant to help with the rest. Matthew's business was ropemaking, and he and his business partner did a brisk trade in ropes and nets for the fishermen and sailors who worked the shores.

"Thank you. I have quite a few that I prepared in advance of the influx of visitors." She turned on the stool and smiled at him, her stomach twisting into such elaborate knots that a sailor would envy them. "I hope it will be a profitable season."

It was on the tip of her tongue to talk about finances. Caroline had long thought that Matthew took more than his fair share, and Arabella always *meant* to talk to him about it—but never found the courage to speak up. She had plans for any extra money she could gain. She wanted nothing more than to set herself up in a snug little cottage of her own. But she hated confrontation, which led to arguing, and then shouting and tears and unforgiveable words.

She was far too worried about disrupting her peaceful life to voice even mild dissonance.

"It's clever of you to plan ahead. And it's fortuitous timing." He pushed away from the doorframe, his chest puffing out. "I have excellent news."

"Really? Were you successful to increase your yarn stock at last?"

"No—though that's still in progress. If we can store more hemp fiber in the warehouse, we can increase our production, and life will be good indeed. No, Arabella, this news is far better than business. I am overjoyed to tell you that Rachel is expecting a child."

"Oh!" She leapt from the stool so fast that it toppled over, startling Shelley and Byron into running for the stairwell. She threw herself against Matthew and wrapped her arms as far as they would reach around his sturdy frame. "Oh, I am so happy for you both."

Rachel and Matthew had been married for years before Arabella had moved into their house, and that had been over a decade ago. They had never had any children, and at this point had no longer expected it to happen.

"Good things come to those who wait, I suppose," Matthew said gruffly as he pulled away, his eyes bright with unshed tears. "Rachel is looking forward to your help."

"My help?"

"Why, we shall need you as a nursemaid, of course. You'll have time, don't worry about that—the babe will arrive in October. Long after the last of the visitors leave. It will be good to have the income this summer from the extra paintings you have done, and then your help after." He grinned at her.

Arabella smiled in reflex, though her stomach pitched. *Nursemaid?* She knew nothing about babies. But her lips were moving, and she heard herself say, "Of course."

Dash it all, why was it so hard to say *no*?

"I knew we could count on you." He squeezed her shoulder and went down the stairs.

Arabella looked down at her work in progress, then at the stack of finished paintings on the table. How many would she need to sell to have enough money to leave her brother's house before the babe was born?

Did even thinking about it make her a terrible sister?

She was terribly afraid that it did.

But October was a long way away. There was time enough to worry about that later. After all, what was the point to dwell on something upsetting when there wasn't anything to be done about it now? It was far better to focus on putting away her paints and getting ready for the party at the Martins' tonight.

With Caroline.

Ah, Caroline.

She was never a source of unhappy thoughts. Except, of course, for the single unhappiest thought of all of Arabella's life—the undeniable, shocking truth, which could never be spoken aloud.

Arabella was in love with her.

It was a forbidden type of love that could never, ever be returned.

Caroline would be horrified if she ever learned of her true feelings. Any decent woman would be, Arabella had concluded long ago, miserable at the thought that she suffered such unnatural desires.

But it didn't feel unnatural, despite the hushed and horrified murmurs that accompanied any mention of such things.

Instead, it felt…lovely.

Beautiful.

Perfect.

If only her love could be returned, Arabella thought she might be the happiest person in Inverley.

It was too bad for her that it was impossible.

Chapter Two

A rabella polished her spectacles and pulled on her shawl before taking her leave of Matthew and Rachel. She let herself into the Reeves' house without knocking and called a greeting up the stairs before settling into an armchair in the drawing room.

George ran in. "Bell!"

She took in the muddy knees of his breeches, the dirt beneath his fingernails, and his wild, gleeful grin. "What have you been up to today?"

"Playing sticks in the sea," he said. "But then Will told me on the way home that he thought he threw his stick the furthest, so I had to wrestle him."

"George Reeve, come here this instant!" Susan appeared in the doorway with a towel and a cake of soap, a look of menace on her normally sweet-tempered face.

He shrieked and ran off with Susan in pursuit, and Caroline appeared at the top of the stairs. "Let us be off, shall we? Susan and Betsy can manage for the evening."

Caroline's dress was plain cambric, unlike the wispy muslins that they both envied on the Londoners who flooded Inverley every summer like the tides. She wore gloves that Arabella knew were shared among the Reeve sisters for occasions like this. There was a patch near the hem of her skirt, but who could notice such a detail when her petticoats fluttered and revealed her ankles as she hurried down the stairs?

Caroline was the most elegant creature that Arabella could imagine. Her chestnut brown hair was glossy and held a curl as easy as anything. Her eyebrows winged away from her eyes in a high arch. Her dark eyes were fringed with long lashes, which Arabella had often cried out that she would kill for when they had been younger. Her high cheekbones and slender nose and firm chin held a classical sort of beauty that Arabella saw on the paintings in the grand houses that ringed round Inverley. They didn't exist on mere mortals.

Except on Caroline.

Arabella did wish there was a way for those worry lines across her brow to be erased for good, as well as the deep smudges of exhaustion under her eyes, which stood out in stark contrast against her pale skin. But Caroline maintained that her family came first, and she would not rest until they were all grown and settled. With her youngest brother, Will, at ten years of age, there was a long time before that could come to pass.

They took one step outside the front door when Caroline stopped. "Do you smell that?"

She did. The faint acrid smell of cheroot smoke.

Caroline sprinted to the back garden, and Arabella waited and listened.

"Jacob Reeve, what did I tell you about such a vile habit? Besides, we haven't any extra money to spare for you to smoke a penny away at your leisure!"

"Aw, Caro, you're no fun at all." Jacob laughed. "Besides, I nicked it, so don't worry about the cost."

"*Nicked* it—oh, Jacob!" Their voices disappeared with the slam of the back door, then Caroline came sailing out through the front again.

"That boy will be the death of me," she said, color high on her cheeks as they set off across town to the Martins' house. She sucked in a deep breath. "But tonight I wish to put the worry of every Reeve behind me."

"This will be a nice evening," Arabella said, darting a look at Caroline's face. It warmed her heart to see her face ease into a smile. "The Martins always set out a lovely supper."

The Martins belonged to a respectable younger branch of an earl's family, having settled in Inverley two generations ago. They had built the largest estate in the area, nestled beside the cliffs overlooking the sea.

Caroline laughed. "It's rare enough that you or I get to enjoy it. I'm sure we were invited with such last-minute notice to even the numbers for their card tables, now that their son is home for the summer. Mr. Martin's desire for whist trumps the usual order of things, does it not?"

With unspoken agreement born from long habit, they crossed the lane and took the shorter route to the Martins' house by walking along the beach. It was cool by the water, and Caroline shivered. Arabella pulled the thin wool shawl from her own shoulders and tossed it to Caroline. She would prefer to feel the chill all night than see Caroline in even one moment's discomfort.

Caroline sighed in relief and rubbed her hands up her shawl-wrapped arms. All Arabella wanted was to be wrapped up inside the shawl with her.

She swallowed. This way lay dangerous thoughts indeed.

Arabella's feet faltered as they approached the house, and she had to force herself through the door. The reason for her reluctance were standing in the parlor. Mr. James Martin was a Corinthian and the eldest of the Martin brothers, overly proud of his high collars and groomed sideburns and skin-tight tan trousers. He also had a fondness for what he deemed to be little witticisms, which were less than witty and more than mean-spirited.

"Miss Arabella Seton is here to grace us with her presence," James drawled, then dropped his quizzing glass. "But *grace* is hardly the word I am looking for, is it?"

His voice was low enough that his parents couldn't hear him, but Arabella felt her cheeks burn.

Caroline glared at him. "I see London hasn't improved your manners. Do recall that we are all respectable adults but I still remember your days in shortcoats. We have known you too long."

He winked at her. " '*Age cannot wither her, nor custom stale her infinite variety.*' You are indeed a treasure, Caroline. I am always delighted to see you. You are as beautiful as ever, and you know how I value beauty."

She touched Arabella's arm to steer her toward their hosts, Mr. and Mrs. Martin, and Arabella concentrated on the warmth of her fingers. "Thank you," she murmured, and slid her spectacles up. She wished she had the courage to throw such retorts around, but was grateful that Caroline was always there for her.

"I swear James exists to torment us," she said with a shake of her head. "Flirting with me, and making sport of you. Wretched man."

After making the round of greetings and introductions, for the Martins had invited a variety of early arrivals to Inverley to their party, Arabella and Caroline were led to their card table.

Arabella bumped into the table before sitting down and her face flamed again as she recalled James's slight, but she pushed it out of her mind and turned her attention to the women already seated with them.

"Welcome to Inverley," she said, while studying the quality of their gowns to try to determine whether she would be able to interest them into purchasing a painting.

Miss Maeve Balfour's dress was made of fashionable silk the color of champagne, and she wore lacy black gloves that Arabella greatly admired. She was beautiful, with rosy-red lips, coal black hair piled high on her head, and a smattering of freckles across her nose and cheeks. Promising for her pocketbook, though Arabella feared her tastes were too expensive for what she could offer.

Miss Grace Linfield wore a simple pink gown that was fetching against her light brown curls, but which spoke of no significant income or pin money. She had a long oval face and a serene smile.

"My mother insisted on visiting for the summer," Miss Balfour said. "She is on an eternal search for relief from megrims, and we have tried many such watering holes—Brighton, Margate, Sidmouth, and now...Inverley."

"The waters here are reckoned to be quite good," Arabella said. "I hope your mother benefits from her time here."

"Oh, nothing pleases her," she said. "We have come all the way from Ireland to England in search of help with no end in sight, and I have started to wonder if my dear Mama perhaps wishes to spend my stepfather's coin without the bother of his presence."

Arabella blinked. This was plain speaking indeed.

Caroline laughed. "Inverley offers plenty of ways for her to part with her money if she so chooses. Everything that you may have already seen in other resort towns, I suppose—donkey rides, sea bathing, spa treatments. I am assured by the brochures that we have all the usual activities here."

Miss Linfield smiled as she broke open a new pack of cards and shuffled them. "It seems you are seeking a more exciting summer than I, Miss Balfour. I am here as a companion to a young lady, Lady Edith, and we are guests of the Martin family for the summer. Lady Edith's mother has charged me with ensuring that she has a peaceful time after the stresses of her first Season."

"I can well understand," Caroline said. "My sisters are rambunctious, and I am hoping they too will settle down for the summer."

"Well, be careful what you wish for," Miss Balfour said with a laugh. "I told my mother I couldn't wait to leave rainy Ireland, and here I am in the corner of England instead of London where I longed to go."

"My sisters beg me to take them to London, but I am afraid our circumstances are such that their curiosity is most unlikely to be satisfied."

"How many sisters do you have?" Miss Linfield asked.

"Two sisters and three brothers, two of whom are still in school. The older ones have dreams that exceed Inverley's charms, I am afraid." Her smile was strained.

"Family is more important than money, or a Season in the capital," Arabella said firmly.

Miss Balfour smiled. "I cannot see any good reason why one cannot have it all."

They were quiet as they played the first round, until Miss Balfour crowed when she won. They were but shilling stakes, but Arabella pushed over coins for both herself and Caroline. Caroline gave her a grateful smile.

"By the way, I heard what that odious toad said to you upon your entrance, Miss Seton," Miss Balfour said as she gathered up the cards for her turn to shuffle. "Is he always so charming?"

Arabella's face burned again. "We have known each other for a long time. James likes to remind me that before I got my spectacles, I often bumped into things. He admires Caroline as much as he derides me."

"A man like that is why I shall never marry," Miss Linfield said with quiet dignity.

Miss Balfour slowed her shuffling. "I too never seek to marry. I didn't expect to find myself in such like company this summer. I suppose Miss Seton and Miss Reeve are beset with suitors?"

Arabella's palms felt clammy. She didn't dare look up from the table. She had been teased long enough by Caroline to know that her face showed every emotion, whether she wished it to or not, and right now she felt sick with worry.

She was *not* beset with suitors. But nor did she wish to be.

Caroline snorted. "No one looks twice at an aging spinster with a passel of the least well-behaved siblings in the entire county. I am content to do my duty for my brothers and sisters and see them well settled instead of myself."

Miss Linfield nodded. "I am devoted to my charge as well."

Miss Balfour tapped a finger on the pack of cards. "What of Miss Seton?" she asked. "Are you the sole one of us intending on capturing a husband one of these fine summer afternoons?"

Arabella didn't dare look at Caroline. She cleared her throat. "I—"

"Oh, Arabella has no interest in a husband," Caroline said as Arabella started to speak.

Wild hope leapt in her heart alongside terror at being perceived, but when she darted her eyes at Caroline, she was looking at the cards in her hand. With a start, she realized there was a pile in front of her as well. She fumbled to pick them up.

"She's a wonderful painter," Caroline continued. "Beautiful seascapes. If either of you are interested in artwork to bring back with you, do look her up on Belvoir Lane."

Disappointment filled Arabella, even though she knew Caroline was being supportive and kind. For once, she wanted to hold onto the dream that maybe Caroline felt something too. That perhaps Arabella wasn't the only spinster in Inverley who felt the pull toward another woman.

She scowled down at her cards, and hardly paid attention to the conversation for the rest of the evening. Her thoughts were in such disarray that she had to be asked twice if she wished for more wine.

A whole barrel might have done the trick, but it would be a scandal for a respectable spinster to drown her sorrows in a bottomless glass, so she demurred. A glass alone would do nothing to help hide the sadness she felt tonight.

❖

Mending never truly ended. The basket beneath the chair in the parlor was forever full of socks to be darned, breeches to be patched, shirts and shifts to be stitched back together at their well-worn seams. Whenever she could, Caroline pressed Betsy and Susan into work, though their focus when mending was attaching new ribbon to their petticoats or lowering the neckline again of their worn out evening gowns.

No matter what Caroline did, the pile never grew smaller.

She picked up a linen chemise and threaded her needle.

Jacob lounged against the doorframe, fiddling with a cheroot in one hand, his other stuck in his pocket. His hair was fashionably long and rumpled, as he had refused the offer of Caroline's scissors for months.

Caroline resisted the urge to roll her eyes. No doubt her little brother thought himself the Lothario of Inverley, but if she didn't hear recriminations from the local matrons, she supposed it was normal enough to allow him to sow his wild oats.

"Do not even consider lighting that in my parlor," Caroline said, eying the cheroot.

"Worry not. I only have the one and must save it for later when meeting up with the lads."

His friends were the same that Jacob had known since they were in leading strings. It was difficult to reconcile the languid men that they had become with the tousle-haired, jam-smeared boys that she remembered running around her house, tin soldiers in one hand and wooden sailboats in the other.

He pushed himself away from the door and strutted into the room, and Caroline hid her smile over the mending. He slouched into the chair across from her, one booted leg stuck in front of him.

Caroline put another handful of stitches into the chemise. "I don't see as much of you as I would like these days."

"Life as a shopkeeper's assistant doesn't suit me as well as I would like, but I have no choice," he said, frowning down at the cheroot that he was twisting in his fingers so hard that Caroline feared the paper would tear and tobacco would be spilt all over the fresh-swept floor. "I work all day, then see my friends in the evening. But it's a good enough life, I suppose."

"There's any number of women in the neighborhood who would be happy to have an offer from you, if you should want to set up your own household."

"I've years ahead of me before I have anything of note to offer anyone. The lads and I must be content enough with dancing above the grocer's shop whenever old Mr. Brown is content to play his fiddle of an evening." Jacob's smile was wry.

Caroline wished things were different for him. For all that she worked to provide a good upbringing for her siblings, it was never enough to give any of them what they truly *wanted*, and she felt the pang of it every day.

There was a knock at the door, and Susan clambered down the stairs to answer it. An unfamiliar voice floated in from the front of the house, and Susan appeared in the parlor doorway with a gentleman following her.

Caroline stared. He was tall and broad-chested, his boots glossier than she had thought possible for even the best quality leather, without a hair out of place on his perfectly coiffed head.

"Excuse me, would you happen to be Miss Caroline Reeve?" His voice was deep and authoritative.

"I am." Her pulse sped up. She wasn't expecting any visitors.

Jacob puffed out his chest. "I am her brother, Jacob Reeve. What business do you have here, sir?"

"I am Mr. Taylor, and I bring good tidings, young man."

Caroline tried not to be intimidated by the crisp lines of the man's suit or the elegance of his bow as she curtsied in return. This man was a stranger. From his appearance, he was a perfectly respectable stranger, but the hairs stood on her neck.

"Please, be seated," she said, injecting as much confidence as she could find into her voice.

"I have been looking for you, Miss Reeve, for quite some time."

Caroline tried to tamp down her fear. He sounded amused, but she found no humor in this visit. She was glad that Jacob was here, and that Susan remained at the door, hesitant to come in and looking ready to flee on an instant's notice from Caroline.

"Now you have found me, Mr. Taylor. What is it you are here for?"

He couldn't be a creditor. Could he? She didn't owe *that* much in town, not even to the grocer. But if it were about money, it would be bankers come to visit, surely? And would a banker wear a coat of superfine that showed no obvious wear, or boots that shone like a mirror?

"Are you aware of your father's relations, Miss Reeve?"

Fear clutched her heart like a vise. Had her father owed debts of honor to this gentleman before his passing?

She straightened her shoulders. Best to get to the point of the conversation as quick as she could, and then she could make a plan. She did well with plans.

"I do not, sir," she said. "We never met the family, I'm afraid. After my father's marriage, they wanted nothing to do with him. I believe they are somewhere in Somerset."

Her understanding was that her father had been meant to marry well enough to support himself, but married for love instead of marrying someone to raise him into grander consequence.

Or into sufficient funds to start his family, though that was less than charitable. She had adored her parents. And while they had lived, they had always kept the family finances well enough together. It was after the fever had struck that Caroline discovered the shallow pockets that remained to their name.

"Your grandfather, Sir Francis, is dead," Mr. Taylor said. "He has left a hefty bequest to his heir's family."

Jacob sat up straight, and Susan leaned into the room, her eyes bright with interest.

"His heir? Then you have the wrong household," Caroline said. "My father was the fourth and youngest son, from what I remember of his stories."

"Why are you here, sharing this news? Why has a solicitor not come to call?" Jacob demanded. "Is this some kind of hoax?"

"Your father's brothers all passed without issue before your father died nine years ago. He was therefore the rightful heir to a baronetcy." He turned to Jacob and bowed. "Which makes you, young man, Sir Jacob Reeve—the current baronet."

CHAPTER THREE

*W*hat?" Jacob half-rose, then crashed back into his chair. His eyes were glassy and his mouth was open like a fish, as unlike his usual air of fashionable ennui as one could get.

Caroline wished, suddenly and desperately, for Shelley or Byron to come mewling their way through her kitchen window so she could clutch one of them to her chest for support.

"Is this true?" she asked. Her hands were gripping the edge of her seat so hard that her fingers hurt.

"I am your second cousin, once removed. I thought I held the title and the holdings for these past few years, but recent investigation proved me wrong. I cede them to you." He gave Jacob a curt nod. "Sir Jacob."

"I didn't know we had any cousins," Susan said, stepping further into the room. She was radiating joy. "Let alone titled cousins. This is *thrilling*."

"Say not a word of this to anyone," Caroline snapped at her, and glowered at Mr. Taylor. "What proof do you have of any of this? How are we to know that you are who you say you are? And how do you know that we are who we say we are?"

He looked affronted. Not accustomed to anyone questioning him, she supposed. Good. Served him right to be interrogated now. What business did he have, barging into houses and disrupting lives and throwing everything into disarray?

"I am a man of honor. Besides, I took the liberty of consulting with Inverley's vicar. He is not the same one as held the post while your parents were alive, but he let me see the books."

"You looked up my parents' wedding records before coming to see us?" Ice ran through her veins, followed by hot fire. "You doubted that they were honorably wed?"

He grinned at her. "As you said—how do we know each other? A wise man finds out the truth first. We were unable to track down your branch of the family years ago. Luck was on our side when we managed to find you now. I wanted to be certain of the connection." He rose and gave them a short bow. "A solicitor is on his way from the Somerset estate to review the paperwork with you tomorrow. In the meantime, I am staying at the hotel on Church Street with my secretary if you wish to find me." He put his hat on his head and strode out.

For once, Caroline experienced complete silence in the Reeve household. She and Jacob stared at each other in shock.

Then Susan squealed and grabbed Caroline's hands, pulling her up from the chair and into a wild swing around the room. "We shall be *rich*! Think of the ribbons we shall buy!"

"No!" Caroline snapped and wrested her hands away as Susan's face fell. "I meant what I said. *Tell no one.* How do we know if we can trust this man? What if this is some cruel jest?"

"Why would anyone jest about such a thing?" Jacob rose to his feet and passed a shaking hand over his face. "Caro—if this is true— it's no jest, but a *miracle*."

"I cannot wait for Betsy to come home! I can tell her, at least. And little Will and George. Why, it will be ever so fun to see their faces!" Susan danced out of the room and hummed her way up the stairs, no doubt to collapse into daydreams in the room she shared with her sister.

Caroline grasped Jacob's shoulders. "Please tell me that you share my reservations about this."

"If what he said is true—I can quit working tomorrow." His jaw was set, his eyes wild. "Imagine, a baronetcy! The boys will think this is capital. And it *is*, Caro! You worry too much. You always have."

"Quit! You shall leave the shopkeeper in a bad position if you leave with such little notice."

He took a step back. "And how am I to explain that Sir Jacob is keeping his hands dirty for the fun of it! No, Caroline. I won't have it."

He stormed out, slamming the front door.

Caroline sucked in a breath. This was outrageous. Her whole family was against her. For surely Betsy would side with Susan and start dreaming of shillings pouring out of the cracks in the walls. Will and George were too young to be anything but excited.

The only person who could keep a secret and who would always be sympathetic to how she felt, no matter what, was Arabella.

Arabella, who knew her better than anyone, who had been by her side since they had been children, who had held her hand as she wept over the loss of her parents, would understand.

❖

Arabella sat on the double-sided swing in the back garden and pushed it into motion with one foot against the wooden stand. She heard the familiar crash of waves pounding against the shore, and crickets chirping from the bushes that surrounded their square of lawn, but she didn't trust that her ears were working properly.

They couldn't be.

If they were, then it meant that Caroline had told her something that made no sense whatsoever.

Arabella gave the swing another push. "I don't understand."

Byron jumped onto her lap and she ran her hand over his sleek grey fur, trying to find comfort. He purred as he curled into a ball.

Caroline leaned in, her face bright, and pulled Byron onto her own lap. "I don't understand it either! It's a mystery to me how Mr. Taylor couldn't find us sooner. I hadn't imagined my father hiding his whereabouts from his own family. I always thought that they wanted nothing to do with us after his marriage."

"No, that's not it." Arabella bit her lip. "I don't understand why you aren't *happy* about this."

Caroline had rushed into her garden where Arabella had been reading her novel. She had been about to offer tea when Caroline had started pouring out this extraordinary story.

Caroline sat back on her side of the swing, pushing it a little higher, a cloud passing over her face. "I'm happy enough about it." Her words were clipped, and she averted her eyes.

Arabella shook her head. "You've been handed what may well be a fortune, and Jacob now has a *title*. This is beyond all wildest imagination." Her mind reeled at the implications of what this meant for the Reeves. "Why, all of your problems are solved, Caroline."

There was a bitter taste in her mouth as she said it. Would that her own problems could be so easily fixed! But for all her dreams and fancies, she had never contemplated the jaw-dropping possibility of someone swooping in and handing over everything she had ever wanted, with no strings attached. She drew her reticule onto her lap and popped a sweet in her mouth. "Ginger comfit?" she asked.

Caroline took one and nibbled on it. "My problems aren't solved. I swore that I would take care of my brothers and sisters until they were settled in life, and I meant it. Fortune or no fortune. Title or no title."

"That is noble of you. It always has been." Arabella paused, searching for the right words. "But this makes all of it so much easier. Money and influence always does."

"Does it? I don't know the first thing about wealth." She sighed. "Maybe we can give it all away."

Arabella hated confrontation, even with Caroline, who knew almost every feeling she had ever had. But she was too surprised to keep her thoughts inside. "I can't believe you are saying this. You, of all people, who have been forced to scrimp and save for years to get by. Now you have enough to purchase anything you have ever dreamed of, and you aren't happy with it?"

Caroline shot a foot out and stopped the swing. "It's complicated, Bell. How am I supposed to trust this man who has appeared out of nowhere to tell us that our troubles are over? Doesn't that seem in the least suspicious to you?"

"It's unusual," she allowed. "But if I had someone tell me I no longer had to rely on Matthew, and in fact I could now choose my livelihood—then I would be ecstatic."

Arabella heard the flatness in her own voice. She was happy for Caroline, dash it all. This wasn't about her life and her issues.

Her *jealousy*, if she could stomach owning up to the truth.

"You think me selfish." Caroline scowled down at the grass.

"No, of course not," she said, stung.

"I can hear Will and George coming home from their lessons with Reverend Thomson. I must be off to tell them." She stalked off toward her house.

Arabella sat for a while in the swing, Byron napping on her foot.

She had always yearned for her independence. She was saving up her coins to eventually move into a little cottage. If she could have all the profits from her watercolor paintings, instead of giving so much to Matthew, then she had a chance at an independent, if modest, living.

But even in these dreams, she would still be working. She would need to continue to paint and sell her seascapes to survive.

It wouldn't be handed to her, like a miracle.

She couldn't understand Caroline's reaction. If it had been her, she would be crying with joy.

She was thrilled for Caroline, she truly was. She *loved* her—of course she wished for her happiness and security. But they were both nearing thirty, and neither of them had ever married, so she hadn't thought that their circumstances would change much. Whenever she thought of the future, it was growing old in a thatch-roofed cottage with the sea salt rusting the hinges on the shutters, watching visitors come and go as Caroline helped herself to a cup of tea in her parlor.

But Caroline probably didn't share that dream. Arabella was starting to wonder if she knew her as well as she thought she did.

Now, nothing would ever be the same.

With a deep sigh, she pushed herself out of the swing and went inside to help Rachel with the chores.

❖

Caroline's head was swimming in all the details that the solicitor, Mr. Jones, had outlined for them as they sat around the table in the dining room. The same table where she hauled out the ledger every week and made her careful calculations about what they could and could not afford.

Today the table had been littered with legal documents and numbers and clauses. It had made her head hurt far more than it ever had when doing the weekly sums. Mr. Jones had even brought the family Bible with him, the front page covered in faint spidery handwriting detailing generations of Reeves and ending with their father's name at the bottom. She opened the book again and traced the names of those unknown relatives with her finger. It was shocking to see on paper that her family *belonged* somewhere other than Inverley.

The result was the same as what Mr. Taylor had stated yesterday. The title was indeed Jacob's. The estate in Somerset was small but doing well. They had a fortune to their name, the details of which were a blur to Caroline, but it was clear that they would not need to worry for money ever again.

Mr. Jones packed the papers into his leather satchel, and Betsy and Susan and Jacob were bouncing with glee. It was unmannerly.

"Will you come for dinner tonight, Mr. Jones?" Caroline asked. "I shall extend an invitation to Mr. Taylor and his secretary as well, of course." That would outnumber the men to the women by one, so she would also have to ask Arabella to dinner. She was glad to have an opportunity to show Arabella how strange the entire situation was.

"I should be delighted. Thank you, Miss Reeve. I look forward to it."

After he left, Betsy let out a high-pitched screech. "We are even richer than I imagined!"

"*I* am richer, you mean," Jacob said with a grin. "It's my fortune as the heir, is it not?"

"You won't let your sisters starve," Caroline scolded him with a swat to his arm.

She tried to hide it from her siblings, but she felt uneasy. She hadn't enjoyed it, but she was accustomed to handling the finances for the family. Now it was in Jacob's hands, and he was barely twenty-one.

She had never relied on anyone to help take care of the family. She had prided herself on doing as much by herself as she could. What would become of her now? What was her role in the family if they didn't need her to provide for them? A spinster running her family affairs while her brothers and sisters grew up had a place of importance. But if her brother was now to take the reins, and if they had a whole new array of Reeve cousins to help, would she be relegated to some relative's attic?

That was Arabella's situation, after all. Although it worked out well enough for her, Caroline didn't know if she would be able to endure the same.

She pushed aside the fear that had her feeling nauseous and told herself to steel her spine. She would have to find another way to make sure she kept her promise to take care of them all, even if everything had turned topsy-turvy.

Caroline took a piece of paper and scrawled a missive across it.

"Betsy, please take this invitation to the inn and invite Mr. Taylor and his secretary to dinner."

"I am not a maid!" she cried. "Send Maisie to town instead."

Maisie was their only servant, and there was far too much work for her to handle in a household of six Reeves. They were all accustomed to helping around the household, and Caroline felt a pulse of annoyance that Betsy seemed to feel too important now to run errands. She narrowed her eyes at her.

"Maisie is tending to dinner. Unless you would prefer to peel potatoes and chop carrots?"

She sulked, crossing her arms over her chest. "No."

"You usually leap at the opportunity to go to town. Go."

Grumbling, she slammed the front door as she left.

Jacob grinned and leaned back in his chair, propping his booted legs up on the table. "I could have gone."

"Jacob Reeve, get those boots off this table!"

Caroline shoved his legs and he laughed as he got up.

"I know, I know I couldn't resist, Caro. Lord of the manor and everything, am I not?"

His boyish enthusiasm was catching, and she smiled. "You've earned your own errand now. Go next door and invite Arabella to dinner, would you?"

Some hours later, Caroline looked around the full dining room table. As this was a special occasion, she had permitted Will and George to dine with them instead of with Maisie, with dire threats to them both if they even considered misbehaving.

The table was laden with savories that rarely made an appearance in the Reeve's larder. There was fine wine instead of small beer, soft bread made with white flour instead of coarse rye, and lamb instead of mutton.

"Thank you for having us to dine, Miss Reeve." Mr. Taylor smiled at her from across the table.

"We have much to celebrate with your arrival, Mr. Taylor. I hope you do not mind being part of the family celebrations?"

"We have a cake for dessert!" George piped up with a look of longing toward the kitchen, and they all laughed.

"A fine occasion, and much deserving of cake," Arabella said to George. They shared a love of chocolate, with Arabella sneaking biscuits and sweets into the Reeve pantry as often as she could while Caroline pretended to turn a blind eye to where they came from. The children loved the ruse.

Caroline gazed at her across the table, and they smiled at each other as their eyes met. She hoped Arabella would see her side of things by the end of the meal. It meant more to her than she could say to have her support.

"You certainly have much to celebrate," Mr. Jones said. "And I am sure you shall have many happy occasions to celebrate in the near future."

"I suppose," Caroline said, uncertain what he meant.

"Forgive me, Miss Reeve, but I was speaking of upcoming nuptials. With three such beautiful young ladies in your family, permit me to say that you shall have no trouble on the Marriage Mart."

"Two, to be sure," she said sharply. "I would be most happy to see Betsy and Susan settled."

"Young Jacob is the heir, and has the title, the estate, and most of the money," Mr. Taylor said as he speared a piece of lamb with his fork. "But I believe Mr. Jones explained this afternoon that each of you have been left with a dowry—a not inconsiderable sum, I may add. You are a family of heiresses."

Caroline blinked. She hadn't followed all of what had been explained earlier. "We each have our own fortune?"

"Why—yes. Miss Betsy and Miss Susan have five thousand pounds to their names, and as the eldest, Miss Reeve, you have a tidy ten thousand. A very nice sum. Any man would be happy to have your hand in marriage."

"I shall *not* be among the green girls on the Marriage Mart hanging about for a husband." The idea filled her with horror.

"But of course you should seek to marry. Whyever would you not?" Mr. Jones blinked and rubbed his hand over his chin.

"I am content to make matches for my siblings and help them to settle into their new lives. My own is out of the question," she said briskly. "Now, gentlemen, can I offer you tea and cake?"

After the men departed, taking Jacob with them to celebrate with a drink at their hotel, the girls curled up in the parlor to gossip and the boys worked off their high spirits by running through the house and whooping up and down the stairs. Caroline and Arabella went to the kitchen.

Caroline put a cauldron of water on the fire. Arabella scraped waste into a pail, then piled dishes on top of each other. She filled the basin with the hot water and picked up a rag and scrubbed it with soap before attacking the dishes, having told long-suffering Maisie to seek her bed.

"Is this the last time we shall do chores together?" Arabella grabbed a clean towel and bumped her hip against Caroline's as she dried a plate. Her tone was light, but Caroline knew her well enough to hear the thread of wistfulness in her voice.

Caroline swallowed. "I never wanted things to change, Bell."

Arabella pushed her spectacles up her nose and dried another dish before setting it on the table behind them. "Be that as it may, change has found you regardless. I cannot imagine Jacob lording it over an estate. Surely you will all remove to Somerset, instead of staying in Inverley."

"I shall never leave Inverley." She stared into the soapy water and gripped the plate in both hands.

"At the very least, you will leave this house. The leaky roof and draughty windows will be behind you at last."

She didn't want to give up her house. Not after a lifetime of treating skinned knees in this kitchen, or hearing the creak of the third stair from the top of the staircase, or doling out sweets in the sitting room to the boys and their friends before walking them to the seaside.

"Perhaps."

She turned to face Arabella, staring deep into her brown eyes, taking in the short fringed sweep of her lashes, wanting to grasp her by the shoulders and to hold onto both her and this moment forever.

Perhaps.

Perhaps this was the last moment she would have in her old life, before everything changed forever. If only she could capture it somehow, press it neatly between the pages of one of her novels, to be opened and stared at later to relive the crackle of anticipation and worry and awareness. The knowledge that soon, everything would be different.

But for now—she could have one last taste of life as she knew it.

She didn't want to just hold Arabella. If everything was going to change, she wanted to throw caution to the wind and press her lips to hers and search for escape. It would be a moment that she could point to later and laugh off, using the stress and confusion of her newly disordered life as an excuse. She hadn't meant anything by it, she imagined saying to Arabella with a little laugh and a dismissive wave.

But that wouldn't do at all.

Firstly, Arabella would be shocked. Maybe she would slap her for trespassing where she ought not dare. And secondly—Arabella deserved far better than to be dismissed.

But then why was Arabella staring back at her, her eyes wide and her full lips parted slightly, as she—*leaned forward*?

Caroline couldn't resist any longer. She put the dish back in the sink and tipped Arabella's chin up with a soapy finger, her heart pounding so loud that she could no longer hear the sea, then bent her head and captured those soft lips from a hundred illicit fantasies with her own.

CHAPTER FOUR

Caroline's whole world tipped upside down. Everything she had ever known flew out the window and nothing felt solid anymore. The one sure thing was right here between her and Arabella, in the soft press of their lips. She clung to it for dear life. She moved closer, her hands tight on Arabella's full hips, her body flush against her own.

If this moment was all that she could have, then she needed to make enough memories for it to last through her lifetime. She darted her tongue into the crease of Arabella's lips, daring to risk as much as she could. She tasted the gin that they had tipped into their tea when they took it into the kitchen with them earlier. Arabella made a little moaning sound that thrilled Caroline and encouraged her to suck Arabella's bottom lip into her mouth before meeting her tongue with her own.

She tried to memorize Arabella's body with her hands, moving them from her hips up her back and then stroking her arms beneath the puffed sleeves of her evening dress. By the time Caroline had settled her hands against Arabella's waist, Arabella was leaning against her, her own hands on Caroline's shoulders, her head tilted back and allowing their kiss to deepen.

A crash sounded from the parlor, and Caroline jerked away. Arabella stumbled and grasped the kitchen table, her eyes wide and shining as she looked up at her. Caroline felt like the veriest cad.

How dare she take advantage of her best friend? How could she have been so foolish to let her own desires slip? Arabella must be horrified.

Caroline managed a little laugh, her heart beating in triple time and her hands clammy as she jammed them into the soapy water. "It's a time for celebration, is it not? Forgive me, the mood of the moment overtook me."

Arabella laughed too, and the tension broke. "Nothing more than I would have expected."

Caroline stepped back and smiled. "Wherever I go, you know, you are sure to have a standing invitation to tea," she said, trying to infuse as much lightness to her tone as she could. "Steeped only once, just for you."

She deserved far more than tea, of course. Arabella was worth diamonds and furs.

Arabella laughed again. "It is the least that I would expect of your new situation."

"But do you see now why I am so concerned about the inheritance? It is the strangest of circumstances, is it not?"

"I understand what you mean," Arabella said, her eyes bright with curiosity. She dried a cup, slowly working the towel around it as she thought. "Why would the former heir be so happy to see the money transferred to Jacob? Mr. Taylor was remarkably at ease tonight for a disinherited baronet."

"Exactly!" She was glad to latch back onto the matter at hand. Anything to keep her mind off that kiss. "I am grateful—but still ever so confused."

"I am determined to get to the bottom of this mystery with you," Arabella said, pushing her spectacles up.

"Together," she said, and was rewarded with a brilliant smile.

They finished up the dishes, listening to the crickets chirp and the sound of the sea crashing upon the shores, and her siblings laughing together.

Come what may, Caroline knew she would miss these moments. All of them.

But especially that kiss.

❖

As the hour neared eleven, Arabella hugged the Reeves good-bye. Instead of slipping upstairs to her second-floor bedroom, she sat outside on the swing in her back garden, the wood cool beneath her thin dress. The waves always sounded tenfold louder at night, but she welcomed the sound, finding comfort in its presence as she tried to settle herself.

Nothing could have prepared her for what had happened tonight.

A heady mix of exhilaration and despair swept through her. The way her mind was whirling, she wasn't sure if she would find sleep at all.

The assembly rooms were still busy at this hour with dancing, and the coffee shops and taverns always bustled with nightlife, nestled in the ground floors of the hotels that hosted visitors accustomed to the later hours of the city.

But their corner of town was on the other side of Inverley, and there wasn't even a whisper of noise beyond the vastness of nature, the waves pounding onto the shore with the occasional call of an owl to interrupt them.

Nature.

For so long, Arabella had considered her desires unnatural. More than wantonness, she had worried it verged on depravity, even though her thoughts had rarely ventured beyond kissing. How could her thoughts stray toward another woman? There might be the occasional discreet rumor or gossip about London folk that swirled around town, but she had never heard of anyone else in Inverley feeling this way.

After years had passed and her feelings refused to dissipate, she had learned to live with the truth of herself. She had vowed never to marry, knowing that she could never be happy with a husband.

She had tested that resolve once, many years ago, and it had ended in disaster.

Arabella pushed the swing and let the cool night air flow through her hair, her emotions as jumbled as the spread of stars above, glittering and sharp in the black sky. Pining for Caroline had always been painful because she knew her love was hopeless.

How many times had she let her eyes drop and pretend her attention was elsewhere, terrified of discovery if she gazed too long in adoration at the object of her desires? How often had she choked back how she felt when Caroline asked if she looked fetching after her sister trimmed her hair, or when she tried on a new bonnet?

She had been so careful for so long that it felt like forever.

It was a shock to discover that the dreams she had about kissing Caroline were nothing like the reality of it. Her fantasy had been a secret confession of love, followed by soft kisses as they held each other tenderly. It was sweet.

The reality had been terrifying. *Mystifying.* Where had that swell of desire come from, urgently pulsing through the lower half of her body, demanding satisfaction? How had her nipples tightened so hard that she was certain they were visible through her dress? How had it all happened so fast, and yet so slowly that she could remember every shift of Caroline's body and every movement of her lips against her mouth? *Inside* her mouth? Her face flamed at the thought.

Her fantasy had been soft and delicate, but the reality had been about as soft as a thunderstorm.

A kiss, however casually Caroline had meant it—and there was no other explanation for it, with no other emotion than the giddiness of excitement—a kiss was something both to treasure forever as the culmination of her earthly desires, and something that slid tendrils of icy dread down the back of her dress.

But it put her in grave danger of wanting more. It had put thought and desire to action, and she had no idea how she could comport herself in Caroline's presence now.

Arabella shivered and unlatched the door. There was light coming from the parlor, where she discovered Rachel in an armchair under a quilt. Byron purred from her lap and Shelley was curled up on the sofa. There were dark smudges beneath Rachel's eyes, and her hair was mussed as if she had lain down and gotten up without brushing it.

"I am so sorry for keeping you awake," Arabella said, a stab of guilt passing through her. It was later than she had expected to stay out, and she hadn't meant to worry her family. "You weren't waiting up on my account, I hope?"

"No, no. I have been having difficulty sleeping these days. I suppose it's the baby. My worries about the baby, I should say. I have been up more often than not over the past few weeks." She rubbed a hand behind Byron's ears, and he yawned and resettled on her lap. "The cats are marvelous company in the dead of night."

Arabella sat down on the sofa, dislodging Shelley. "Are you feeling well enough? Is there something I can do for you?"

"It is very kind of you to offer, my dear. I am so grateful that you have been here in the house, and that you will be here to help after the baby arrives. I cannot imagine doing this alone."

Arabella was glad that there was but one candle lit on the mantel. She knew her face betrayed her emotions, and she felt hesitant about the idea of taking care of a baby. It wasn't something that she had wanted for herself. But she couldn't add to Rachel's fears and uncertainties at this time. The middle of the night was no time to talk about something like this.

"I'll always support you," she said, because that much was true. She loved Rachel and wanted the best for her. But why did it have to come at the expense of her own life? Why did her brother always expect her to give so much of herself? She tried to push the uncharitable thought away.

Matthew ambled down the stairs and clasped her shoulder. "Arabella! Do you have any news to share of the Reeves' situation?"

Rachel perked up. "Yes, do tell. It's ever so interesting. They have been our neighbors ever since we purchased this house upon our marriage. I could never have imagined such a thing happening to them."

Arabella could hardly give a satisfactory recounting of the evening when her thoughts were so wrapped up in the single moment of kissing Caroline.

"Mr. Taylor and Mr. Jones were perfect gentlemen, and very kind in their attentions to the family at dinner. Very complimentary."

"Caroline is far above you now, I suppose," Rachel said. "It will be a hardship for you, I am sure. I know how close you are."

"We will still be friends," Arabella said, but she felt a pulse of alarm.

"Oh, yes, but you shan't be invited to the same places now. No more dancing above the grocer's shop for *her*. She will be too grand for such things."

Arabella supposed that must be true. The thought rankled.

"Well, I have been up very late already and must seek my bed," she said, forcing a smile onto her face. "I hope you are able to get some rest soon, Rachel."

Matthew squeezed Rachel's hand. "Thank you for keeping Rachel company, Arabella. You are always such a help. I'll go make some tea, Rachel, shall I?"

Arabella went up the stairs, listening to the murmur of their conversation and the clink of kettle and teacups. She had never felt more conscious of the fact that this was *their* house and *their* tea and *their* moment. Expecting the birth of their child, increasing their family.

Arabella lived here, but it wasn't her life that was being lived here. She was a support for her brother's life.

She brushed her hair and drew on a cotton chemise, and her jumbled thoughts cleared.

She wanted her own life. Not simply a change in location, though she still craved her independence and a cottage by the shore. But she wanted more moments like the ones she shared tonight with Caroline, doing dishes and taking care of things for family.

And yes—more kissing.

Like a real relationship.

Like the marriage that she always said she didn't want.

But maybe it wasn't marriage with a *man* that she wanted.

Oh, but this was outside the realm of her wildest fantasies. In her dreams there had only been kissing. But a proper relationship, two women being in love together and setting up house—well, it was out of the question. Even for her, as lost in daydreams as she often was.

Pure nonsense.

She touched her fingers to her lips, which throbbed at the thought of the kiss.

Or was it?

CHAPTER FIVE

The Inverley assembly rooms were open three evenings a week during the summer months for dancing. In the mornings and afternoons, it offered cards for the gentlemen and tea for the ladies and was one of the most popular places in town due to its fine views of the beach.

It was considered terribly romantic during the evenings to walk the terrace that circled the building and listen to the ocean. Fanciful ladies swore they could feel the very mist of the sea on their faces as they strolled, but Caroline knew it was to disguise the glow of perspiration from their exertions—dancing, or otherwise.

They didn't have anything new to wear—Betsy and Susan hadn't been able to wait that long, begging Caroline to go dancing from the very day that Mr. Taylor had arrived to tell them of their good fortune. Not one week had gone by, but Caroline had grown so tired of their whining that she had acquiesced.

Besides, it had always bothered Caroline that she had never been able to provide a night of dancing at the assembly when she knew how much they had always wanted to go. The attendance fee had always been outside their means.

The people dancing tonight should be people who knew them. Surely their neighbors would not look down on their faded muslins or turn up their nose at the sight of a patch or two. It was still a week or more before a stream of fashionable visitors would start to descend upon Inverley, so they should be safe from the worst of sneers.

"Behave," she warned her sisters. "I mean it."

They were too old for a governess, and too wild to be trusted with a companion—even the most dragon-faced matron would despair of the pair.

Mr. Singh, the master of ceremonies, was standing inside the door. He was a tall dapper man of middling age who had moved to Inverley from India fifteen years ago. He called upon all new visitors who wished to visit the assembly to ascertain whether or not they were respectable enough to join the dancing, and he took it as a matter of personal pride that the assemblies were well-attended and that not a single set lacked sufficient partners to make a merry round of it. He was beloved by the townsfolk.

"Good evening, Miss Reeve. Miss Susan. Miss Betsy." He nodded at each of them. "Are you passing by on a fine evening stroll?"

Caroline swallowed. "We were hoping to join you in this fine establishment to dance tonight, Mr. Singh."

Betsy jangled her reticule. "We have more than enough coin to purchase an evening of pleasure, I do assure you."

Caroline wished nothing more than for the cobblestones to part and for her to sink right through them. She had thought that their recent turn of fortune would be enough to assure them entry everywhere, but the look on his face told her all she needed to know. Not even their new bank balance had rendered the Reeves good enough to mingle with socially.

She felt even worse at the sympathy that shone from Mr. Singh's kind eyes. "I regret to inform you that the rooms are full tonight."

Caroline knew it for the rejection that it was, and she was grateful that no one saw them as they were turned away. The rooms weren't full. They never were at this time of year.

As they walked back down the street toward home, the girls complaining mightily, she turned back to see Mr. Singh wave another couple inside.

Shame tasted bitter in her throat.

If she was meant to be the head of this family, she was doing a terrible job. Her parents had trusted her to shepherd her siblings through life, and she couldn't even give them the smallest of opportunities to mingle among people of their new station.

"We shall have to come back earlier next time, before the crowd is too large," Susan said. "It shall be the easiest thing in the world to arrange dinner an hour in advance."

"Next time it will not be any easier for us to gain entry," Caroline said, trying to gentle her tone. "It is not the crowd that deterred Mr. Singh from letting us in. It is reputation. How many times have I told you to behave like ladies in public?"

"This isn't Almacks!" Betsy contested. "We are *quite* good enough for a small-town assembly, I am sure of it!"

"You have the proof of it before you, Betsy. We are indeed considered not good enough."

"Well, who wants to dance in a stuffy room filled with bores!" she cried.

Susan glared at her and jostled her arm. "I do," she said. "What about what *I* wish?"

Betsy stopped in the middle of the street, hands on her hips. "Are you both blaming me?" she asked, her voice shrill.

Caroline sighed. "Betsy, you have been sneaking around with any man you can find."

"Susan is as bad! And you may not engage yourself with men, but you are even worse, Caroline! You have no emotion at all—you are a spinster with no heart!" She picked up her skirts and ran down the street, leaving Susan and Caroline to follow.

"I haven't engaged in any undue intimacies, Caro," Susan muttered, scowling. "I swear it."

They walked the rest of the way home in silence.

Caroline took her worries to bed with her and fretted all night. It wasn't just the problem of what to do with her sisters that weighed on her, but the accusations that Betsy had lobbed at her.

Passionless.

No emotion.

No *heart*.

It wasn't true. She yearned to snap back that although she had known passion, she also knew discretion.

That wasn't exactly the message she wished to give to her sisters.

Yet—why was it that she felt guilt-free when she had indulged in her own affairs, but she was as censorious as the master of ceremonies toward Betsy's?

And where did her confused kiss with Arabella fit into it?

The night brought her no answers, but the next morning she sent a note round to Mr. Taylor's hotel.

Mr. Taylor was as easy in his manner as ever as he sat down in her parlor and agreed to a cup of coffee and a fresh biscuit.

She hated to rely on anyone, especially someone outside the family—and yet, he *was* family. He was their cousin, and he had dropped them into this mess. The least he could do would be to help guide them through it.

"Do we have any female relatives who might be up to the task of readying us for Society?" she asked without preamble.

"Ah, changing your mind that you can do it all by yourself?"

It stuck in her throat to admit it, but she forced out the word. "Yes." She sighed, then recounted the story of the previous night. "If we cannot even gain entry to the Inverley assembly rooms, how will I ever get the girls to London to secure the future that I dream for them?"

"There are always gentlemen agreeable to a fortune," he said gently. "They are not always found at dancing halls or evening balls."

"Yes, I have seen them—with their slick smiles and sly words. I want better than a fortune hunter for my sisters." Caroline hesitated. "I wish them to have a love match, if possible. But I would settle for them not ruining all their chances at matrimony before they have been heiresses for a scant week."

"And you can't give them that opportunity without shaping them up into young paragons. I see how it is."

"Turning them into *paragons* is more ambitious than I would dare dream. I would be happy if they learned even the smallest degree of decorum."

"I am sad to say that there is no such female Reeve up to the task. I have not yet married so I have no wife to help out. My mother is indisposed, and my aunts have their hands full of their own unwedded children. I wish I had better news for you."

Disappointment stabbed at her. Without a female relation to sponsor them, society would be overwhelmingly difficult to navigate. They might be able to muddle their way through Inverley for the summer without courting ruin, but it would be next to impossible to get to London for the next Season with nothing but their own notoriety to recommend them.

"Thank you, Mr. Taylor."

He settled his hat upon his head as he rose. "It has been a pleasure, Miss Reeve. May I have the pleasure of seeing you again soon?"

Drat it all, but he was charming. And he was a favorite of Jacob's these days. And most importantly of all, he was family. "Do come by tonight for dinner, Mr. Taylor—that is, if you have not tired of our provincial dining habits. I know you could get a finer cut of beef and cup of claret at one of the eating establishments in town, but we do enjoy your presence here at the house."

"I should like nothing better. I consider myself ever delighted of the good fortune that has reunited the family, Miss Reeve. Until tonight."

CHAPTER SIX

Jacob grinned. "It's perfect, Caro!"

The house to let was the corner building in a row of shiny new townhouses that were built in what Caroline had been assured was the London style, which she knew nothing about but had impressed Jacob mightily when the banker showed them inside.

Although Will and George would need to share a bedroom, the house was spacious with big bay windows that opened onto a gorgeous sea view, a scant hundred feet to the sand.

Maybe it was too grand.

How would she find enough staff to manage the household? How would she even learn to direct a staff of more than a single maid who had been with them forever?

Terror gripped her, and she clasped her hands behind her back to hide how much they trembled.

"Perhaps we should look at other options—"

"Do forgive me, Miss Reeve," Mr. Taylor interrupted, "but I believe you could make do with such small quarters, considering the snugness of your previous establishment. I'm afraid I have already reviewed most of the available lodgings in Inverley over the past few days, and this is the largest that you would be able to find on such short notice."

Small quarters? Caroline glanced up at the soaring ceiling. She supposed that to some, having but two parlors and a dining room that must also be used for breakfast were a sign of mean quarters indeed.

To her, it was palatial.

"You have already looked?" she asked.

"Inverley is a charming place, and I would feel dreadful for abandoning you when I have met the long-lost family at last. My secretary and I have decided to stay here for a few weeks. Perhaps a month. We shall be renting rooms from a widow at the edge of town—pickings are lean for two old bachelors, I suppose."

She flushed, remembering that Jacob was now the happy inheritor of his wealth. She could not help but wonder what his circumstances were like now.

"Mr. Taylor is right," Jacob said. "This house *is* small, isn't it? Maybe we could look at something further from town, with its own land? I heard that Captain Smith was looking to let his manor. This townhouse is nowhere near good enough for the likes of us now."

When he had entered the house, Jacob had been all smiles and excitement. But now that Mr. Taylor had said his piece, he was sneering.

"We should be grateful to find something as well located as this one," she said. Jacob seemed chastened, but she couldn't be sure if he would take the first opportunity to roll his eyes at Mr. Taylor behind her back.

She tried to find charity in her heart. Jacob had no father figure beyond the age of eleven. Now Mr. Taylor with his starched collar and shiny guineas and crisp sense of authority had come into town, given him wealth beyond his dreams, and shown him attention—of course he would become Jacob's new hero, capable of no wrongdoing in his eyes.

She knew she should be grateful to Mr. Taylor—Jacob did need help settling into his new role and new life. He was woefully unprepared for his new responsibilities.

But still, Jacob's cavalier words stung.

"Perhaps we don't need to move yet." Caroline felt uneasy about putting money down anywhere. It was still hard to believe that it was theirs to spend.

"I realize we have only just met," Mr. Taylor said, "and we are not so close in relation, but I feel compelled to urge you to reconsider. Your family has risen in consequence to the point that your current dwelling—forgive me, it pains me to criticize—is unreasonable for you to live in. Your brother is a baronet. You and your sisters are heiresses. You cannot continue to dwell in such straightened circumstances, with but one maid-of-all-work."

"Thank you for your input." She tried to put as much dignity as she could into the words.

He was right, of course. She hated to admit it, but she was letting her pride get in the way.

Besides, staying where they were meant staying in the house next door to Arabella. After that kiss, how could she continue to put temptation within such easy reach? It would be good for them both if she moved away from Belvoir Lane, if that was how Caroline was going to start reacting around her best friend.

Better to be safe than sorry, and what could be safer than this three-story house across town? There were no plump women with big eyes and a cute snub nose lurking around these parts for her to lust after. This was her best bet to put the kiss behind her.

"We shall lease it," she announced, and began to settle the fee with the banker.

"For how long, Miss Reeve?" he enquired.

This was an establishment meant to rent out to visitors. It wasn't permanent. Where would they end up? When would they have a true home again? Her heart hammered as the future loomed ahead of her, full of so many unknowns.

"I suppose for the summer."

"I recommend month by month," Mr. Taylor said. "It gives you flexibility to make your decisions."

"Yes—and that means we could decide to remove to London on a moment's notice!" Jacob exclaimed.

London? Caroline felt dizzy. Everything was happening so fast.

Mr. Taylor laughed. "Hardly London, my boy, not in these months. The stinking heat of the city, the tedium as everyone is out at their estates, or places like this—you ought to be grateful that you grew up here. Many pay good coin to spend their leisure hours here."

Jacob muttered that he was indeed grateful.

"Well," Caroline said, striving for some modicum of control again. "Now we have lodgings. I suppose next we need servants, and food for the larder."

"And to arrange a housewarming party," Jacob said brightly. "The parlor is large enough for dancing, is it not?"

"That it is. You also need new clothes to match your station," Mr. Taylor said, grinning at Jacob. "I can't take you to White's wearing what you've got on now. You need the best of everything, my boy. We should go to London and set you up—all of you," he said, turning to Caroline. He put up his hands as she started to protest. "For a visit, mind! I am not suggesting removing to the capital."

"Inverley will do well enough for us," she said, ignoring Jacob's hiss of displeasure. "We need no London fashions."

Of course they needed a new wardrobe. She didn't like to admit that Mr. Taylor was right, yet again.

"You say that now, but the cream of society has not yet descended from London, and you will be mixing with them soon," he warned. "You may well change your mind."

"If I do, then we shall arrange a trip to London later. No need to do it now."

"I can see you are an intelligent young lady, unlike so many who I have encountered in London and elsewhere. Many such young ladies, ill-educated and ill-informed, enjoy a man guiding them. But I can tell you are no such young miss, are you? Forgive me, I should have behaved better." His eyes were warm and sincere.

"That's how Caroline is," Jacob said dismissively. "She is always trying to tell us what to do."

Mr. Taylor narrowed his eyes, and the warmth was gone in an instant. "Miss Reeve is your eldest sister, and from what I can tell, she has done an excellent job in raising you. You ought to respect her authority, whelp."

Jacob wilted under his stare, and Caroline felt a little more charitably inclined toward Mr. Taylor. Perhaps he was not so pompous after all.

When Caroline and Jacob returned to Belvoir Lane, Jacob shouted out their news as soon as they were within the door.

The family was gathered in the kitchen. Maisie was stirring soup in the cauldron over the fire for dinner, and there was leftover cake on the table.

"You're going to get chocolate all down your sleeve," Caroline warned Betsy, nudging her elbow off the table.

Betsy tossed her hair. "Will it matter? We cannot keep wearing these rags now that we have riches."

Caroline drew in a deep breath and took in the scene before her. Betsy was wearing her bonnet indoors and at the table, which she liked to do on occasion because she thought it made her look fetching. Susan was idly picking at a broken nail. Will and George were punching each other in the arm as they fought over the last of the cake.

Poor table manners.

Poor attitudes.

Ill-fitting and old-fashioned clothing.

This was the family that now had a fortune to its name? They would be barred from every respectable drawing room in the land, let alone the assembly room and the promenades of Inverley.

She blew out a breath. The Reeve family had a lot of work ahead of them. And they needed her to take charge, like always.

"We need a plan," she announced. When no one paid attention, she grabbed a wooden spoon and thwacked it against the table. Silence fell. "I *said*—we need a plan."

"What kind of plan?" Jacob asked, tilting his chair back and propping his feet on the table.

"Boots off the table," she snapped. "We need a plan to fit into society."

Betsy and Susan stared, and then collapsed on the table in peals of laughter. "*You* saying this!" Susan gasped. "Why, it is too funny. You've never cared a pin for society."

It was true.

"Besides, we have a grand new house now! We need no *plan* when we have money, consequence, and rooms a stone's throw from the sea."

"Good society is more than a fashionable address," she said. "Jacob, you ought to speak with Mr. Taylor and ask his opinion of what to do. Perhaps his secretary could help you to understand your responsibilities. You have much to learn about your station, and an estate to run." She hated to admit it, but Mr. Taylor was his best bet for success.

He frowned. "I don't know if I need to hobnob with a *secretary*."

Caroline ignored his protest. "Boys, I will engage a governess and a tutor for you straightaway. You have plenty to learn before you attend school. Betsy and Susan, I will engage a chaperone for you, or find a sponsor to help us enter Society."

"A chaperone!" Betsy wailed. "We shall never have a moment's fun ever again!"

"If you prefer to call her a companion, you may. But someone will have to vouch for your good behavior, or you shall *never* enter the assembly rooms, no matter how rich we are."

Jacob stood up. "I am the head of this family now! It's my title that protects us all. I don't know if we need all this fuss and bother, Caro."

"*I* protect you all," she snapped. "Do not ever forget that I made a solemn vow to our parents to provide for you and to see you all settled. Your title and our new wealth offer us some shelter, but it is I who must uphold my duty to protect you."

He stammered, then sat back down.

"Now. Is it clear to everyone? We all need lessons, and training, and guidance, before we can even *think* of accepting the humblest invitation to tea. We are Reeves. We will pull through this the way we have pulled through everything else—together."

Caroline looked at the crowd of sulky faces around the table and hoped she was right.

❖

It was midafternoon and Arabella's wide straw bonnet kept the worst of the sun from her face. It was a fine day for drawing on the cliffs. She filled her lungs with the fresh sea air, salty and clean. Sunlight glinted off the water like crystal, dazzling her sight if she stared too long at the waves.

She was glad to have an excuse to be out of the house. Her mornings were spent selling paintings from the front parlor, but today Rachel had decided to sit with her while she sewed baby clothes, excited to talk about the upcoming few months and all the arrangements that they would have to make.

The way Matthew and Rachel talked, it seemed like they had decided that Arabella would become a nursemaid and eventually a sort of governess to the child.

She wanted to help her family. Truly, she did. She was willing to help with the marketing and chores and errands after she moved to her own home, and to sit with Rachel when she was feeling overwhelmed, and to help take care of their child. But she didn't want every day of her whole life to revolve around the baby, and she worried she wouldn't be strong enough to say no if Matthew asked.

She tried to clear her head. After all, it was a beautiful day, and the rock where she was perched was one of her favorite vantage points.

If she faced east, she saw the sea lapping the shores of the pebbled beach.

North featured the majestic sweep of the widow's manor house, fanciful and forbidding. Whether her paintings of it sold depended on whether the buyer was interested in gothic spires and spiky iron fences, but the house intrigued people year after year. She always made sure to have fresh paintings of it in her inventory.

South was lush with fields that covered the hills, wildflowers poking their way through weed and underbrush, with narrow walkways carved into the cliffs.

West was the town, with its charming shopfronts and neat rows of houses. If she craned her neck, she could see the townhouse that the Reeves had moved into last week. She had helped them pack up their belongings and had given directions for the wagon coming up the lane as Caroline had been busy hassling Jacob into finishing up his share of the work.

Arabella hadn't been able to look Caroline in the eye. Not since the kiss.

Her fingers tightened on her pencil.

Byron settled low into the grass, waiting for Arabella to raise the pencil so he could pounce at it. It was how she started most of her drawing sessions, as he was her constant companion no matter where she worked. She darted the pencil back and forth between his paws, careful not to let his claws ruin her paper, and when he had enough of the game, he flopped into the grass and curled up for a nap.

It didn't take her long to fill a few pages with rough outlines of the views, with notes about color and composition. She would spend the next few days painting them in her attic, but she liked to have the landscape in front of her while she composed the images.

Caroline came striding up the hill with her skirts clutched high in one hand, her other hand on her bonnet to prevent a wind gust from blowing it off her head.

"Bell!" Caroline peered down at her drawing. "You are so talented. As always." She sat down on the grass and Byron yawned and stretched before curling up on her lap like a cushion.

Arabella envied the cat as Caroline stroked him. The strength of her physical reaction startled her—her skin tingled, and her lips felt dry, and she was hard-pressed to keep her papers in her lap instead of tossing them to the wind and throwing herself into Caroline's arms.

She swallowed. "Were you looking for me? Or taking a walk?"

"I stopped by your house to see you, and Rachel told me you had come up here to sketch."

"I thought that you would be too busy these days for company, so I haven't stopped by your new house."

The truth was that Arabella had been avoiding her for the first time in their lives, fearing that their encounter would be awkward. But as Caroline sat there cuddling Byron, her brown hair blowing across her face, the sea breeze seemed to take any awkwardness away with it. Arabella felt herself relax.

Caroline groaned. "Busy is not the word. I am more exhausted now than I was before, despite the fact that I have not prepared a single meal, done an inch of scrubbing, or put one stitch into the mending. Instead, I have been arranging the furnishing rentals, interviewing servants, and discussing curriculums with the new tutors."

"Is Mr. Taylor helping you?"

"I hate to admit it, but I could not do any of this without his help. He has been…well, I suppose I ought to say *invaluable*." She said the word as if it was distasteful.

"Perhaps we have been wrong about him."

"Perhaps. But the situation is still so dashed suspicious." Caroline sighed. "And there is one thing he cannot help me with."

"Oh?"

"Betsy and Susan want nothing more than to be launched into society. I might be reaching for the stars, but I think they have a chance at a respectable match."

"What are you going to do?"

"I am trying to find a sponsor who will help me with the girls. But Mr. Taylor knows of no such woman. He was unable to suggest any aunts or cousins or family that we have." She frowned. "Is that not odd?"

"Decidedly odd," Arabella agreed.

Byron opened one eye and meowed.

"Byron agrees that Mr. Taylor is an enigma," Caroline said with a laugh.

He meowed again, then leapt onto Arabella's lap and butted his head against her sketchbook. She rubbed beneath his chin, then picked him up and nuzzled the top of his head as she thought about Caroline's predicament. It didn't make any sense to her.

"I'm not sure what I'm going to do," Caroline confessed. "I need help."

Caroline *never* asked for help. Worry flitted across her face, and she was working her bottom lip with her teeth in a moment of vulnerability that Arabella rarely saw. Caroline was always confident and charging ahead with a plan. She never seemed to need anyone.

She knew who she wanted Caroline to need. *Her*.

But if she couldn't have Caroline, she would still do anything in her power to help her.

"I know what you should do," Arabella announced.

"What?"

"Write to your new cousins directly. You showed me the family Bible. There were scores of names written in it—and most of them were women, remember? That was why they had to go back a generation or two to find Mr. Taylor and give him the baronetcy in the first place after your father and his brothers had passed. Mr. Taylor must be overlooking someone in his family. A gentleman may not know the niceties of such a thing, after all. You could ask for their direction from the solicitor, could you not?"

Arabella's heart hammered. Suggesting to go against a family member felt almost treasonous to her, especially when she herself had such a hard time standing up to her own brother. She had no intention of sowing discord among the Reeves.

She felt like a hero when Caroline beamed at her.

"You always have the right idea, Bell. I don't know what I would do without you."

Didn't Caroline know why she was always so eager to help? Wasn't it clear from her face? The longing and the love must be as naked as the day in her eyes.

Caroline's face was bright, her bonnet tipped back, her strong, capable hand stroking Byron.

She wanted that hand on *her*. Stroking *her*.

Arabella decided thinking things through wasn't helping her. It never had when it came to Caroline. She leaned down and pressed her lips to Caroline's, savoring her sweet gasp and then the touch of her tongue against her own, the warmth of her face from the sun and the scent of the sea mixed with her lemon soap.

It wasn't as dramatic a kiss as the one they had shared after dinner. This was lighter and sweeter and shorter, a little more like her fantasy kisses, but the sizzle in her belly told her that it stoked her desire all the same.

Caroline blinked up at her, her lips parted and her eyes round, and Arabella settled her skirts around her as she sat back down on her rock. "A kiss to settle the agreement," she announced. "The knights of the round table did such things with King Arthur when they committed to a quest. I read it in my most recent novel. This is like our own quest. Instead of knights, we are spinsters. Armed with books and teacups."

Was it convincing enough? She thought it unlikely that Lancelot had touched his tongue to Arthur's while swearing fealty, but then what did either of them know about history? All she knew was that she wanted to sneak as many kisses as she could this summer, under whatever guise she could manage them.

Caroline's lips twitched. "And the unknown sponsor is the dragon? It could well be. That reminds me—it's Thursday. I may have moved across town, but it gives you no excuse to forget about me."

"Forget about you?"

"My weekly novel. From the lending library." Caroline poked her knee. "You didn't bring me anything yesterday. You always brought me one on Wednesdays."

Arabella stared. "But you can afford your own subscription now."

She shrugged. "It's not about the cost. I like the recommendations."

An absurd warmth spread through her heart. "They have staff there who can recommend anything you wish for you."

"They aren't *you*."

Caroline gazed into her eyes, and the warmth spread until her body was hot and tingly. Thank goodness for the breeze, or she would be set aflame.

"There's always next week," Arabella said.

She would always be there when Caroline needed her.

And maybe, if she were very lucky, she would be able to get what she needed, too.

Chapter Seven

After a lifetime of pencil nubs and paper scraps, it was the most luxurious thing in the world for Caroline to put a pen that someone else had sharpened to a crisp white paper from the fanciest stationer in town. It was a marvel to send out invitations via a servant who had no more pressing task that day but to invite friends to meet her at the bathing rooms at eight o'clock the following morning.

After some deliberation, she had invited Arabella and the women they had met at the Martins' card party several weeks ago—Miss Maeve Balfour and Miss Grace Linfield.

Miss Linfield picked up the chalk and wrote their names on the granite board near the door, putting them in line for the next available bathing machine. It was early enough that they shouldn't have to wait long, as Inverley boasted four machines hitched to horses that plodded into the sea as often as one could wish between the hours of seven in the morning to two in the afternoon. Though Arabella told them it would be a squeeze to have all four of them at once, Miss Linfield had confessed to nerves at the concept of dipping and Miss Balfour had firmly declared it to be settled—they all would go together.

Caroline ordered a round of sea tonic for them all, pleased that she had more than enough coins tucked in her reticule to pay for a dozen such excursions.

Miss Balfour wrinkled her nose. She was as elegant as she had been at the Martins', even in her flannel wrapper and her silk bathing cap. "Could we not have a strong cup of tea instead?"

Arabella smiled at her. "You don't sound enthused. Did you not say that your mother was here to partake in the health cures? Has she been enjoying the tonics?"

"She is as enthusiastic as I am not," she admitted. "Mama is rigorous about bathing every morning in the waters. She even enjoys being toweled dry by cloth that had been previously soaked in sea salts, which I think sounds unnecessarily harsh on the skin." She examined her hands. "I cannot countenance such a thing."

"You have come all this way and ought to be trying everything," Arabella told her, taking a glass from the attendant. "I'm sure the tonic has wonderful properties."

Caroline grinned. "You recommend it, Bell, even though I know you never tried even a sip before?"

She blushed. "You know I have been in finest fettle my whole life and never saw the need."

Miss Balfour touched her tongue to the tonic. "I'm not sure I have the wherewithal for this."

Miss Linfield braved a sip, then peered into the glass. "It's not so bad," she said, but doubt was in her voice. "Rather…sulphuric."

Caroline downed hers in one gulp. "That's the way to do it. It's medicinal, after all. Not something one must savor." Thank goodness for that, because it was the most bitter thing she had downed in all her life. Like Arabella, she had never bothered with the tonics before.

"Not the most ladylike approach," Miss Balfour said. "But you make a good point." She tipped the tonic down her throat with a shiver of revulsion, making a sound that had them all laughing.

"Well, we must follow suit," Arabella told Miss Linfield, and with a count to three, they downed theirs as well amid the encouragement and laughter of the others.

"My eyes are watering," Miss Linfield gasped. "This is more rigor than I was expecting for such an early morning." She dabbed at her lips with a dainty handkerchief.

"I think a ginger comfit is in order," Arabella declared. "I carry them at all times. They should clear away the taste." She passed round her reticule and they each withdrew a paper-twisted sweet.

"Exactly what we need," Caroline said, unwrapping the comfit. Arabella was always so thoughtful.

Arabella's tongue darted out to catch sugar dust from her full bottom lip, and Caroline couldn't stop staring.

"It is lovely of you to invite us, Miss Reeve," Miss Linfield said. "I have been enjoying the novelty of Inverley very much, though I thought to see you and your sisters at more events these days."

Caroline snapped her attention away from temptation and back to the matter at hand. "We intended to be. But we were turned away at the assembly rooms last week. Miss Linfield, Miss Balfour—I invited you here because I wish to know you both better. But I also thought you might be trusted to give me an honest recounting of what people are saying about myself and my family, so I can be prepared for the worst."

It was their turn for the bathing machine, and in an excited flurry they were escorted by an attendant down the shore where two sturdy draft horses waited. They were hitched to a tall wooden structure with four sturdy walls, two windows, and not much inside except for two narrow benches—just enough space for the four of them and the two dippers who accompanied them.

"Does Inverley not have any scandal papers?" Miss Balfour asked once they had settled in, tucking elbows in against each other in a comfortable sort of squeeze.

"There's no need," explained Arabella. She was seated snug against Caroline, who was in a fever of awareness from the curve of her hip and thigh that pressed along her own. "Word of mouth is more effective at getting the news out long before a gossip rag could ever be typeset."

The bathing machine lurched forward, the horses pulling it steadily into the sea. "What is the worst they are saying about us?" Caroline asked, pitching her voice over the noisy churn of water from the huge wheels.

"Are you sure you wish to hear?" Miss Linfield asked, darting a look at the dippers.

Caroline smiled. "Mrs. Green and Mrs. Harris know my sisters as well as I do."

"Aye, that we do," said Mrs. Harris. "I've known Betsy and Susan since they were wee nippers, and Jacob has been known to hang about my Alice from time to time. Suppose he has no such time for her now."

Miss Balfour leaned in. "Well, if you must know… I was at the assembly last week, and the tale of your fortune was on everyone's lips." She hesitated. "The word of mouth is that excepting its eldest member, the Reeve family is droll—but vulgar."

Caroline let out a sound of dismay, and Mrs. Green patted her knee. "There, there."

"Well, at least *you* weren't called vulgar," Arabella comforted Caroline.

"I also was left out of *droll*," she said, and was surprised at how much it stung. "Am I so cheerless?"

The bathing machine continued to lumber along, her stomach pitching worse than if they were on a boat. Echoes of Betsy's accusations sounded in her head. *No emotion. No heart.* Was that what the whole town thought of her?

"You aren't cheerless at all." Arabella took her hand. "You are a delight and a credit to your family."

Her hand was warm and soft, and Caroline stroked her thumb against her palm. Arabella was such a dear—always present, always comfortable.

"Who will excuse our vulgarity? Are there *any* prospective suitors for my sisters among the visitors who are here?"

Miss Linfield considered the matter as she adjusted her bathing cap. "There are a few eligible gentlemen that have been introduced to my charge so far. Perhaps Mr. Smith would do for one of your sisters? He is an easygoing man, likes to fish. But Lady Edith considered him rather dull. Forgive me, if your sisters truly are vulgar, I am not sure how high you can aim," she said apologetically. "I don't imagine any of the titled gentlemen may do."

"My sisters are more high-spirited than anything," Caroline said firmly. "They are good girls at heart. This gentleman might do for Susan. But who for Betsy? She's the one I worry about. She has grown frightfully ambitious, talking about how she will be the one to make the most advantageous match of the summer. I cannot tell if it is fancy or not."

"Mr. Worthington is newly arrived in town. Again, he isn't titled, but he is very respectable. A widower, with two children."

Caroline felt Arabella stiffen as straight as a board, but when she glanced over, she was staring out the tiny window at the sea. Her jaw was set and she was scowling. Perhaps she was nervous now that they were approaching the dipping.

Miss Balfour tapped her finger against her chin. "Your Mr. Taylor is handsome," she said. "Mightn't any of you consider him?"

"I would expect he needs to marry more money than any of us have as a dowry, given that he has been disinherited by Jacob," Caroline admitted, feeling a pang of guilt. But it was an interesting prospect. If they could trust him, and she had to admit that he had shown no evidence to the contrary, then he would be a fine suitor for Susan. That wasn't a bad plan at all.

"What about Mr. James Martin?" Miss Balfour asked.

Miss Linfield bit her lip. "If I may, I would like to stake a claim—my mission from Lady Edith's mother is to see her engaged to Mr. Martin by the end of the summer."

"Better her than my sisters," Caroline said with feeling. "I have the unfortunate impression that he would court me if I gave him any encouragement. But worry not, Miss Linfield. I do not hold him in any sort of esteem."

"Well, he has a brother, hasn't he? Maybe he would do instead?"

"And don't forget my Alice for Jacob now, mind," Mrs. Harris said with a wink at Caroline.

"All this talk of gentlemen is tiresome," Arabella cried, startling Caroline, "when there is *nature* all about us!"

They stopped, and Mrs. Harris opened the door to reveal the sea swirling around them. She dropped a ladder into its depths but simply leapt out herself, followed by Mrs. Green. "Come now, ladies. Two at a time for the dipping."

Miss Balfour gave Caroline a little push. "You invited us, so you get the pleasure of going first."

Miss Linfield nodded, her face pale. "Yes, do show us how it's done, Miss Reeve."

Caroline looked at Arabella. "Shall we?"

They drew off their wrappers, and Caroline saw Arabella's lush figure in her bathing dress before she disappeared into the water. The sea was gloriously cool, splashing up to Caroline's breastbone and

Arabella's neck. Arabella had left her spectacles back at the bathing house with her day clothes, and her eyes were larger than ever without the glass over them. Her eyelashes glittered with sea spray. She was giggling with Mrs. Green as she was tipped back and under, shaking her head after she emerged and blinking the water from her eyes.

She was gorgeous in her unfettered joy.

Caroline wanted to be the one to hold her like that. She wanted her own arms around Arabella's waist, with nothing but ocean all around them and pleasure on their minds.

But it was a bad idea. Arabella was too dear to her. And even if she were not her best friend, she would *still* be off limits. Caroline could never afford the blow to her reputation if her desires were discovered.

If her sisters were considered vulgar because of their wild flirtations, what would people think of *her* if they discovered her true inclinations?

Mrs. Harris put a strong hand on her shoulder. "Time to be dipped, if you're ready," she said, and Caroline allowed herself to be led down under the salty water, the coolness reaching between every finger and toe and strand of hair, deep in a world where sound was dimmed and feeling was heightened and only this very moment existed. She was raised up and out at the moment that her lungs were wanting air—Mrs. Harris had been doing this for many years—and was dipped several more times before she and Arabella climbed back into the carriage and Miss Balfour and Miss Linfield took their turns.

"People think us vulgar?" Caroline asked as they settled themselves, watching Miss Balfour throw herself into the dipper's arms, laughing uncontrollably, which made Miss Linfield relax and laugh too.

Miss Linfield came up from her dip, sniveling a little, eyes wide, hair escaping from her cap.

"I may have heard the same," Arabella admitted, shifting on the bench. "I hope you are successful to get a sponsor from Mr. Taylor's family."

"All I wish is for Betsy and Susan to get their feet wet in the shallows of Inverley society, where things are safe enough if they misbehave, before we remove to London."

"London?" Arabella said sharply.

"Jacob is set on it, and none of the family wishes to be apart right now."

❖

Arabella had lost all pleasure in the morning.

Before the dipping, the day had been full of laughter, and she had been delighted with the new friendship of Miss Balfour and Miss Linfield. She had nestled beside Caroline in the bathing machine and enjoyed the closeness of her body.

But then Miss Linfield had mentioned Mr. Worthington in her list of suitors. It hadn't been a name she had expected to hear.

Now all four of them were in the bathing machine with Mrs. Harris and Mrs. Green, rumbling and splashing their way back to the sandy shore, and Arabella was aware of every discomfort that had seemed a mere trifle before.

Her eyes ached without her spectacles and her blurred vision frustrated her.

Her back throbbed against the unyielding wood bench with every movement of the horses.

Her temples pounded with the laughter and chatter that surrounded her, along with the creaks and groans of the wheels, and the water slapping up against the machine.

Instead of the fresh sea air, her nose was now filled with the odor of damp wood and horseflesh.

"This has been such a delight!" Miss Linfield announced, her face shining, her earlier apprehension having dissipated. "I cannot believe I had the nerve to do such a thing. I must recommend it to Lady Edith. There is *nothing* quite so invigorating, is there?"

"I commend your bravery, dear Miss Linfield. Shall we prolong the pleasure and have tea in the charming little shop next door?" Miss Balfour asked.

Oh no. No, Arabella wanted nothing more than to leave this outing behind her.

"We would love to," Caroline announced for both of them.

Arabella was more comfortable after being toweled dry at the bathing house, and dressed again in her soft cotton shift and cambric day dress, her spectacles once again putting the world to rights all around her.

She still would have preferred seeking her bedchamber and cuddling Shelley and Byron to soothe her, because far beyond the pain in her temples was the ache in her heart.

Their kisses obviously had been nothing to Caroline, for her to speak so casually of London. When had she set her sights on the capital?

The tea shop next to the bathing house was dainty and delicate. Floral paper covered the walls, and there were flowers and lace everywhere one looked. It was picturesque enough that Arabella's paintings of it always sold very well.

It was nothing like the neighborhood bakery that Arabella preferred to frequent, where she was accustomed to picking up the daily bread for the Seton household and the occasional addition of chocolate biscuits for the Reeve boys.

As they were settling into a table near the window, a deep voice spoke. "It is my luck to see such a bevy of beautiful young ladies, sitting together as pretty as a painting."

Arabella dropped her reticule on the floor.

Mr. Worthington.

It was not every day that one's past caught up with one.

Especially not in the form of one's former fiancé.

CHAPTER EIGHT

Mr. Worthington looked as well as ever. Little details showed the passage of years—the cut of his hair, the style of his sideburns—but his eyes were as serious as ever, and his manner of dress remained neat and practical instead of fashionable. She had worried for so many years that she would see him again, but that worry had long faded over time. It made the shock even greater now, when she least expected to see him.

He must have read the silent appeal in her eyes, for he hesitated, then bowed to them as a group without acknowledging Arabella.

"I am Mr. Worthington and would be pleased to make your acquaintance. If I may be so bold, I believe I may know who you are already—you are the talk of Inverley, Miss Reeve."

It was gauche to have introduced himself, and he had the grace to look embarrassed. Arabella realized he must have expected her to greet him and introduce him to her friends, but she was fixed in place as if made of stone, her tongue locked.

Caroline's smile didn't reach her eyes. "Thank you, sir. If you may excuse us, I am in the midst of a private conversation with my friends."

"Of course. Do forgive me." Instead of returning to his table, he settled his hat on his head and walked out the door.

"How very odd," Caroline said.

Miss Linfield frowned. "He is one of the gentlemen I mentioned to you as a prospective suitor—Mr. Worthington, the widower."

"Well, I thought his manner strange. The way he had stared at us! It was most peculiar. If he had not taken the hint, I daresay I would have started to go on about the best home remedies for one's menses."

"If you had, you would surely have earned your rightful position among your sisters as vulgar," Arabella told her, unable to stop laughing. She was trembling with relief now that Mr. Worthington had left.

Whatever was he doing in Inverley?

Miss Balfour snorted. "That would have been inspired, Miss Reeve. Though I would like to know your remedy, if you have one. I suffer dreadfully, you know."

"All I can suggest is a hot compress and a strong cup of tea," Caroline said apologetically.

"I am grateful that I am a mere lady's companion," Miss Linfield said. "I never need to find a reason to fend off male attention. Quite beneath any gentleman's notice."

"I never *escape* their notice," Miss Balfour said. "It is tedious in the extreme. You know, perhaps we may be able to help each other."

"I would appreciate your help with my sisters," Caroline said.

"I am sure Lady Edith would be delighted to meet Betsy and Susan," Miss Linfield said. "They can be assured of a friendly welcome when they do make it to the assembly rooms. Lady Edith would find your sisters' reputation to be dashing."

"Are you sure you do not have any desire to be courted or wedded yourself, Miss Reeve?" Miss Balfour asked.

"None at all."

"Then why do we not agree to come to each other's rescue when faced with such burdensome interactions? You said you were planning to be at more social events, did you not?"

"I will be attending many of the same," Arabella said. "If the Reeves are there, then I wish nothing more than to support them."

The idea of mixing more often in society filled her with dread. She had never been popular and hated the idea of seeing James sneer at her in public. She also quaked at the thought of seeing Mr. Worthington again.

But she would do anything for Caroline.

Miss Balfour studied them for a moment before speaking. "If I can trust you not to fawn over every handsome face that comes into a room, then I shall be sure to ensconce myself beside you at every opportunity. That way I could be assured of a sensible evening. There is nothing more annoying than a swooning miss in one's midst when one is trying to hold a reasonable conversation."

Arabella smiled. "I hereby promise that if I ever see an earl making calf eyes at you from across the assembly rooms, I shall put a halt to his attraction by tripping you into the buffet."

They all laughed.

Miss Linfield leaned in. "I promise that if I ever see a handsome man pestering any of you for a dance, I shall come over and make such dull conversation that he shall fall asleep." She nodded. "Men hate it when women talk about science, for example. I have dissuaded several unsuitable young men from my charge with this tactic."

Caroline smiled. "Are we all such dedicated spinsters here?"

Miss Balfour nodded. "If I may be frank—I much prefer the company of women. In *all* manners of speaking."

Miss Linfield poured her another cup of tea, a serene smile on her face. "Indeed, I believe we share the same inclination. It is a lovely thing to be among friends who properly understand one another, is it not?"

Arabella froze. Could this mean what she thought it might? Could these women be like *her*?

Caroline gaped at them, but she also leaned forward, her eyes bright.

Miss Balfour said, "I do think you catch my meaning, Miss Linfield. Now, if we are to be friends, I insist on being comfortable. Please can we agree to address each other by our given names?"

And in no more than the moment it took to add a splash of milk to a cup of tea, Miss Balfour became Maeve and Miss Linfield was Grace.

Arabella felt much better as tea was served than she had upon exiting the sea. Maybe it was the hot brew warming her from the inside—but maybe it was the warmth of friendship that settled over her like a cozy blanket.

Maybe society need not be so terrifying.

Maybe with the right people by her side, it could even be…fun.

She peeked at Caroline, who was talking to Grace and gesturing with a cucumber sandwich in hand, and her heart swelled.

It could be more than fun.

If only she had the courage to reach for what she wanted.

And if only Mr. Worthington could leave well enough alone.

❖

"The militia have returned to the barracks across town," Betsy announced with a dramatic flounce into an armchair in the drawing room. "The militia, Caro! Even you must be delighted."

"Oh?" Caroline slipped the page she had been writing on under a book. She had been making a list of prospective suitors for her sisters. Given the lack of red-coated gentlemen on it, Betsy wasn't going to be receptive to her suggestions.

"You may have turned your nose up at the local boys that courted me before we inherited, but the chance to have an *officer* as a husband! This shall be the making of us all." She propped her chin on her hand and gazed out the window that overlooked the street, clearly dreaming of strong arms and chiseled jaws and marching drills.

"The militia have been stationed outside of Inverley for three years."

"Yes, but they have been away on training for months, and Susan and I have missed them so. Do you not see what a grand opportunity this is for us all—including you?"

"I have told you time and again that I am not interested in soldiers. I am not interested in marrying. At least not until every last Reeve is well settled, and Will and George have years ahead of them before that happy occasion." The last thing Caroline wanted was for it to be bandied about town that she was too proud of her new station to consider their local militia. That was nowhere near the truth of why she never wished to wed.

She thought of Maeve and Grace and Arabella, and her mind reeled again at what they had tacitly revealed at the tea shop yesterday. Did they all truly share the same reason for spinsterhood?

"Why must you be so stodgy?"

"I'm not stodgy. I'm responsible."

"Caro Lamb would have been best pleased with an officer," Betsy muttered.

"For the last time—you are not to base your life on a woman whose main goal is to ruin herself over a poet. Why do you even wish to be like her?"

"I wish you were like her," she snapped. "Then you would understand me."

"I want to understand," Caroline said softly. "Tell me what you need me to know."

Betsy had always been difficult, and Caroline had never known best how to handle her. All too often, she thought of the dreadful fever that had taken their parents, and had almost taken Betsy too. She had been ill for days after their parents died, lying there wan and listless. The doctor that they could hardly afford had told them to prepare for the worst. Her pale face had haunted Caroline's nightmares for years afterward. But maybe she had indulged her too much over the years. Maybe if she had been stricter, Betsy would be better behaved.

Her heart ached. All she wanted was for her brothers and sisters to be happy.

Betsy rose from the chair and paced about the room. "Caro Lamb understands passion. There is nothing in the world so grand as love, and she grasps at it with both hands and refuses to let go. She's an inspiration!"

"She's a married woman who had an ill-advised affair with Lord Byron, who now scorns her affections at every turn. Where is the happiness in that?"

"Love is more important than reputation."

"Luckily for you, you can have both," Caroline said. "You need not ruin yourself to prove that you have a love for the ages. You simply must marry after finding the right man." She hesitated, but decided it was best to be frank with her sister. "I have heard that people are calling the Reeve family *vulgar*. Do you have any idea why rumor mongers may be calling us so?"

Betsy crossed her arms over her chest and narrowed her eyes. "If anything dire should happen—and I am confessing to *nothing*—then I could run off to Gretna Green with my lover, and the papers would be all agog at our grand romance. It would be wonderful. There are far worse things than common vulgarity."

Caroline wanted to weep. Her little sister, caught up in a situation that she knew far too little about. "But what if he is a scoundrel who leaves you before taking you to the altar?"

"Then I shall be considered notorious and fascinating forevermore, and invited to dine out on tales of my heartbreak." She shook her head. "But these are rumors. I have done no more than kissing, Caro. I swear."

"You have the chance at a decent match if you don't throw away your name."

"I wish my name to be associated with more than being a girl from Inverley who did nothing of interest and sat out every dance not pre-approved by her older sister."

Caroline snorted. "You have been reading far too many novels."

"Well, if marriage is so worthwhile, why aren't *you* snapping up any of the men who look your way?"

"I told you—"

"Stuff and nonsense!" Betsy cried. "You know perfectly well that with our new circumstances, you need not be so *involved* in order to make good on your promise to take care of us all. We are all grown now, except for Will and George. And if you are worried about a suitor not wanting the boys underfoot, they will soon be sent to Eton and not a bother to anyone except on holidays."

Panic clutched at Caroline's heart. Did her siblings feel like they didn't need her anymore? "I have no plans to marry. But I want to see you and Susan as respectably wedded as can be, and I wish to help Jacob settle into his new responsibilities as best I can."

"What makes for a *respectable* union?" Betsy rolled her eyes. "It sounds dull. What do you consider to be the ideal for such a suitor?"

She thought for a moment. "It should be someone dependable. Reliable. Someone who makes you laugh. Someone who understands you, and wishes to do nice things for you, and who treats you well. Someone who looks at you like you're the only one in the room."

Caroline stopped short, the hairs on the back of her neck tingling. It sounded an awful lot like Arabella.

Betsy sighed. "That sounds bearable, as long as he has dashing good looks and a fine sense of iambic pentameter. You cannot expect me to wed a man without literary sensibility."

"There is more to life than poetry."

"You say you want to be there for us—but you just want to meddle. If you thought so highly of marriage, you would do it yourself and leave us well enough alone," Betsy snapped before she stormed up the stairs.

Marrying might solve all of her problems. It would give her a partner to help raise her brothers, and if she chose the right man, it would give them better standing in society which could help her sisters find better husbands. Guilt roiled in her belly, but she knew she couldn't do it. Not even for the family.

Besides, she didn't want to rely on someone else. She had managed well enough this far, and she would see her duty completed on her own. As she had vowed to her parents.

The next morning, Mr. Taylor strode into the parlor, his color high beneath his starched collar. "I see, Miss Reeve, that you have taken matters into your own hands."

Caroline set down her pen, in the middle of making a list of what they needed from the draper, as well as a strict note to the modiste instructing her to ignore every plea that her sisters were sure to make for a high hemline. "I beg your pardon?"

"My aunt, Lady Margaret, has arrived in Inverley this afternoon. She claims to have always wished to try the waters of Inverley—and is asking me what on earth is this mysterious missive that she received from a distant cousin that she knows nothing about?" His tone was cool. He stood in the doorway, as she had not invited him to sit, nor was she inclined to if he had decided to visit her in a temper.

Caroline had taken Arabella's advice and had written to several ladies whose names she found in the family Bible, but she had received no letters in return. It was most interesting that one of them had decided to come to Inverley straightaway. "Why hadn't she heard of us? Did you not tell anyone in the family about us?"

"I wished to spare you," he said, his cheeks reddening. "At least until you settled into your new life. I thought it would be overwhelming to have a gaggle of Reeve relations swarming around Inverley, as feckless as your own branch."

She laughed. "Are we all cut from the same cloth?"

"Every last one of us is born and bred from trouble." Mr. Taylor grinned at her, his temper dissipating. "All except for you and I, of course. We are the sensible members, are we not?"

"And yet you are but a Reeve by distant association."

"Well, Lady Margaret is here now, so you shall all have to meet her." He frowned.

"Is she truly unsuitable as a sponsor?" Caroline asked. "I apologize for writing to her without telling you—but we do need someone to help us."

"I would describe her as the terror of a thousand debutante balls."

She was impressed. "Is she so fearsome?"

"You may judge for yourself at half past three when you call on her today. She will be expecting you in the tea shop next to the hotel."

As it turned out, Lady Margaret was far from fearsome.

She was an elderly woman with short grey curls, her skirts in last century's fashions, and her cheeks reddened with poorly matched rouge. But her eyes were bright and curious, and from the moment Caroline ushered Betsy and Susan into the tea shop, she was all smiles and laughter, delighted to meet them and roundly telling off her nephew for failing to introduce them sooner.

She dithered over ordering her tea, harumphing over the fact that the waiter may *say* it was the same brew to which she was accustomed—but one never knew anything for sure when one traveled, after all, and it mightn't be the same whatsoever. How was one ever to tell? A nice green tea was suitable for the afternoon, if not too hot. But then again, not too cold either, as she told the waiter severely, beckoning him back as he had started to leave, not too cold at all!

"We are so pleased you decided to visit us in Inverley, Lady Margaret," Caroline said once everyone had a dish of tea in front of them. "You are wonderfully strong to brave the journey from Somerset." She bit her lip. Had she known Lady Margaret's age, she would never have suggested that she be their sponsor. "I hope you will not trouble yourself to think of London on our behalf, with its late hours. We would not dream of inconveniencing you."

"Oh, but I know everyone, my dear. And I do so love London. It has been years since I've been to the city. Certain nephews seem inclined to coop up their relations," she said, rapping her fan in front of Mr. Taylor's teacup, "but there is nothing I love more than enjoying a glass of ratafia while watching the young people dance. This will all be great fun!"

Betsy urged a biscuit on Lady Margaret. "Did my sister mention that there are *officers* in town, ma'am?" she asked, her voice as sweet as the sugar that Lady Margaret liberally laced into her teacup.

She gasped. "Officers! Why, my dear—there could be no greater honor than to be a military wife. We shall see you settled at once!"

Betsy grinned at Caroline. "I should like nothing more, ma'am. I shall be ever so diligent in following your instruction."

"*My* instruction!" She laughed. "You young things shall be teaching me a thing or two, I do not doubt it! It is always the way."

"You may be able to see why I told you that none of our relations were suitable," Mr. Taylor murmured to Caroline as he refreshed her cup.

She glanced at Lady Margaret, who was in raptures with Susan about the latest bonnet styles, and how sensible it was to buy up as much ribbon as one could get one's hands on if the color was right.

"She is nice," Caroline said, loath to admit that he had been right—again. The evidence was all in his favor. She would have to tell Arabella that their suspicions about Mr. Taylor had no merit to them. When she looked back at all he had done for them, his counsel had always been sound, and he had been nothing but kind and accommodating.

If he was the honorable gentleman that he appeared to be, then she should consider him as a potential suitor for one of her sisters, even though he had shown no partiality toward either of them. There was still plenty of summer ahead for feelings to develop.

"Do not mistake me. There is no one kinder than Aunt Margaret. She does know everyone, and is accepted everywhere. Doors would open to her that would otherwise be closed to you and your family. In many ways, she would be an ideal sponsor. But as to the other half of the coin which you are chasing, as a *chaperone*…"

Lady Margaret was patting Betsy's hand and assuring her that she would do all in her power to see her wedded this very summer. "In my day, you know, we didn't scruple at the means! The end result was quite good enough for us. I do believe I can get a man trussed up to the altar faster than my Peggy can pluck a goose for Sunday dinner."

Mr. Taylor sighed and moved closer to Caroline. "I call her the terror of a thousand debutante balls not because she is awful. But because she will stop at nothing to see a match go through. And I mean nothing," he said grimly, his voice now so low that it was difficult to hear him. "Mamas despair of her methods, but daughters all love her when all is said and done and they have a ring on their finger—even if they had their skirts over their ears to get it."

"There's nothing better than a suitor with a sizeable pocketbook," Lady Margaret was telling Betsy, "and an even bigger—"

"Caro, didn't you say we may go shopping?" Susan called out, her face bright. "May we go tomorrow with Lady Margaret?"

"I am afraid we already made a commitment to visit the modiste with Miss Balfour," she said, which was a bald-faced lie. She hoped Maeve would prove agreeable, as the girls seemed to be in awe that a woman of such fashion would accompany them.

"Nicely done," Mr. Taylor murmured with a smile.

She frowned at him. "I can't imagine what you mean," she said as she gathered up her sisters and sailed out the door.

How was she ever to launch her sisters with a chaperone like this?

CHAPTER NINE

The fog was a reliable presence in Inverley. It rolled from the sea into town in the dark hours of earliest morning, once every fortnight. Sometimes it was no more than a damp chill swirling around one's ankles and it dissipated by dawn. Other times it was so thick that it was difficult to see to the end of the street, and it overstayed its welcome through the day.

It happened a good deal more often than the brochure writers were wont to admit, as the evidence of fog negated their claims of a good healthful seaside air. Arabella presumed the visitors to be tucked up in their hotel rooms and manor houses and rented townhouses, playing desultory hands of cards by candlelight and tsking over the promises they were sold of a beatific summer seaside town.

What visitors were not doing on foggy days was purchasing seascapes from her brother's front parlor.

Arabella lugged the hinged sign proclaiming *ART FOR SALE* inside, the painted wood slick under her fingers, and propped it beneath the pegs for bonnets and cloaks. Matthew was generous to give her the use of the front parlor every morning to sell her art. The room had a big window that she could throw open and sit at with her easel to entice people inside.

There was a knock on the door, and she whirled around to see Mr. Worthington enter the parlor. He took off his hat and shook the water from it before tucking it beneath his arm and bowing.

Arabella's heart leapt into her throat faster than Shelley jumping to the windowsill. The blood rushed to her head and she felt a moment's dizziness. She supposed it had been too much to dream that maybe she wouldn't see him again.

"Forgive me for calling unannounced, Miss Seton. I took your direction from the woman working in the tea shop where we met. She told me that you sell your artwork here."

He came no closer, which she appreciated, and instead stood there by the cloaks.

"I sell my paintings here every morning, but I've closed up for the day," she said, pointing to the sign that she had brought inside. "It's too wet to welcome visitors."

"Am I simply a visitor?" he asked. "I thought perhaps I might be considered a friend."

Once upon a time Mr. Worthington had indeed been a friend. He was also the finest painter she had ever met, creating sprawling historical canvases that were displayed all over Bath. She had been in awe of his talent, and swept up by his charm and good looks, and had ignored every nagging thought that she would not relish his touch if she were to accept his hand in marriage.

Oh, how young she had once been. Nineteen and away from Inverley for the first time in her life, on a year-long visit with her aunt and uncle.

Emotion closed up her throat. For a moment, she wished that Rachel or Matthew were home, and she could insist on shielding herself with family, but perhaps it was better this way. She had never told them about Mr. Worthington, and she would be hard-pressed to explain his presence in the parlor. It was beyond scandalous to entertain a gentleman behind closed doors. But she longed to delay the discussion that he seemed determined to have, and wished nothing more than to avoid this wretched awkwardness that had her wanting to wring her hands.

"I am surprised to hear you say it," Arabella said finally. "After all, the last time we spoke was when I broke off our engagement." She swallowed. "It was not well done of me."

"A lady has the prerogative to change her mind."

Arabella remembered calling on Mr. Worthington the day after she had permitted certain liberties. They had enjoyed an unexpected half hour of privacy after he had escorted her home from a dance, and his attentions had been kind, thoughtful, and welcomed. He hadn't known that the reason she encouraged his touch was because she had needed proof that it could erase the desire for Caroline's.

It had done nothing of the sort. Instead, it had confirmed that her passions would never be for a man.

The next day, she had paid him a scant five-minute call to tell him that their engagement was over, and the day after that, she had returned to Inverley.

"I owe you an apology, Miss Seton. I should never have subjected you to such treatment. You deserved the sanctity of the marriage bed, and I was presumptuous in the extreme. I cannot fault you for ending things."

"I do not blame you in the least," she said, which was entirely true.

His smile was rueful. "I hope that eight years has lessened the sting for you as much as it has for me. Without the loss of you, I would never have gained the hand of my dear Lucy nor had the joy of my two daughters."

"Lucy?"

"Ah. You knew her as Miss Smith, if you may remember. I am sad to say that I am a widower of five years now."

Miss Smith had been a sweet girl that Arabella had often sat next to at church. "I am sorry to hear of your loss," she said.

"Thank you. My daughters were devastated, and so was I." He frowned down at his hat.

Arabella sighed. There was no putting it off. She welcomed him into the parlor, but he declined to take her offer of tea. She hoped it meant that his visit would be short.

"Why are you here?" she asked.

"My doctor recommended Inverley after a bout of lung infection this past winter. I certainly don't mean to make things awkward for you. So much time has passed that I didn't even recall that you were from this part of England. When I saw you in the tea shop, I thought I should pay my respects, but you looked so horrified when I approached. I tried not to single you out for attention."

"None of my friends know that I was once engaged," she said. Especially not Caroline. Her tales of her long-ago year in Bath with her aunt and uncle had been light and silly, focusing on mishaps at private balls or tripping over one's hem.

She hadn't told anyone about secret kisses that failed to stir her heart. She had been lucky that no one had found out her indiscretion because she would never have been able to bear marrying, even had she been caught. Her name would have been ruined.

She had lived with that fear for years after returning to Inverley. Every letter from her aunt and uncle in Bath would send her into a panic, and it was a long time before she accepted that her secret was safe.

"Is this your art?" He gestured at the table spread with her paintings. "I remember you showing me your sketchbooks in Bath, but I had never seen your paintings. They are fine."

Heat crept up her throat. *Fine.* Arabella remembered when her aunt and uncle had brought her to London for a week that long ago summer, when Mr. Worthington's work had been accepted to the Royal Academy. They hadn't known about the engagement, but they had known she admired his work, and they had thought a trip to London was a treat for a girl who had never been to the capital.

She had stared up at his work in awe. They had earned well-deserved praise from everyone walking through the Royal Academy, where his work was hung at eye level amid the hundreds of paintings on display. She could still remember the vividity of color, the bold brushstrokes that lifted off the canvas, the emotion, the composition. The brilliance.

And this man said her local watercolor seascapes were *fine*.

"I am proud of them," was all she said, struggling not to sound defensive.

"As well you should be. I must take my leave of you, Miss Seton. I do hope my presence here will not cause you undo distress. May I have leave to claim acquaintanceship the next time we chance upon each other?"

It was nicely done. She felt churlish at the thought of refusing, so she nodded. "Are you here for long?" she blurted out.

"I have not yet decided. I am renting rooms for several weeks, but if the air is agreeable then I may extend my stay."

Arabella balled her hands into fists and went outside after Mr. Worthington left. With fog swirling as opaque as walls, it felt private in the garden. Like the world had dwindled to nothing but herself and the crash of the waves.

In many ways, she worried her world *had* dwindled.

Her life in Inverley was the same as always. The same views, the same paintings. Her year in Bath had been a whirlwind of a different life, but it was so long ago that it almost felt like it had happened to another person, and it had brought her no more happiness than she found here in Inverley.

Being confronted with Mr. Worthington again was bringing all of her old dreams to the fore.

Dreams of finding something that belonged to *herself.* Dreams of finding someone else to love, someone to cut the desperate ties that she had to Caroline, whom she knew she could never have. It hadn't worked, so she had tucked away most of her other dreams.

Dreams of marriage.

Family of her own.

A *home* of her own.

The swing was wet, but she brushed the worst of it away with the edge of her hand and sat down, not caring if the damp overtook her skirts and soaked her to the skin. The metal was cold beneath her palm as she gripped the chain and pushed the swing with her foot.

The very best part of a heavy fog was that it was easy to cry and hide the evidence of it. She let the tears mix with the droplets on her cheeks, blurring her vision as they collected on her eyelashes, and she let her head drop to rest against her hand on the chain.

She felt the emptiness of the house next door like a hollow ache in her chest.

No more Reeve children shrieking and playing in their garden and tumbling their way into her own, grabbing for Shelley and Byron, clambering over the swing and hollering their successes over their siblings.

No more chats with Susan and Betsy, commiserating over their beaux and looking over the new ribbons that they had always been so excited to show her.

No more nightly talks with Caroline, with glasses of elderberry wine in hand.

She hadn't wanted things to change.

But the change wasn't all bad, was it? Arabella stilled the swing. After all, there had been one very interesting and *very* welcome development since the Reeves had inherited.

Kissing.

Frequent, charming little kisses that she and Caroline were finding as easy to exchange as currency.

Delightful kisses, stirring up her heart.

They had never had *that* before.

And kissing had never felt like that in Bath with Mr. Worthington.

An idea swirled in her head like the fog creeping up her skirts. She wanted Caroline. And she wanted all her old dreams. Why settle for the opportunity to exchange kisses when she craved so much more? Why not *try* something?

The conversation that they had in the tea shop with Grace and Maeve had been revelatory. It had opened the door to opportunity that she had never thought she would have.

This was going to be risky. But the prize was suddenly tantalizing.

Determination settled over her like a suit of armor.

Or at the very least like a chain mail chemise.

She pushed away from the swing and raced up to the attic. Realizing that her dress was wet, she yanked it over her head and wrapped her chemise-clad body in a shawl that she kept folded at her desk. Shivering, she pushed her spectacles up her nose and thudded her sketchbook open to a fresh blank page.

The Rules of Pursuing an Heiress.

Arabella stared down at the spiky black words that flowed from her pen. Did she *dare*? She was just a shy spinster with a reticule full of ginger comfits. Bearer of sweets and library books, not wedding rings.

But she had read plenty of novels. She had seen friends fall in love and get married and move away. She had heard romantic stories of visitors whose gallant suitors proposed to them on the beach or on the bluffs. Her own year in Bath had ended in an engagement.

She should know *exactly* what to do to secure Caroline's affections.

A frisson of delight shivered up her spine as she thought of courting Caroline. Wooing. Pursuing. Why not become her suitor in truth? Or—better yet—her *suitress*?

The very idea was shocking. But oh, so tempting. All she needed was to find the confidence to reach for what she wanted. A lifetime of shyness hadn't earned her the life that she yearned for. If she wished to gain something different, she needed to screw up all the courage that she could muster in order to seize the moment.

She tapped her pen against the page and thought about how gentlemen pursued ladies. Could she not do the same?

She wished there was a guidebook she could consult on how to do the thing correctly, and wondered how gentlemen got their best advice. Probably from other gentlemen at the clubs. Arabella didn't have access to such things.

She knew that it wouldn't work at all if she followed the advice for a woman to pursue a gentleman. Why, Caroline would find it ridiculous in the extreme if she should feign a sprain and have to be carried into the Reeves' townhouse, fainting and sighing away and encouraging tender solicitations.

She certainly couldn't drop her handkerchief in the street and expect Caroline to pick it up with any hint of romance—she would be laughed at for her carelessness if she tried such a thing.

Simpering over her every conversation and agreeing with her every word would cause Caroline to wonder if she had become ill.

She thought some more, then decided to begin with the basics.

Rule 1. Be charming, attentive, and ever present.

That was easy enough. Inverley was tiny, and she had already promised to be at any social event that Caroline attended.

Rule 2. Bring gifts during at home hours.

She could always find an excuse to drop by the Reeve house, whether it was visitor's hours or not. As for gifts…well, that might be harder, now that Caroline could buy anything she needed. But she was certain she could think of something.

Rule 3. Dancing.

Her throat tightened, knowing it was something they could never share together. She lost herself in imagination for a moment, her hand on Caroline's hip, her other hand clasped in hers, music playing and eyes only for each other.

However, if they couldn't manage to dance together, there was plenty to do at an assembly where dancing occurred. Fetching wine. Plying her with a fan. Perhaps sneaking a liberty or two beneath the starlight.

Rule 4. Take her for a stroll or a carriage ride.

The best she could manage there would be to rent a donkey on the beach or to rent out the bathing machines again, so she scratched that part out. At least Inverley offered plenty of walking opportunities.

Arabella considered other ideas. But she was no writer of either poetry or love letters, preferring to read instead. Feats of bravery or prowess were out of the question with her shyness.

But she thought that her list was a good beginning.

She closed the book and let her thoughts run wild. Her shawl dipped low over her shoulder, and she pulled it back up, imagining it was Caroline's attentive touch, and she sighed.

If Caroline was open to the same sort of desires that she had, then the reward could be rich indeed.

CHAPTER TEN

The next two weeks were a whirlwind.

Lady Margaret may have proven to be a ditherer and a gossiper. But she also proved to be a source of encouragement that Caroline hadn't anticipated. Every morning, Mr. Taylor walked Lady Margaret to the townhouse where she beamed at Betsy and Susan through etiquette lessons and advice on decorum, all the while rhapsodizing about the men they could expect to have on their knees by the end of the tedium. It was more than enough to make both girls behave.

They learned the different depths of curtsies appropriate to rank, which spoon to use for soup, and how best to stifle a sneeze in company.

Dresses and shoes and fripperies were delivered in droves, to the extent that Susan's bedchamber resembled nothing more than a shop than a bedchamber. Clothing was piled high on every available surface and bulging from the wardrobe. Caroline sought out Susan and Betsy, who were arguing in the back parlor over the correct address for a duke in the admittedly long odds that one might appear in Inverley and be smitten with one of them.

"Susan, what is happening in your bedchamber?" Caroline asked.

Susan grinned. "Isn't it wonderful? Our wardrobe shall be the envy of all."

"But your room is now so filled with everything from fans to umbrellas that you have nowhere to lay your head at night."

She shrugged. "Betsy and I shared a room together at the old house, and we decided we could make do again here. After all, the rooms here are ever so much bigger. It's well worth it to have the extra storage for our fine things."

"You'll never have time to wear them all."

"Yes, we will," Betsy said indignantly. She poured the contents of her reticule onto the table. "Look at all of our subscription tokens." She picked up a handful and let the stamped metal circles and crisp printed cards slip through her fingers. "We have enough for a full summer's worth of entertainments—the lending library, the music hall, the theater, and the promenade. I calculated how many events we could possibly squeeze in, and purchased a change of outfits for each one."

"One outfit *per event?*" Caroline reeled at the expense.

"I think I was quite frugal, if anything. Why have money if not to spend it?"

Caroline had no reply to that.

Lady Margaret launched an impressive siege on the master of ceremonies. She insisted on visiting Mr. Singh every afternoon, Caroline by her side, as she waxed eloquent about all the improvements she saw in the Reeves since her arrival. Her conversation heavily featured the many illustrious lords and ladies she had met over her decades of socializing in London. Caroline was impressed by her dedication to link the Reeve family to greatness, even though she wasn't sure she believed half the tales.

At first, Mr. Singh remained firm in his decision. After a week of persistent petitioning, however, he relented.

"I should be happy to welcome the family to *one* assembly," he said. He sighed. "If I may say so, I would be hard-pressed to deny entry to the talk of Inverley at this point. Everyone has been asking after the Reeves."

Caroline tried not to feel intimidated now that the wheels were in motion. There was no turning back now. After they returned home after receiving the much-coveted approval, she asked Lady Margaret, "Do we have a chance? The whole town knows we are nothing more than the Reeve family of Belvoir Lane."

Lady Margaret patted her hand. "People will buy anything you wish to sell them, my dear. Especially if it entertains them. And a nobody becoming a somebody is *always* high entertainment. You have nothing to worry about."

The evening of the assembly was welcomed with great reverence in the Reeve household. Betsy insisted on speaking in nothing but whispers all day, for fear of straining her voice before she had a chance to wear it out by talking and laughing all night. Susan selected and discarded no fewer than five outfits. Even Jacob was more animated than his customary air of ennui allowed, as he practiced the quadrille with Betsy up and down the hallway.

Caroline stared at herself at the mirror as her new maid Lucille trussed her hair into tight ringlets wound around tiny white flowers and seed pearls.

"It's all the rage, miss," Lucille assured her, when Caroline mentioned that it wasn't the most comfortable hairstyle she had ever worn. "You can't think of the pain and the trouble. You must focus on how very grand you look!"

Caroline supposed she did look grand. She hadn't purchased the amount of clothing that either Betsy or Susan had, but her evening dress was new and made from the most beautiful fabric she had ever worn. Lucille draped an amethyst necklace around her neck, the stones small and dangling from fine loops of silver chain.

Unlike the rest of her ensemble, this wasn't new.

The necklace had been her mother's.

She was almost breathless as Lucille fastened the clasp, reluctant to have someone else touch the precious heirloom. It was almost certainly worthless in terms of the money it would fetch, but it had value beyond diamonds to her.

Oh, that her mother and father could see them now. Their daughters and their son dressed in finery, with coffers filled beyond their wildest imagination. How her father would have laughed! How her mother would have been proud.

Caroline swallowed. For them, she would make sure the evening was a success. She had sworn to see her siblings settled, and she would reach as high as she dared in society in their honor. She needed to be in control tonight, no matter what.

For all her years in Inverley, she had never set foot in the assembly rooms, and she was delighted to see how fine it looked inside. It was spacious, with swaths of white curtains at the open windows, and crystal chandeliers dangling from the ceiling, and an inlaid wooden floor that was so shiny that it was a wonder that no one ever slipped while dancing.

Caroline's plans to shepherd her siblings about the room and gain introductions to the best that Inverley had to offer were wrested from her in an instant.

Lady Margaret propelled Betsy and Susan with remarkable speed toward a group of militiamen, claiming that they ought not waste a minute when officers could be dancing attendance on them instead of on other ladies.

Jacob and Mr. Taylor ambled toward a group of men who seemed ready to abscond to the cardroom.

Caroline felt the sting of betrayal. She brushed her thumb over the amethyst hanging at her throat. Maybe her family didn't need her to take care of them anymore. Maybe they would have been fine all along without her trying to watch over them so closely. Maybe she had overestimated her importance.

For an instant, she contemplated running for the door.

Then she saw Arabella.

Adorable, reliable, sweet Arabella.

She had her nose in a cup of wine and was talking to Grace and Maeve. Her dress was the same one that Caroline had seen her wear on countless occasions over the years, but it was no less charming for being well-worn. It hugged her bosom and clung to her hips in a way that always made her forget how to breathe for an instant.

Caroline loved how Arabella spoke with her whole body, using every inch of herself to paint a picture with word and gesture as precisely as she applied her brush to paper. Watching Arabella made her feel calmer, and she paused to look her fill before making her way over to her.

She must have hesitated a fraction too long, however, because suddenly everywhere she turned she saw a male chest. A half dozen men swarmed near her.

"May I fetch you a glass of orgeat, Miss Reeve?"

"You look ever so beautiful tonight—may I tell you that your complexion is a credit to the fine sea air?"

"Are you free to dance? Miss Reeve, has any man been lucky enough to claim your hand for the first set?"

It was impossible to tell who said what, as they jostled for position around her.

Caroline frowned. "My two sisters, Betsy and Susan, are here at the assembly rooms as well," she said. "I am merely accompanying them tonight. I would love to have the pleasure of introducing them to you." She strained her neck to try to peer around the wall of shoulders, searching the crowd for her sisters.

"So modest! Miss Reeve, you are elegance personified with the humbleness of a saint."

She wondered if the master of ceremonies would take it amiss if she stepped on a few toes. Accidentally, of course. "I assure you, gentlemen, I am not the one you are looking for—"

One of them grasped her hand and kissed it, tugging her forward enough that she lost her balance. "Such pretty manners! Come, Miss Reeve, the dance floor beckons!" He urged her forward, and, in a daze, she followed him. "Your sisters are stars, Miss Reeve. But stars are but pale imitations of the sun, which I now dare to hold in my arms."

"That turn of phrase would be most pleasing to my sister Betsy. She adores poetry."

"I hope such a preference runs in your family."

"I share it not," she said firmly.

"There you are, Caroline!" Arabella popped up beside them and grabbed her arm. "I do apologize for interrupting, Lord Hanbury, but I must have Miss Reeve's opinion on something important. Please do come with me."

Caroline allowed herself to be pulled away to where Grace and Maeve awaited, giving a sympathetic smile over her shoulder to the man who had tried to dance with her.

Maeve held up her glass. "The true enjoyment of the night is not the dancing, but the fact that they do not serve watered down wine here."

"I might say the same if I could boast of my own glass," Caroline said. "Arabella, thank you so much for rescuing me." She gave in to impulse and swept her into a tight hug, burying her face in her honey brown curls before taking a safe step back. It was too dangerous to stand so close to her, when all she wanted was to give her a kiss to properly thank her.

"You are well deserving of a glass of wine. I shall go fetch one for you." Arabella disappeared into the crowd.

"Arabella is a good friend to you," Maeve said, sipping her wine. "Very devoted."

"Arabella and I have been the best of friends for years. Decades, even." Did Maeve guess at the intimacies in which they had engaged? What surprised her was that she longed to say something. To be seen, and heard, to give voice to her desires.

Grace sighed. "It must be wonderful. I left my family to go into service early in life, and have been a companion or a chaperone for so many years that I doubt any of my childhood friends would recognize me."

"I don't know what I would do without Arabella."

It was the bone-deep truth.

She paused, not wanting to examine that thought too much.

They were grown women, nearing thirty, and sworn spinsters. They shouldn't be a danger to anyone—especially not each other.

Except Caroline wasn't so sure about that.

Arabella felt dangerous indeed these days.

Dangerous. And delicious.

Maybe those kisses meant more than something silly and fun between friends. Maybe Arabella felt the pull between them the same as she did.

Her skin felt like it was sizzling, and she plied her fan.

All she knew was that she was willing to find out more.

❖

There was a crowd around Arabella as she waited in the refreshment area for a glass of wine to bring back to Caroline. So far, her plan was working better than she could have hoped. She had performed her first task as a suitress by rescuing her lady from the perils of an unwanted dance, and now she was well on her way to completing her second task of procuring refreshment.

She had even earned a hug for her efforts. The evening could not be more perfect.

Arabella rose to her toes, annoyed that she was too short to see around the room. She pushed her spectacles up and moved around a tall gentleman to be rewarded with the sight that she was seeking.

Caroline was still standing with Maeve and Grace, and oh— how she sparkled. Somehow Arabella hadn't expected it, being long accustomed to seeing her in her old evening attire, which had boasted little embellishment. But tonight, Caroline sparkled from the jeweled pins tucked in her hair to the cluster of beads on the swell of her bodice, down to the pearls gleaming from the scalloped hem of her skirt and the crystals embedded in her dancing slippers.

She sparkled from head to toe, but no jewel could compare to the brightness of her eyes.

Arabella didn't care about London lace or French fripperies. Caroline was the prettiest woman in the assembly rooms and had more elegance and grace in her little finger than most of these other women had in their whole bodies.

The attendant gave her a glass of wine. Arabella turned toward the room and bumped into Mr. Worthington.

"Miss Seton, what a pleasure it is to see you."

Her pleasure in the evening dimmed, and she struggled to keep a smile on her face. "I hope you are enjoying yourself, Mr. Worthington."

"Might I have the pleasure of a dance?"

"I do not think it wise." Dancing would draw attention to their acquaintanceship, and she didn't want to explain to anyone how she knew him.

"Not even for old time's sake?" He smiled at her, and she remembered the good times that they had enjoyed. He was a wonderful conversationalist, and they had talked for hours about art and music. She had felt very worldly during her year in Bath. It was altogether too odd to see him in provincial Inverley.

"I am afraid not, sir."

"I hope I can convince you at another time, then. I would be happy to rekindle the friendship what we once had."

"Perhaps." She sipped the wine, wishing for nothing more than to flee.

"I thought I ought not rank myself too poorly and give up just yet." He smiled. "I hope you would not begrudge me my efforts?"

Arabella bit her lip, then shook her head before taking her leave of him.

Drat her cursed shyness. She knew she should have said no right away, but it was so much easier to let things happen and to handle the consequences later. He mightn't be in Inverley long enough for her to see him again anyway, so what was the harm in allowing him to believe that she would say yes to a dance?

Her face burned. The last time she had tried that with Mr. Worthington, she had allowed things to go much too far before finally saying no.

She needed to work on being less passive.

A suitress wasn't passive. She needed to have confidence. Like Caroline did. Caroline was the strongest person she knew, determined to do right by her family no matter the circumstance that they found themselves in. She would do better to follow her example.

But she had to admit that the extra wine also helped, so she took another healthy gulp before she made her way back to her friends.

She thrust the half-empty glass at Caroline. "I'm sorry, I was woolgathering and forgot myself."

Caroline laughed as she accepted it. "This isn't the first wineglass we've shared together of an evening."

"You deserve better now, to match your new finery," Arabella teased her. "Soon you shall have a snooty London maid and you shall flounce around your new townhouse forgetting about your old ways and your wardrobe of fustian and twice-turned-up hems."

Caroline's smile was rueful. "My London maid started this morning, in fact. She was the one who persuaded me into this hairstyle."

Caroline might be a confirmed spinster, but she was gaining as much attention as her younger sisters, if not more—after all, Betsy and Susan were as silly at a ball as they were anywhere else.

Caroline no doubt would be giving them a scold when they returned home.

But for now—well, was it not enough to simply enjoy the magic?

James strolled up to them, and Arabella bit back the sound of dread that crawled up her throat. All of the well-to-do were here, and he probably missed the indulgences of London more than most.

"Caroline, you have never been in finer bloom. I swear, you grow lovelier each time I see you," James announced, picking up her limp hand and bringing it to his lips. He smirked at Arabella. "We can see who the *belle* of the ball is, can we not, *Arabella*? It is not in the name, to be sure."

"Leave off," Caroline snapped. "Why must you be so odious?"

He shook his head. "Here is how I can tell that you are newly arrived to your fortune and to your elevated station. Your sense of wit is not yet refined to town ways. Worry not—I can guide you to a better understanding of your position."

He edged his way between Caroline and Arabella.

"If these are town ways, I need no guide as I want no part of them."

"And if she did need one, then perhaps I would be better placed to offer my services." Mr. Taylor appeared as if conjured by magic, broad-shouldered and tall, his face somehow full of patronizing warmth as he looked down his nose at James. "Miss Reeve is my dear cousin and I owe her all the support and guidance in the world."

Arabella supposed she should feel gratitude to anyone who delivered a set-down to James, but all she felt was annoyance. What was Mr. Taylor doing here?

Whisking Caroline away for a dance, apparently. In no time, she was on his arm and he was leading her to the floor, talking to her in earnest.

James sniffed. "Your bosom friend would be better off with me, you know."

Unwillingly, she leaned in. "Why? What news do you have of Mr. Taylor?"

He shrugged. "What news does anyone need when one can tell everything by the cut of his coat and the style of his hair? Anyone with that low of a collar in such high society is not to be trusted."

"Sartorial displeasure does not replace news."

"You know, if you had more looks or fortune, the two of us could have rubbed along quite well together," he said thoughtfully, grinning at her. "You have more spirit than one might give you credit for at first."

Arabella grimaced. "No, we would not have. I remember your poor behavior over the years all too well."

She was surprised that the words came to her so easily tonight. How many years had she wished for the courage to snap back at him when he was being awful to her? This suitressing business was working wonders for her.

He laughed. "Boyish high spirits, nothing more, Miss Seton. Though I confess, Caroline's peerless beauty is what has captured my heart. Imagine a match with my fortune and her pretty face. Compelling, is it not?" He winked and left.

Arabella lost herself in thought, watching Caroline spinning around the room with Mr. Taylor.

Maeve touched her arm. "You are pining," she pronounced.

Arabella was startled. "I beg your pardon! I am doing no such thing."

"Are you not? Your eyes tell a different story. Has no one ever told you that it is unwise to wear one's heart on one's sleeve? It makes it rather difficult to hide one's inclinations in such a situation."

She forced herself to laugh. "Is it no wonder that I should look at the dancing with such longing—me, who hasn't been asked a single time all night?"

"Ah, so you are pining over no one in particular, is that so?"

"Exactly so." It was a bold-faced lie.

"I thought you weren't interested in marrying?"

"A dance is no declaration of matrimony. And you told me that you also have no interest in men, yet I saw you twirling as merrily as anyone else earlier."

"Very true." She smiled. "I apologize, I did not mean to pry. Forgive me, Arabella, I am too accustomed to speaking my mind." She paused. "Please know that you are always welcome to do the same with me. I am a true friend to any who share our persuasions, and I am an excellent confidante."

Arabella's gaze sharpened as the man who had tried to dance with Caroline earlier was now escorting her onto the terrace. "Thank you, but I must go," she said to Maeve, and then pushed her way toward the terrace in unfashionable haste.

Once outside, she spotted them easily. Lord Hanbury had cornered Caroline against the balustrade, speaking to her with far too many gesticulations. Her arms were crossed over her chest as she leaned away from him.

Arabella rapped her fan on his shoulder and he sprang away from Caroline.

"I say, what is the meaning of this! Oh, Miss Seton again, is it?"

"Yes." Lord Hanbury was a middle-aged man who frequented Inverley every summer and who purchased a painting every year for his mother, and she liked him apart from his current predilection for the woman that she wanted to become her lover. "You have my dear friend's attention, but I am afraid I have need of her, my lord."

"I was explaining to Miss Reeve all the charms of my estate in Suffolk. A great many sheep, you know—important to explain the provenance of such a noble creature—very possible that Miss Reeve might have a particularly vested interested now, you see—"

"Unfortunately, all I see is that I have rent my hem, and I need dear Miss Reeve to come to my aid. Please do let us be off to the retiring room."

She grabbed Caroline's hand, and they rushed away up the narrow stairs. Caroline burst out laughing as they entered the empty retiring room. "That was well done of you, Bell. You came to my rescue yet again."

Pride swarmed over her. She had done it. Maybe it wasn't so hard after all to be confident. "I took our pact in the tea shop seriously. I intend to honor it."

"No gentlemen allowed," Caroline said happily. "I should be delighted to embroider it on my reticule for the world to see."

Caroline glanced around, then pulled her in for a kiss. Arabella's toes curled inside her evening shoes and she wrapped her arms around her neck, wanting to hold her close forever. She hadn't danced a step but her thighs trembled as if she had spent the whole night whirling across the assembly room. Caroline's lips were soft but the hand on her lower back was firm and possessive, and it flooded her with warmth. She angled her head back as Caroline trailed a series of kisses across her lips and down to her jaw.

"That was a thank-you sort of kiss," Caroline said after they pulled apart. "For services rendered."

Arabella was delighted.

More kissing.

Suitressing had been the very best idea she had ever had.

CHAPTER ELEVEN

Their new townhouse probably wasn't large by London standards, but to Caroline it felt cavernous. Everything was strange. There were new servants living in the attic, and more staff than she had ever had to manage before. There were new routines to get used to.

Dinnertime pouting, however, hadn't seemed to change a whit with their new location.

Will scowled into his pudding. "It isn't home," he muttered, stabbing his spoon into his jam roly-poly. He always had a complaint about something when he was overtired, and it had been an exhausting month for all of them.

"It's home now, darling," she said.

But it didn't feel like home to her, either. Where were the mended cloaks hanging from the hook in the hallway and billowing in the breeze of the open door? Now their cloaks were all shut away in cupboards without a patch to be seen. There was no sprawl of George's toys, or errant bonnets on the side table, or a thousand other things that she never had the time to put away, but which had made the old house feel comfortable.

"I miss where we were *before*." Will's voice was plaintive.

"Tell me what you miss most about it, and I shall see if I can rectify it."

Caroline had packed up his tin soldiers herself, and his favorite sticks for throwing in the sea, and his collection of seashells and stones from the sandy shores. What else could a boy of ten years be missing?

"I miss Shelley." His lip jutted out. "And Byron."

Truth be told, she missed them herself, much as she had always complained to Arabella about Shelley sneaking around on market day. "I could arrange for us to have a kitten."

"Don't want a kitten. I want Shelley and Byron!" His voice raised in a petulant whine.

"Let's take a walk to town tomorrow and visit Bell. You know wherever she is, Byron at least is sure to follow."

Arabella. That was what *she* missed most about the old house. Her constant presence, popping in as often as Shelley had.

The next day was sunny, and Caroline was happy to see the wood sign outside of Arabella's house which meant that she was selling her paintings. A couple of visitors were gathered in her parlor, their dresses bright and fashionable, murmuring over Arabella's array of watercolors.

Caroline stepped into the room, everything suddenly dim as her eyes adjusted from the bright sun, and she grinned at Arabella from across the room. Arabella's answering smile filled her with joy.

"Hi, Bell," Will announced as he streaked past her, doubtless in search of the big wooden swing with the hope that the cats were snoozing in the back garden.

The pair of visitors were occupied looking over the seascapes.

Caroline strolled over and peered at them too. "The colors are marvelous, are they not?"

"And the composition is most striking." One of them started to flip through the paintings and stopped when they saw the widow's gothic mansion. "How intriguing."

"The house must be haunted," Caroline said. "Look at those spires. Can you not imagine a ghost or two wandering around them in the moonlight?"

"Miss Reeve has a very active imagination." Arabella glared at her.

"That does sound interesting," one of them said. "I love it. It will look wonderful in my sitting room." She paid for the painting and the pair left.

"You can't just tell people the manor is haunted, you know." Arabella started to tidy the pile of paintings, putting them back into order.

"It sells more paintings," Caroline said, shrugging.

"I don't want my work to sell based on sensationalism. I want them to sell because they're good art." She was staring down at her work, her shoulders hunched up, and Caroline was surprised to see how upset she was.

"I'm sorry, Bell. I thought the whole point was to generate income."

"Yes, that's the goal. But I want my work to *matter*."

Caroline felt a jolt of uncertainty. How had she missed how much her painting meant to Arabella? She had always known her to be passionate about her art. How many times had she lain in the grass on the bluffs and stared up at the sky while Arabella stabbed her brush at her easel, back in their childhood days?

But she had thought now that Arabella was an adult, the paintings were a simple means to an end.

"You're right. It does matter," Caroline said quietly. "Your work is excellent." She meant it. She had always loved looking at Arabella's paintings.

"Any accomplished young lady can do as much, if not more." Her voice was stiff, and she was still gazing down at the thick paper instead of looking at Caroline, so she knew she had made a grave error. "It's not like proper art. Like oil paintings."

Caroline glanced out the window to make sure that no visitors were on their way in, then stepped over to Arabella and took her hands in her own, reveling in her touch despite the barrier of their gloves. "Your work is full of charm and spirit and color. When I look at the seascapes, it's like I'm standing right there at the shore. And most importantly —what you do makes people *happy*. Did you see the look on that woman's face when she purchased the painting? She was full of joy. You're a wonderful artist."

She grasped Arabella's face in her hands, slowly stroking her thumbs along her cheeks, then dipped her head down and kissed her. There was desire in the way that they moved against each other—she felt the heat of it in her blood, and the urgency between her thighs—but there was so much more. Caroline felt the sweetness of it flood through her body. Behind the touch of their lips lay the years of caring for each other, the knowledge of each other at their core.

Caroline broke away. "That was an apology kiss. Between friends. All the rage in…um, France."

Any excuse would do at this point, no matter how silly or how thinly veiled. But they were going to have to do something about this. And soon.

Arabella squeezed her hands, then pulled away, pink flooding her cheeks.

"Were you on a morning walk through town?" she asked, busying herself again with making sure the room was neat and tidy for the next round of visitors.

"Will missed the cats," Caroline confessed, relieved that they weren't looking so intensely at one another.

Arabella laughed, and the tension in her shoulders eased. "Shelley has been meowing in your garden every morning, looking for you all."

Will came in, carrying Shelley close to his chest.

Arabella smiled at him. "Would you like to bring Shelley on a nice long visit to your new home to help you get settled in?"

Caroline started. It was a generous gesture. But then why was she surprised? It was typical of Arabella to be so kind.

"Won't he miss Byron?" Will asked, but his eyes were big and shining and he clutched Shelley tighter.

Arabella shook her head. "If he doesn't like it with you, then he is always welcome to come back here. After all, your sisters named the cats, and they have belonged almost as much to your household as they have mine over the years."

"Thank you," Caroline said as they got ready to leave. She tried to put all of the meaning into it that she could, but words didn't seem like enough, so she squeezed her hand and hoped that could help convey the depth of her gratitude.

"It's a big adjustment for them, isn't it?" Arabella asked softly. "For Jacob and the girls, it's a madcap adventure and a dream come true. But for Will and George, it's the upheaval of all they've known."

How was it that Arabella saw it so clearly, when Caroline was struggling to make sense of it all?

But she was always a sensitive soul. Arabella was always there to help, always ready with a kind word or action. It had taken her time away from being her neighbor to realize how precious that was.

She was quiet on the walk back to the townhouse, Will chattering her ear off as he held the wicker basket which contained the plaintively meowling cat.

When they arrived at the townhouse, all was in total pandemonium. Two wagons were outside, a burly man was demanding payment from one of her footmen, and Caroline could hear arguing from the open front door.

Inside the house, Susan squealed when she saw Shelley streak out of the basket. She nabbed him and nuzzled her face into his orange fur. "My favorite poet," she crooned. "Oh, Caroline, how wonderful!"

"What's going on?" Caroline demanded.

"George has managed to have a spot of fun, is all."

Caroline sprinted to the parlor where most of the noise was coming from.

George was beaming at a table laden with every sort of sweet imaginable.

"Young Master George bought out the bakery," Miss Anderson, the new governess, intoned from the corner. Her face was pinched and pale.

The table heaved under piles of boiled sweets and frosted cakes and quivering jellies and latticed fruit pies. Long loaves of bread stuck out of baskets, and mounds of buns were heaped high on plates. There were clever sugar sculptures and ribbons of bright candy. It was an explosion of color and fanciful shapes everywhere Caroline set her eyes

Will gasped and threw himself at his brother, hugging him tight. "This is miraculous!" he cried, and grabbed a fistful of cake.

The aroma of sugar, cocoa, and jam was overpowering in the small parlor, even with the window opened. Several interested sparrows hopped on the windowsill, waiting for an opportunity to snatch up breadcrumbs, and Shelley crouched low, tail twitching as he watched the birds.

George was steadily making his way through the pile, taking a bite of a pie here and sucking on a candy there, his entire front sticky. He was either oblivious to the trouble he was in or trying to make sure he had his fill before finding out what punishment awaited him.

Miss Anderson was wringing her hands. "We stopped in for a licorice twist—a *single* licorice twist, mind you, as Master George had been so good with his lessons today—and then the young master strode up to the baker, calm as you please, and said he would take the whole lot! The baker could *not* be stopped once he started packing everything up—he said he was perfectly aware of the Reeve fortune and was more than happy to guarantee all his sales in one fell swoop for the day, so he packed up everything into wagons and even carried some of it over himself. That's him outside now, demanding payment. He was overjoyed, miss, saying he was going to close up shop for a few days and take a little holiday."

She looked as if she might faint.

The boys continued to feast, smeared with powdered sugar and cream and chocolate.

"You cannot eat any more," Caroline snapped, pulling Will and George away from the table. "You shall be sick. This was a terrible use of money, George Reeve. Other people must do without while you stuff yourself senseless and leave the balance to rot! What were you *thinking*?"

His eyes were wild, torn between the table that was the culmination of all his boyhood dreams, and Caroline's face. "I wasn't," he confessed. "But, Caro, we can afford it! Easily! Jacob is always saying how much money we have. Betsy and Susan bought enough clothes for a dozen people. Why can't I spend any of the money?"

"Because you are a child, and it is my responsibility to buy you all that you need." She thought of what Arabella had said about the boys, and how everything had changed for them overnight with little understanding of what it all meant. She gentled her tone. "You know that I will always take care of you, and I provide you with reasonable treats on occasion. But this is not *reasonable*, George. It's wasteful. So much of this food will not be enjoyed by anyone now. The money is gone, and so will the food be, so who is the winner here?"

His eyes filled with tears. "I'm sorry," he said, his voice low and trembly, but she heard it all the same. She passed a hand over his hair, rumpling it. He was still so young.

"Now, you are to go to your room." She called for Maisie, who, like the rest of the servants, was hovering just beyond the parlor, and told her to give both boys a good scrubbing to rid them of all traces of sugar and flour.

She bit her lip, then thrust a note at the fascinated footman hovering at the door. "Please take this to Mr. Singh and tell him that we shall be happy to provide the assembly rooms with a feast tonight."

Miss Anderson gripped her arm as she passed by to follow Maisie. "You may wish to pay a visit to the toy shop too, miss."

Lord above, it never ended. As long as there was a Reeve in the house, trouble was soon to be found.

Caroline sighed, then shook her head as she strode outside to settle the payment with the baker.

❖

Arabella stabbed at the paper with her brush, slashing a violet swath over the waves. She was hunched over her table in the attic, working on a series of storm paintings. She knew from experience that the drama of the wind-tossed waves and threatening clouds would sell well. She was lucky that Inverley showed to advantage in every type of weather, whether the ocean was tranquil or heaving.

The past few weeks had seen a steady stream of sales. It promised to be a profitable summer, but she still wasn't sure that she would have enough at the end of it to purchase the cottage that she dreamed about. If she didn't give so much of it to Matthew every month, she thought she might have enough but those thoughts were uncharitable. He and Rachel provided so much to her, and contributing to the household in return was fair.

Arabella felt at loose ends as she finished up her painting and set it aside to dry. When the Reeves had lived next door, there was always something to do. If she wasn't painting or helping Rachel, then she would wander over to the Reeve household and occupy herself there. Caroline always appreciated her company, whether they were doing chores together or walking to town on an errand or brewing up a cup of tea for a comfortable chat.

She hadn't understood the hole that their absence would leave in her life, even though the Reeves had moved but a half mile away.

But there was more to her life than painting and neighbors, wasn't there? Her day didn't have to feel empty if she couldn't spend the rest of her afternoon next door.

In fact, there was something important that she had meant to find out more about.

Ever since the day in the tea shop with Maeve, Grace, and Caroline, Arabella had been fascinated about the idea that she might not be the only one in Inverley who fancied other ladies. Maeve had certainly seemed to notice Arabella's interest in Caroline at the assembly rooms last week.

The idea of putting anything into words terrified her. And yet, she had found the courage to pursue Caroline in earnest, and she had even found the words to stand up to James at the assembly rooms. She should be able to find the courage to confess her feelings to a friend.

The rooms Maeve was renting with her mother were located a few streets from Caroline's new townhouse, and were not in the first state of fashion. It surprised Arabella when she knocked on the door and waited for the maid to bring her outside for a walk, because Maeve was one of the most fashionable women she had ever seen in Inverley.

"My mother fancies that a sea air is healthful, but a *direct* sea air is ill advised by her doctor. She didn't dare choose anything too close to the water itself, though she enjoys bathing every day," Maeve explained as she left the house with Arabella. "The lodgings around here were snatched up so fast that we had the devil of a time settling on a precise location."

Maeve's walking dress was a fine muslin the color of amber and was very fetching on her. As they walked to the beach, Arabella admired it. How much easier it would be if she had been smitten with Maeve upon seeing her at the Martins' card party!

But she had made her decision to follow her heart, as complicated as it was proving to be.

"Thank you for agreeing on such short notice to go walking together," Arabella said. "I am looking forward to getting to know you better."

Maeve laughed. "Are you? I thought you were more inclined to stay close to your old friendships. One in particular, if I may be so bold."

Arabella was glad that she was short enough to duck her head and hide her blushes under the cover of her bonnet. "It is bold indeed," she said, her voice hardly above a whisper.

"Then why are you squeaking like a little mouse? I promise, Arabella, your confidences are safe with me."

The beach was long and there was plenty of room to walk, but it wasn't private. There were a few dozen people strolling on the sand, a dozen more eating pies and nuts near the vendors' stalls. A swarm of children shrieked their way up to their knees in the water. Arabella guided Maeve away from the crowd, along a shady cove and past a group of boulders, to a spot of sand where she and Caroline had enjoyed many quiet conversations together.

"We can unroll our stockings here without any concern of the gentlemen seeing us," Arabella said, and slid off her shoes and stockings. "No one ever comes here."

"I certainly don't wish the gentlemen about," Maeve said cheerfully.

They stood together as the waves lapped at their ankles. Arabella wiggled her toes in the sand and tried to find the courage to say the words that she felt in her heart. They were so loud inside of her that she felt sure Maeve could hear them anyway.

"I fancy Caroline," Arabella blurted out

It was only three words, but the enormity of them dizzied her.

Maeve grinned. "I rather thought you did. I love being right. Does she fancy you back?"

"I'm not sure." She thought about their last kiss. "Perhaps. At least a little."

"Are you going to do something about it?"

"I'm trying to."

Arabella explained her suitress plan, which had Maeve doubled over in peals of laughter. Her delight made it easier for Arabella to speak. There was no censure here, just easy acceptance and support.

Arabella hadn't realized how lovely it would feel to confide in a friend. She had never thought anyone would listen to such ideas without turning their back on her, and it meant more than she could say to know that Maeve was as trustworthy as she had claimed to be.

"I swear, Inverley is the most diverting place I could imagine," Maeve said, wiping tears from her eyes. "This is wonderful. Well done, Arabella. So what is your next step?"

Arabella kicked her foot into the froth of an oncoming wave, splashing water onto her skirt. "Next step?"

"Well, you've established that you wanted more kisses, and you've received more kisses. What are you going to do now?"

Arabella slowly exhaled. "I hadn't thought about it." Her dreams had revolved around indulging in the moment. Thoughts of the future and where kissing might lead to were frankly rather terrifying.

"Have you talked to her about how you feel, or about what you want?"

"No! I couldn't."

"Maybe you should try it. You need to look out for your own heart, after all. Make sure she values you as much as you value her. If you want more than kisses, then you should be open with her."

"But what if I lose her?" The idea was devastating.

"What kind of relationship do you want? One where you give everything and follow her lead? Or do you want something truly equal, where you are both partners?"

A relationship. Partners. That sounded like heaven.

"I don't know. I sought to win her affections—but didn't think through what it would mean apart from the physical side of things."

"You are more than a suitress. You're her best friend. Hopefully the two of you will work this out and become lovers. But if you say nothing, how will you ever get there?"

Arabella nodded. "You're right. I need to talk to her."

The idea filled her with trepidation, but she reminded herself to be brave. There was no other way to reach for her dreams.

CHAPTER TWELVE

The curricle in front of the townhouse was canary yellow and polished to a glossy shine. Caroline knew nothing of horses, but even she could see that the pair of bays hitched to the curricle were perfectly matched, down to the stars on their foreheads and their white forelocks. She and Susan were making their way home after visiting the shoemaker, and Susan cried out in delight and rushed down the street to see the horses up close.

A group of young bucks that Caroline didn't recognize surrounded Jacob, slapping him on the back, their congratulations so loud that she could hear it up the street. Her heart sank, but then she noticed he was having words with Mr. Taylor, who looked a good deal more reasonable than his mischief-making friends.

"Wherever did you purchase such a rig?" Caroline asked. "Or such horses? Surely not in Inverley!"

"Of course not in Inverley," Jacob said. "These fine fellows took me to London on a lark yesterday on the mail coach, and I came back today equipped like the gentleman that I am."

An exhausting journey, but not impossible for a young man burning up with ambition.

"London?"

"Is it not natural that a baronet might make use of a curricle?" he asked in injured tones. His friends added agreeable voices to his own, nodding and swearing up and down that it was true.

Caroline exchanged a look with Mr. Taylor.

"I was saying to this young buck that he has no stables for such beasts."

"Maybe I ought to be away to London in it again, then." He darted a look at Mr. Taylor. Caroline's heart ached to see the desperate ploy for attention from his hero, which he was trying to hide under a poorly constructed arrogant mien. "It could fit two."

"You shall remain in Inverley until it is time for you to be in London," Mr. Taylor said. "Or until your sister gives you leave. You still have much to learn from your tutors here."

Jacob thrust the reins at a footman. "Being a bloody baronet isn't much fun then, is it?"

"Watch your tongue, Jacob Reeve," Caroline snapped.

"I've heard worse," Susan piped up.

Caroline didn't even wish to ask where. She turned to the footman. "Would you be so good as to drive the curricle to Martin House and to ask them to please keep it for the meantime while we make arrangements?" She hated to be indebted to the Martins, but they were the only ones that she knew had stables to spare. Drat Jacob and his foolish impulses. "This is the height of folly," she said to him.

"It wasn't that expensive," Jacob muttered, before rattling off a sum that made her head spin. "On the curricle alone," he clarified. "The horses were a fair bit more, but one *must* have horses!"

"*If* one can feed and keep them!"

"You are rushing into things, young cub." Mr. Taylor slapped his gloves against his palm. "You are but twenty-one and have your whole life ahead of you. You must learn to think before you act. These rash purchases might gain you accolades and a round of drinks at the tavern with the lads, but it doesn't suit your new station. You need to be wise."

Jacob scowled at the pavement. "Yes, sir."

"Into the house with you both," Caroline told Jacob and Susan. Two of Jacob's friends followed them, and the rest tipped their hats and sauntered toward town, no doubt in search of less tame entertainment than a house call.

"Thank you for speaking some sense to Jacob," she said to Mr. Taylor once they were alone.

"Of course. I feel a sense of responsibility to your family, which I do not take lightly. After all, I am the one who brought all of this to you with your new situation. Jacob is family now."

"I appreciate it. Thank you." She hesitated, hating to ask anything from anyone. But Mr. Taylor had proven time and again that he was trustworthy. "Please could I ask a favor? If you could keep an eye on Jacob—he is young and spirited, but he could get into trouble with the wrong influences."

"Anything for a Reeve," he said, and followed her into the house.

Betsy was already holding court in the parlor with Lady Margaret and the pair of Jacob's friends. Also seated with them was Lord Hanbury, who Caroline recognized from the assembly rooms. A bouquet of fresh roses was set on the mantel, no doubt courtesy of one of the bucks, and a box of sweets was opened on the table amidst half-empty cups of tea.

Caroline realized by the censure in Lady Margaret's eyes that their at-home hour was already half gone. It was hard to remember that there were particular hours for receiving visitors, so accustomed she was to people coming by her house as needed.

Susan snatched up a chocolate nonpareil and squeezed next to Betsy on the sofa, enthralled by the attention of the men before them.

"I was charmed to have the opportunity to dance with you at the assembly last week, Miss Reeve." Lord Hanbury adjusted his cravat.

She darted a glance at Lady Margaret. It wouldn't do to mention in front of their sponsor that Arabella had cut the dance short, almost before it had even begun. "It was a pleasure, my lord. Have you had the opportunity to dance with either of my sisters? Susan is so accomplished at the quadrille."

Susan, in fact, was a disaster on the dance floor, but was so cheerful about it that gentlemen seemed to overlook her missteps.

"I am sure she must be, with such a fine example of a sister to look up to."

She wanted to roll her eyes, but Lady Margaret was making encouraging gestures and nodding at her, so she managed to smile.

"Miss Reeve is a lovely dancer," Lady Margaret said, reaching over and patting Caroline's hand. "She is a fine example of any sort of accomplishment you could imagine."

That was an even worse fib than the one Caroline had told about Susan. She could see why Mr. Taylor hadn't considered his aunt to be the best choice as a sponsor, given that her lies were so thin.

Mr. Taylor smiled. "There is no finer accomplishment than good sense, and Miss Reeve certainly has it in spades."

Caroline considered having a maid fetch the headache powder for her throbbing temples, but instead a footman arrived and said the very thing that was guaranteed to help her to feel better. "Miss Seton is here, ma'am."

Arabella wandered into the room. She hesitated when she saw the crowd already gathered in the parlor, but she held her chin high and approached Caroline. "I brought flowers," she said, thrusting a bunch of daisies at her.

Caroline's heart clutched. She knew where they grew. How many afternoons had she sprawled on the hill with Arabella when they were ten, plucking petals to tell their fortunes, and making flower chains so they could crown each other?

One of Jacob's friends sneered. "One hates to contradict a lady, but those may be better classified as weeds, are they not?"

"I picked them on the way here," she said, her voice calm.

"They're charming," Caroline said firmly. "In fact, daisies are my favorite flower."

"They have a sort of rustic appeal," the man said. "But nothing like the hothouse roses I procured for you."

The roses were showy. Betsy had already plucked one and wore it in her hair.

"There is nothing more breathtaking than a cultivated rose from the greenhouse," Lady Margaret announced, shooting a hard look at Caroline.

"I am more of a wildflower type," Caroline said.

"We spinsters are known to have unusual tastes," Arabella said.

Lord Hanbury spluttered. "Miss Reeve is hardly a spinster—barely past the first blush of youth—why, I never—"

"It's true, in fact," Caroline said. "I have long considered myself a spinster. Perhaps that is why I prefer a hardy wildflower to a delicate bloom." She grinned at Arabella.

A maid brought a vase to the parlor, and Arabella arranged the bouquet of daisies with as much as care as if they were the rarest flower in England instead of the most common.

Caroline felt better than she had all day. She had missed Arabella's frequent presence in her home, popping over with comfits and books, sitting down with the boys and listening to them talk about the different slugs they had found in the garden that morning. She missed telling Arabella everything and hearing her calm advice and soothing words. She wished nothing more than to pull her into the other parlor and tell her all about Jacob's foolishness with the curricle, but then again, she couldn't bear for Arabella to realize how out-of-control her siblings had become. It didn't reflect well on her.

"I have something else for you," Arabella said, and held up her reticule. "I went to the lending library today."

"You brought me a book?"

"It is Wednesday, is it not? Of course I have a new book for you."

Caroline drew it out of Arabella's reticule and flipped it open. It was a romance, which wasn't an unusual choice, but the way Arabella looked…She was the picture of innocence, her eyes wide behind her spectacles. That face was incapable of hiding a lie, and she could tell there was a plan churning around in that charming mind of hers.

"Meet me at the bluffs," Arabella said. "Tomorrow at noon."

How could she say no?

❖

The next day, Arabella was early and walked the cliffs alone, waiting for Caroline. She tried to breathe deeply to calm herself down—after all, if Inverley's sea breezes were the healthful cure-all that the brochures claimed, then surely they could help calm her nerves?

It was time to admit to herself that her plan to woo Caroline was incomplete.

There had been more kissing, but Maeve had been right. She needed to think about what she wanted *after* the wooing was successful.

Her breath caught when she saw Caroline walking toward her.

"You're not drawing today?" Caroline asked when she reached her.

She had often invited Caroline to sit with her while she painted, but that wasn't why she had asked her here this afternoon.

"Too overcast."

The skies were grey and the water was choppy. Arabella's dress was whipping back and forth against her legs in the wind.

"It's going to rain," Caroline said, glancing up at the sky.

"That means there is no one around. Only us." She took a deep breath. "It can't just be me that has been feeling this way?"

Caroline's eyes gleamed, and the corner of her mouth turned up into a sly smile. "What way exactly, Bell?"

Did she dare? No more excuses, no more meeting each other's lips as if by chance. The crash of waves roared in her ears, or maybe it was the blood rushing through her, drowning out all other noise.

No one was here.

It was safe.

Except for her heart.

CHAPTER THIRTEEN

Arabella couldn't deny herself any longer. She took another step forward, her body pressing against Caroline's narrow frame, which she had hugged and held in so many circumstances over the years. Laughing. Whispering. Grieving. Celebrating.

And more recently, with the fierce pulse of pleasure beating between them.

She touched Caroline's face with her fingertips, light and slow, moving from her temple down the hollow of her cheek, and brushed her thumb near her lip. She stood on the balls of her feet and pressed her lips against hers, and heat and warmth flooded her at the sweet contact.

The rain started suddenly, drenching them within a minute, and they jerked away from each other. The ribbons on Caroline's bonnet drooped, and her dress was slick against her body, but there was a wild joy on her face. Arabella laughed, happiness welling up inside her, drops of rain collecting on her spectacles and making Caroline a blur of shapes and colors, but it didn't matter. She knew it was her.

She would *always* know it was Caroline, sight be damned. She knew her scent, her pace when she walked, the feel of her body, the sound of her very breath.

Caroline eased the spectacles from her eyes and dropped them into her sodden reticule. She moved close and swept her into her arms, providing enough heat to ward off the chill of the summer storm.

Caroline dipped her head again and kissed her, then trailed a sweet succession of kisses along her jaw and down her neck, the crown of her head bumping Arabella's chin, but that was all right with her.

Everything felt all right now.

Caroline raised her head, and that dear sweet face that meant the world to her shimmered, a haze of woman and rainfall and all her fantasies blurring into one perfect moment.

The skin on her forearms prickled with the cold air, and her gown grew damper by the moment.

"Our first kiss when we were washing the dishes wasn't an expression of celebration, was it?" Arabella asked.

"No, I suppose it wasn't," Caroline admitted. "Neither was the apology kiss. Or all the other kisses."

"They truly *did* kiss at King Arthur's court—but perhaps not quite the way I kissed you that time," Arabella confessed.

"Why have we never thought to do this before?" Caroline asked, and Arabella didn't need her spectacles to know that there was a glimmer of humor shining in her eyes.

She wanted to say that she had thought to do this a thousand times or more but couldn't bring herself to pledge her undying love and devotion here on this blustery hill.

She squelched the confession down, knowing it was too much to hope that Caroline felt anything close to romance. They would always be friends, after all. This was simply an icing of desire, a light coating of pleasure as temporary as the rainfall. Nothing more.

But she couldn't deny that there had been *nothing* before.

"The cherry orchard," Arabella said, breathless. "Do you remember?"

They had been sixteen on a hot day in August, and Mrs. Reeve had tasked them with picking enough sour cherries from a neighbor's orchard for pies. It had been two summers before Caroline's parents had been stricken with fever.

"We picked enough cherries for the pies, and plenty more for our mouths," Caroline said. She was frowning, lost in memory. "I remember it was a lovely afternoon." She glanced up at the rainclouds, which were easing a little. "Almost as unlike this one as could be."

"I had cherry juice all down my dress, and I was distraught, worried about the scolding I would get from my mother when I returned."

Caroline grinned. "And then I helped strip you out of your dress so we could soak it in the river that wound through the orchard."

Arabella took a deep breath. "While we were scrubbing it, and laughing, I turned to you—"

"And you looked at me," Caroline finished softly. "I remember. You *looked* at me, and you leaned in, and I thought I knew what you wanted—but I was so afraid."

"I was never sure if you realized," Arabella said. Joy filled her heart. She hadn't been alone in her desires. "I wasn't even sure I knew what I was doing."

"I should have kissed you then."

Happiness crashed inside her chest as loud as the waves on the shore, sending a shiver down her spine, and she threw her arms tight around Caroline. She leaned her head against her shoulder and delighted in the feel of her arms around her waist.

Caroline kissed the top of her head, and Arabella hid her grin against her shoulder. This was a moment she had longed for. Forever.

"Where do we go from here?" Caroline asked, resting her chin on her head. It felt as if it had always belonged right there.

A dozen thoughts danced in her head. Dinner. Strolling along the promenade. Secret glances and clandestine touches at the assembly. Stolen kisses at night. But stolen kisses didn't feel right—that reminded her too much of Mr. Worthington and her broken engagement.

No, between herself and Caroline, there would always be kisses freely given and received.

And more. Somehow, there had to be...*more*.

Confused thoughts of naked skin and sweet lips and the curve of Caroline's breast flashed through her mind's eye, as well as plenty of things she had hardly dared to ever dream about.

She swallowed. "Maybe we should retire somewhere to dry off first?"

In fact, Arabella thought she would be happy to strip off her soaking wet clothes here and now, and tumble around the sodden ground and learn the ways of pleasure at once.

Caroline's eyes gleamed. "Let's go to the hot baths to warm up."

"You're rich enough to draw up a hot bath in the privacy of your own home," Arabella pointed out.

"I may be, but *you* are not, and I am not yet beyond the delight of taking advantage of the amenities here in Inverley that I could never enjoy before. Indulge me," Caroline said, her voice low and rough with need, and Arabella shivered. She certainly wished to indulge.

They made quick work of the bluff's descent, hand in hand as they found their footing among the muddy rocks, the gravel path so wet that the pebbles pressed hard against the thin soles of their shoes.

Arabella knew they must have appeared a sorry sight to the attendants at the baths, but she watched in admiration as Caroline strode up to them as if she were a queen and paid for access to the bathing pools.

An attendant helped them to disrobe, passing them each a thin flannel wrapper. "We have no other customers today with the weather being so poor. I shall put your dresses to dry before the fire. They are so fine they should dry in a trice. The rain should cease by then too, I daresay." She was a comfortable matron and promised to bring steaming cups of tea and chocolate biscuits to enjoy in the bath.

There were individual rooms for both cold and hot baths, but as they knew they would be private no matter where they decided to be, they chose the larger one with room for two dozen or more women.

Light came in from the high windows, hazy from the rain outside and the steam that curled from the surface of the pool that ran the length of the room. Intricate mosaics were laid in the floor, bright ceramic shards depicting fanciful sea creatures.

The stone along the wall of the pool was carved a few feet beneath the water, so one could sit along it and be submerged up to the chest if one was tall and elegantly proportioned like Caroline. The water reached the top of Arabella's shoulders.

Caroline sat and draped her arm along the edge of the bath. "Come here."

Arabella nestled against her, resting her head against Caroline's arm, cradled in the nook of her elbow. She lifted her legs and settled her thighs over Caroline's. The warm water lapped at their skin, and all she wanted was to follow the trails it left on Caroline's body with her tongue. Caroline pressed lazy kisses against the crown of her head and her temples, with one teasing kiss on the tip of her nose when she raised her head.

Instead of raindrops, now there were beads of sweat on her skin. When she glanced down at her chest, she saw that it was flushed and rosy from the heat. Fog steamed up her spectacles from the heat, and she tucked them to the side of the bath.

It was time to ask Caroline what she wanted. What she expected. Where this could go. But Arabella found herself faltering at questions about the future, so she sought refuge again in the past.

"When did you first know about yourself?" Arabella asked, moving closer against her.

"The cherry orchard," Caroline said with a little smile. "I had never had a thought about a woman before that. But I did, many times, afterward."

That was an unexpected pleasure, and Arabella sighed at the romance of it. "I've known since we were thirteen. It was always you, you know."

Caroline kissed her forehead. "That is so sweet."

She thought about what Maeve had said. If she wanted more than kisses, the key was honesty. She needed to tell Caroline the one secret that she had kept from her, except for the fact that she was in love with her. She didn't have the courage for that secret yet.

She took a deep breath. "I was engaged during that year I spent in Bath."

Caroline sat upright, dislodging Arabella's head from against her arm. "Engaged!"

"I was too ashamed to tell anyone in Inverley, because I broke it off the week after I accepted the proposal." She splashed at the surface of the water and decided to tell her everything. "My suitor was the gentleman that we met at the tea shop. Do you recall? He was the one who so rudely interrupted us?"

Caroline blinked. "*That* man? He is the one you were engaged to?"

Her tone was disapproving, and Arabella laughed. "He didn't intend to be rude. He thought I would introduce him, but I was too shy to breathe a word. Mr. Worthington is a great artist. If there was any man who could compel me to marry him, it would be him. Being an artist's wife would open so many doors, you know. If we had married, I may have gained some renown in Bath. I'll never know for sure."

Caroline drew Arabella close to her again. "Do you ever wish you had said yes?" she asked softly.

"I suppose sometimes I wonder what could have been," she admitted. "But I knew I could never be happy with a man, so it wasn't fair to marry. I was happy to return to Inverley and settle into spinsterhood."

Caroline tipped her chin up and kissed her. "I am very glad that you returned. I missed you awfully that year."

"I missed you too."

❖

Caroline had never guessed that Arabella had ever been engaged. The idea of it filled her with worry. A husband could give her so many opportunities that Caroline never could. If Arabella had entertained such a thing once, perhaps she would again now that Mr. Worthington was in town.

But then who was here with her in the baths now, the hot water coaxing sweat from her brow and confidences from her lips? At least for now, Caroline was the winner.

She had an armful of Arabella, but it wasn't enough. The baths had been a good idea to warm up, but being in proximity to the sweet press of Arabella's breasts in her wet shift had her priorities changing fast to finding them a bed.

"My house is empty," she told Arabella. "Susan and Betsy are on an outing with Lady Margaret. Jacob is with Mr. Taylor. The boys are at the vicarage. Even the servants have the afternoon off today."

"You finally have space for yourself," Arabella said. "How wonderful!" Her lashes swept up, and Caroline saw the mischief in her eyes. "Is there time for a friend to visit?"

"You know more than most how much I value friendship. Certain friends may consider themselves as intimate *there* as they ever were on Belvoir Lane, you know. I am aiming for a shocking lack of pomp and circumstance, much to Betsy's wails to the contrary."

This summer everything had gone head over heels with the reversal of fortune and popularity and now...*this*. Arabella was an anchor to her old life. If her new life overwhelmed her, there was always the comforting familiarity of Arabella's smile. She could always remember where she came from when she was in Arabella's arms.

It was an enormous relief.

But not as much a relief as it was to finally be in the privacy of her bedchamber with Arabella, and knowing that their desires were about to be fulfilled.

"You're so beautiful," Caroline said, and was startled to see Arabella scowl.

"I am not, and you know it," she said. "How many times have I complained about my nose and my glasses and these cheeks?" She pinched her cheek and made a face.

"Hmmm. I see beauty." She drew a finger from Arabella's temple down her cheek and tipped up her chin. Arabella stared up at her, her lips parted slightly. "Your cheeks are like a hothouse peach, full and sweet. Your lips are the coral of the inside of those seashells we used to collect when we were younger. Your eyes"—Caroline tipped her spectacles down—"are wide and expressive and beautiful. Like sea glass."

Arabella sighed and swayed a little, and Caroline moved her hands to her hips to steady her, then to press against her. "I have many other words to describe you," she said, "but I wonder if perhaps there is something else I ought to be doing?"

"Oh! Perhaps there is."

Arabella kissed like it was second nature, but Caroline suspected it was her first intimate encounter. She knew that Arabella was a dreamer at heart. How often had they been somewhere together and Arabella had tucked herself in a corner with her hand propped up under her chin, watching events unfold before her? Caroline expected her to be passive and thoughtful as she seduced her.

But she couldn't have been more wrong.

She was shocked when Arabella took a step back and whipped off her day dress, then shucked off her stays, chemise, and stockings, until she was standing in the middle of the bedchamber as bare as nature intended. She folded her spectacles and put them on a side table, then turned to face Caroline.

"I've waited quite long enough."

Arabella in the nude was glorious. Her body was full and generous in its proportions, her breasts plump with taut pink nipples, her hips wide and her belly soft. Caroline wanted to know if she tasted as sweet as she looked.

Caroline laughed and gathered her in her arms, adoring the feel of her smooth skin and round bottom beneath her hands. "You are a delight, Bell. But I want to make sure you're comfortable. If you are nervous, we can get beneath the covers."

"I certainly am not. There's no reason for modesty with what we're doing." Her grin widened, and her happiness was contagious, filling Caroline's heart. "Besides, I want to *see*."

Arabella might have been a little clumsy without her spectacles, but she more than made up for it with wholehearted enthusiasm. She tugged off Caroline's clothes almost as fast as she had her own, and then pushed her onto the bed.

Loving Arabella turned out to be no different from anything else they did together—they knew each other so well that they were able to communicate with a look. Not that it was the only way Arabella communicated.

A lick at her breastbone caused a gasp. A touch at the swell of her breast gave way to a deep moan. Caroline caressed her shoulders and sucked her nipple into her mouth, trying to be gentle, but Arabella's body moved under hers with abandon as she cried out in pleasure. She flung her arms above her head and wrapped her legs around Caroline's waist.

Caroline was glad there was no one at home, not even the servants. Arabella wasn't a lover for a quiet moment in the corner of a ballroom—she was proving to be as lusty as a sailor kept too long at sea.

Which suited Caroline perfectly.

"Tell me when you like something," Caroline murmured as she kissed the valley between her breasts. "Or when you don't. I want to make sure that I please you."

Arabella's face was shining, and she nodded.

Caroline was content to spend an eternity on Arabella's breasts, licking and tasting and teasing her nipples, but before Arabella said anything, Caroline could tell by the movement of her hips that it wasn't going to be enough.

"I want more," Arabella whispered, then buried her head in Caroline's shoulder. "I need more."

"Your every wish shall be fulfilled."

Caroline smoothed her hand over her waist and down her hip and had barely touched her thighs when they fell open for her. She cupped Arabella, feeling her damp warmth beneath her palm, and she kissed her long and hard as she made sure that Arabella was accustomed to her touch before she moved her fingers against her core.

Nothing had ever felt so wonderful.

Caroline stroked her finger against her opening, and then slid inside. She loved the little sigh that came from Arabella's lips as she entered her. Caroline gently moved again and found a rhythm with her fingers that lead to a long, heartful moan from Arabella.

Arabella urged her to go faster, gasping her name as she arched her hips and ground herself against Caroline's hand, giving one high keening cry as she found her release and relaxed beneath her.

After a moment, Arabella stirred, and she nudged Caroline off. She moved on top of Caroline, moving her hands eager and fast over her body, as if this might be a dream that might end too soon.

Caroline's head fell back as Arabella kissed her way down her throat and nipped at her collarbone, then covered her breast with her mouth. Arabella slipped a hand between her legs and Caroline was delighted that she was as vocal when giving pleasure as she was when receiving it. Arabella made a breathy sound of wonder as she explored Caroline's quim with her fingers, and then gasped louder than Caroline did when she eased her finger inside.

Waves of pleasure rocked through her at Arabella's touch, and the sweet ache inside of her built as Arabella moved her fingers deep, her weight pressing her against the bed. Caroline held her tight as her gratification reached its peak, sending her body into spasms of relief.

A long moment passed as she tried to collect herself afterward.

Sexual release was always wonderful, but this was something new for her. This emotion welling up inside of her, filling her to the point where she thought she might burst from it—she wasn't sure what she felt, but it was raw and uncomfortable.

She didn't know how to explain it, but she wanted to cry.

She never cried.

She shifted on the bed.

"What's wrong?" Arabella sat up, gazing down at her with concern on her face. "It was my first time, you know. I hope I wasn't too—well, I hope it was—" She was fumbling her words, her brow furrowed, and Caroline felt wretched that she had done anything to make her think that she was anything less than perfect.

"You were amazing," Caroline said. "That was a beautiful experience." She sat up and blinked back her tears, drawing in a deep breath. "We shared something incredible. There is nothing wrong."

"Are you sure?"

"Absolutely. Now come here." She drew Arabella back into her arms, pulled the sheet over them, and stared up at the ceiling as Arabella relaxed into sleep beside her.

Right now, she wanted Arabella to feel as wonderful as possible after her first sexual experience. That *didn't* include Caroline weeping and piling her problems on her. Arabella always listened to her, and supported her, and helped her through her problems. She was worried that she was starting to depend too much on Arabella, and she didn't want to take advantage of her sweet nature.

It was time that Caroline made sure that Arabella was treated like the treasure she was.

She also very much wanted to be the woman that Arabella clearly adored. She knew Arabella saw her as strong and confident.

She couldn't bear to see that light in Arabella's eyes dim as she realized that Caroline was floundering in her new role, that she was losing control of her brothers and sisters as they ran amok through Inverley with their new fortune.

She wanted to be strong. She wanted to be able to protect Arabella. Most of all, she wanted to be the type of woman that Arabella deserved to be with.

CHAPTER FOURTEEN

Arabella saw Caroline the next afternoon at the promenade. She paused before handing her shilling to the attendant who guarded the entrance to the private mile-long walk beside the shore. Caroline was with her sisters, Lady Margaret, Grace, and Lady Edith, and they were talking together near one of the benches which lined the gravel path.

Caroline was as striking as ever, her dark brown hair caught up in a shining net of silver thread and pearls, one elegant hand resting at her throat as she listened to Grace speak. Arabella might have been the one lucky enough to lay with her, but seeing Caroline dressed in her finery, shiny in the sunlight like a newly minted penny, surrounded by fashionable ladies as if she had always belonged among them—well.

It put things into sad perspective.

It reminded her that she *didn't* belong.

She still struggled to stand up to James, or to the men who pushed their way around Caroline to pay court to her. She still felt tongue-tied and shy. Inconsequential.

She may have gained entrance to a lover's bed, but what claim did she have in the daylight?

"Madam?" The attendant caught her attention, and Arabella dropped the coin into his hand and hurried onto the path.

They had agreed to meet this morning with her family and with Grace and Lady Edith, Arabella reminded herself. This had been the plan even before their intimacies yesterday. She had been invited. This wasn't a craven effort to comb the streets of town and fling herself in Caroline's path, begging for attention.

Begging to be noticed.

To be touched.

Even though that was exactly what she had wanted to do since their passionate interlude yesterday.

Seeing her today threw her senses into disarray. How was it that they had set the bed aflame with passion, and now they were to behave as if nothing had happened?

But suitresses didn't beg. At least, Arabella didn't think they should. She should hold her head up high, with confidence, even if she didn't feel confident inside. After all, this magnificent woman had chosen *her* to cavort with. That was worth something. Wasn't it?

This was merely an afternoon like so many others that Caroline and Arabella had spent in each other's company, with the exception that instead of strolling along the sandy shores of Inverley for free, they had chosen the gravel path reserved for those who could afford it. It was but ten feet difference. Arabella eyed the metal chain that separated the promenade from the beach. She was worth no more or no less as a person, regardless of the side of the chain she walked.

Caroline smiled when she saw her. "Arabella! Now that you are here, you have made the afternoon perfect."

Susan and Betsy rushed up to her and started chattering about the minutiae of their life as if she would be as fascinated as they were about their new teacups that were so fine one could almost see the tea through the china, or the fancy spoons that were stamped with the mark of a famous London silversmith. She relaxed in their presence, as familiar with them as if they were her own sisters, and she met Caroline's eyes over their heads.

Being among them felt like home.

Betsy, Susan, and Lady Edith fell into their own conversation of poetry and novels, assuring one another that poetry was by far the better entertainment, and that none of them enjoyed gothics, deriding them as silly. And yet in the same breath, Betsy encouraged Lady Edith to walk with them the next day to have a view of the great and terrible widow's mansion that all of the Reeves thought was absolutely *positively* haunted.

"Then we will pay a visit to Arabella's house to look at her artwork," Betsy said. "I know the perfect painting for you to take home with you, Edie—she has a wonderful one of the widow's manor! One shivers to look at it. It is ever so dramatic!"

Edie instead of Lady Edith, was it? The Reeve girls were quick to be so familiar, but Lady Margaret seemed to encourage the friendship.

Caroline said, "You will not be disappointed, Lady Edith. Arabella's paintings are the finest in Inverley."

Lady Edith smiled at her. "The Reeves have been telling me of your accomplishments since I met them, Miss Seton. I look forward to seeing your paintings."

She was a polite young lady, and Arabella smiled at her and Grace. "You and Miss Linfield would be very welcome to stop by any morning."

"Now, shall we stroll?" Caroline asked Arabella.

Arabella hesitated, then took Caroline's hand and patted it into the crook of her elbow. Not because there were any gentlemen about, jostling for an opportunity to escort them—but because she wanted to. Because she could.

Because Caroline gave her the sweetest look when she did.

"I would love to," Arabella said. "Let us go the full length of the walk and admire the view at the pier."

They quickened their pace to pull ahead of the group.

It wasn't enough anymore to look for moments like this one, enjoying a publicly affectionate and appropriate touch of hand upon arm that nevertheless lit her senses on fire.

"Thank you for suggesting we walk together," Arabella said. "I wanted to speak to you in private."

"Of course. You're my best friend, Arabella. We will always have time together to talk."

Best friend.

Arabella squeezed her friendly hand on Caroline's and tried not to notice how warm and snug it was against her friendly bosom.

But a flame of annoyance flickered inside. She was feeling decidedly *unfriendly*.

They reached the edge of the promenade and turned onto the pier that jutted into the sea. The breeze picked up once the water was churning on both sides of them. It blew a fine spray on their faces and ruffled their skirts about their ankles. Caroline licked the salt from her lips, and Arabella felt her lower belly tighten.

They had left their party long behind them, and there was no one else walking this far on the pier. Private enough for her purposes.

Arabella cleared her throat. "I thought perhaps we were getting a little beyond friendship yesterday."

"Yesterday was wonderful, Bell."

But the look on Caroline's face was pinched, as if something was bothering her. Arabella wondered if it was related to how she had acted yesterday after they had made love. The experience had been wonderful, but then Caroline had seemed to pull away from her.

"I want more," Arabella said. "Not just—sex." Her mouth was dry as she stumbled over the word. It was the first time she had ever said it aloud in her life. There had never been a need for it. Until Maeve and Grace had come to Inverley, she had doubted she would ever talk of such things to anyone.

Caroline wouldn't meet her eyes, instead gazing out to sea as they made their turn at the end of the pier and headed back to the promenade. "I can make a dalliance happen, Bell. Give me enough time and I can plan for a few hours here and there, for us to be intimate."

Arabella frowned. "I don't want to *plan* for it. Can't we see where this takes us naturally?"

"Where could it possibly take us?" Caroline looked at her then, her face full of surprise.

"I don't know. All I know is that I care about you. Deeply." *I love you, in fact,* she wanted to say, but didn't dare. Not yet. "I want to be on this journey with you. I want to explore what we could be. What we could have."

Arabella could hardly believe that she was saying this. For so many years, she had passively allowed her brother to arrange life around her, letting her own life pass her by without putting out a hand to stop it.

It felt grand to think that there could be something else. Something unexpected. Something new.

She felt free.

"I've never done this before," Caroline said after a pause. "I have had brief affairs with visitors. Never anyone from Inverley, and not for more than a week or so. Nothing more than physical attentions."

"I am worth more than that," Arabella said with as much dignity as she could muster, and was relieved when Caroline relaxed into a grin.

"You are worth the world and more," she said quietly. "I care for you too, Bell. That's why I'm nervous. But...I'm willing. If you want to see how things will unfold, then I will follow along with you."

They were back on the promenade now, and among their party. Caroline joined Betsy and Susan, laughing over some story they were telling Lady Margaret, and Arabella hung back for a moment.

It was overwhelming, saying how one felt.

But when she thought about the reward...well. It seemed well worth the risk of reaching so high.

Arabella turned toward the row of vendors who lined the promenade where it abutted the beach, intending to purchase a tray of sweets for the group, and smacked her face into Mr. Taylor's shoulder. She stumbled, and he hoisted her up by his stalwart arms.

"I do beg your pardon, Miss Seton! You are such a slip of a thing, I hardly saw you. My most sincere apologies."

She squinted up at him as she adjusted her spectacles. This was flummery, she was sure of it. She may be short, but she knew perfectly well she was judged as no slip. At least he was kinder about her stumble than James would have been, so it was a point in his favor. "The fault was my own, sir. I daresay you overlooked me in your haste to pursue Miss Reeve—a common occurrence these days."

That surprised a laugh out of him. "I did hope to stroll for a moment or two with your party," Mr. Taylor admitted.

Caroline had told her that she no longer harbored any suspicion about Mr. Taylor, but Arabella wasn't so sure.

She placed a hand on his arm and veered him away from Caroline, attempting something akin to a simper. "Are you missing the belles of London? I am sure the capital has plenty of lovely ladies."

"Ah, but the ladies in present company are incomparable," he said.

"Do tell me how you are enjoying Inverley?"

"I like it very well. It has much to recommend it."

She didn't miss how he gazed at Caroline as he spoke.

"Yes, the air is considered very fine here. Have you gone bathing yet?"

"I have and liked it exceedingly. Very bracing to be in the water first thing in the morning before one has broken one's fast, is it not?"

She would have to advise Caroline to avoid the shores at dawn. "I hear you have been spending time with young Jacob Reeve. How is he taking to things?"

"He needs some town bronze, but I am happy to take him under my wing. He's a fine young man."

Perhaps Mr. Taylor was what he appeared to be—a charming gentleman enjoying his new connections, and who was perhaps a little too interested in Caroline for her liking.

The thought was depressing.

"Miss Reeve is out of your reach," she told him, deciding to be frank.

He blinked. "I wasn't aware that she had expressed any particular preferences. But for what it is worth, I agree with you. Miss Reeve is a jewel, and far above my touch."

She wished she felt reassured.

❖

When Arabella arrived home, she was surprised to see Mr. Worthington taking tea with Matthew and Rachel. She gawked from the doorway of the parlor, one glove still on and the other dangling from her hand.

"Arabella, do come in," Rachel urged her, a fresh teacup already in her hand. "I knew you wouldn't be too long. Didn't I tell you so, Mr. Worthington? I am so glad you agreed to wait, sir."

Arabella slowly removed her other glove and tucked them both in her reticule. She tried to collect her thoughts as she worked the knot out of the bow of her bonnet.

She sat down next to Matthew and accepted the cup of tea from Rachel. "It is very nice to see you again, Mr. Worthington."

It wasn't quite the truth. She didn't mind seeing him, but she decidedly did not enjoy seeing him in her home with her family.

"I was strolling through town and thought that viewing your watercolors would be a charming way to spend a quarter hour, but alas I did not find you here. Your sister-in-law very kindly invited me to stay."

"I display my work in the mornings," she said, sipping her tea. She was sure she had told him this when he had first visited her.

Matthew frowned at her. "But the paintings stay right here in the parlor," he said. "I can unfold the table and put them out in a wink. Hardly any trouble."

"Oh, I wouldn't ask for such a thing. I would be happy to come by another time. I don't wish to disturb anyone."

But Matthew was already setting up the table. He drew out a stack of paintings and set them down with a thwack that had Arabella wincing. "It's a wonderful business," he said, tapping the stack. Arabella warmed to hear the pride in his voice. "Did you know you could squeeze a crown from someone for such things?"

Arabella took another sip of tea. Of course he was interested in the finances.

Mr. Worthington seemed interested too. "Indeed? My opinion is that they could be sold for more, if you were so inclined. Forgive me for being so bold, but I am a painter myself, and I know the value of such skill. I would have set the price at a pound each."

"If I sold them for so much, I wouldn't sell half as many," Arabella said.

"Ah, but you would only *need* to sell half as many to turn the same profit. It would free your time up for other things."

"I like painting. I do not seek to spend less time on it."

He smiled at her. "I do understand the passion of one's calling."

Matthew stared at the paintings and stroked his beard. "This is something to think about, though, Bell. Mr. Worthington makes a very intriguing point."

Mr. Worthington took his leave of them not long after, and Arabella sighed in relief.

Rachel pulled out a basket of baby clothes that she was working on and threaded her needle. Arabella sat beside her and took the next piece of clothing from the pile.

"Does this not make you want a brood of your own, Arabella?" Rachel shook out the baby blanket that she was hemming.

Arabella's needle poked through at the wrong place in the tiny shirt that she had picked up. "No." She yearned for family, but she didn't yearn for a baby of her own.

"I hesitate to pry, but we are family and I want the best for you. I thought there was a little sense of familiarity with Mr. Worthington today. I was wondering if perhaps you had a certain interest there?"

"I will stay a spinster forever," Arabella said, trying to sound firm. She didn't want a husband. She wanted a snug cottage by the sea. But she couldn't bring herself to say it. It would be a shock to Rachel to hear that she wanted to leave.

"I am the greater for your spinsterhood. I so appreciate you being here for me." She smoothed her dress over her belly, which was swelling to the point that had Matthew hovering and waiting on her at every opportunity when he was at home. "But if you ever did marry, I would be the first one to congratulate you. It can bring one so many blessings."

Matthew picked up a sock that didn't even cover the palm of his broad hand. "That it does."

Arabella cast her thoughts to another situation that would be sure to distract Rachel. "Matthew, do you not have business associates in Somerset?"

"I do."

"I am asking because that is where Mr. Taylor is from. Jacob's new estate is there, and the source of the Reeve family's newfound fortune. I know nothing of the area."

Rachel leaned forward. "Somerset? How very interesting. One doesn't wish to gossip, but I must admit to being very curious about the whole situation."

Matthew sat down and tossed the sock back onto the pile. "It has been some time since I ordered supplies," he said. "I suppose it would do no harm to write and place a fresh order, and at the same time ask if he has any news of this fellow. I do have a powerful strong curiosity. The Reeves lived next door for so long that I consider us particularly connected to them."

"Thank you. I know it would put my mind at rest to know more about where they come from." Her mind churned with guilt. She had brought it up knowing he would offer to do exactly that. What kind of sister was she to ask favors, while she was planning to leave the household? It didn't seem right.

"Mr. Taylor seems to be a gentleman. I saw him at the tavern the other evening and he was a fine, sporting fellow. But I would do most anything for the Reeves, as close as we have been over the years. Caroline Reeve is a good girl, and has been a fine friend to you, Arabella."

"I have missed seeing the children running about," Rachel said. "They brought a liveliness to our corner of the neighborhood."

"We should have them over for tea," Arabella said.

She hadn't thought that her family might miss the Reeves as much as she did. They had often had dinners and teas together. She and Rachel had hung up laundry with Caroline and their maids on washing-up day, and Matthew had always been willing to do any repairs on the cottage for Caroline, including the year that the roof had to be rethatched. Rachel had helped mind the younger children often enough.

The Reeves had been part of all of their lives. Not just hers.

"Oh, I'm sure we couldn't." Rachel pursed her lips. "They are used to finer accommodations than Belvoir Lane could offer them now. We couldn't ask them to condescend to visit us."

"I can and I will," Arabella promised. "The Reeves are not stuffy. They are not any less inclined to take tea in our parlor than they were two months ago."

"I do miss hearing all the latest news from Betsy and Susan," Rachel confessed with a smile. "I know those girls are not always considered quite the thing, but they have such a charming manner when they are in spirits."

"They screech something terrible when they're laughing, but they're a kind pair," Matthew said. "They never failed to help out when you used to ask them to bring lemonade down to the docks to quench our thirst on a hot day."

Arabella smiled into her teacup. Betsy and Susan had always leant a willing hand when it meant hanging about the shore and watching the burly rope makers at work. She doubted their newfound wealth had dampened their enthusiasm.

❖

Lady Margaret's presence in Inverley had improved the Reeves' standing in society to the point that invitations overflowed the silver salver that they kept in the hallway. Betsy tried to argue that she could find the time to attend up to five invitations in one evening, if she stayed but a fashionable quarter hour at each event, and wanted to send back a positive reply to every invitation.

Caroline held firm and told her that she was only to accept invitations if she could guarantee her presence for a polite amount of time. "We do not want our name to be associated with flightiness and poor manners," she told Betsy during one of their many arguments.

"I'm not flighty!" Betsy cried. She was sitting on the edge of Caroline's bed as Caroline finished attending to her hair. They were expecting Lady Edith and Grace for an afternoon visit, and they were due to arrive any minute. "I can manage my time well enough, thank you very much."

"Why do you even wish to exhaust yourself at so many soirees?" Caroline fastened her earbob and met Betsy's eyes in the mirror.

"I have a great many new acquaintances. I don't wish to slight any of them."

New acquaintances. Caroline feared she meant new suitors.

"I don't doubt it, but no one will be slighted if you decline an invitation when you have already accepted another."

"Any sister with proper feeling in her heart would warm to my plight. We have all we could wish for now, but you aren't letting me enjoy any of it!"

Caroline willed herself not to lose her temper. "You have enjoyed plenty this summer, and I am delighted for you to enjoy more. Within reason."

"Reason! That is hardly the way I wish to live my life."

Caroline gazed at Betsy with her hard eyes and set mouth and crossed arms. She could remember when she had been born, a scrappy howling infant with plenty of spirit in her. She knew her fears, her hopes, her worries. Or at least...she *had* known them. Betsy had become more of a mystery the older she was, and while Caroline had always expected them to become closer once she was grown, it felt like they only ever grew further apart.

Caroline had spoken to Lady Margaret about her concerns about Betsy's behavior, but she had merely twinkled at her and sang that everything was well under control for her little ducklings.

Sometimes, Caroline wished for nothing more than to take back the moment where she had ever written to Lady Margaret to ask for her sponsorship.

"Is there someone in particular that you hope to see at these soirees?" Caroline asked.

Betsy raised her chin. "There might be," she said. "He's wonderful."

There had been many men who Betsy had declared wonderful one minute, and then tedious beyond measure in the next.

Caroline's mind raced. If Betsy truly had set her cap for someone, was he good enough for her? Would there be scandal? Knowing Betsy, he was unsuitable in every way. He could be a gambler, or a rakehell. Or he would ruin her and crush her heart. Caroline would rather run a man through with a sword than see him hurt her sister, but try as she might, she could not wrench his name from Betsy.

"I can't wait to leave this family!" Betsy snapped instead of answering. "I hate being interrogated at every turn, without any trust from anyone. One day, I shall have a ring on this finger and leave forever—or I shall leave my finger bare and find my own way in London!"

She stalked out of the room.

There was a knock at the front door. Betsy and Caroline went downstairs, where Susan was already impatient enough to throw the door open instead of waiting for a servant to open it.

"Edie!" Susan cried. "You must see our new frocks that were delivered today."

"You will think our new dresses divine," Betsy assured Lady Edith, tossing her curls and avoiding looking at Caroline.

In a giggling swarm, the three of them went upstairs.

"They have taken to calling Susan's old bedroom the Reeve Fashion Emporium," Caroline told Grace. "It is the utmost folly. Do you ever wish to throw up your hands and walk away from your position? If my sisters were not family, I would be tempted to do exactly that."

Grace laughed and settled herself next to Caroline on the sofa in the parlor. "I would be in a very sorry state if I were to leave my employment at a moment's notice, I'm afraid. But Lady Edith is a good girl. Not so many trials and tribulations as some girls give their companions."

"I fret over my sisters when I am not there to watch them in person. I worry about what they might get up to."

"Have you thought about hosting more events, where you could control who is invited and what happens in your own home?"

Caroline blinked. "Jacob did tell me that he wished to have dinner and dancing here as soon as we settled into the house, but I have been so busy that I forgot every word about it. That is a fine idea. I can prove to anyone who still looks down on us that we are surely ready for high society. I will issue invitations straightaway."

It would be a pleasure to entertain friends at home and to serve them with the niceties that she hadn't been able to afford before.

"I have been thinking a great deal about our conversation in the tea shop," Caroline confessed after she poured the tea.

Grace smiled. "I have thought of it too. I am so pleased to find myself among friends. I have lived in many places as a companion or a chaperone, and I have not often found myself among like-minded women."

Caroline stared down at the array of cakes on the tea platter. "If I may ask, have you ever had a—well, a proper relationship before?" She lowered her voice. "I mean, with another woman?"

"I have. Twice, in fact."

"How have you managed such a thing? I've never had a relationship before. I have had friendships, and I have my family, but I've never really had a lover. Not long term."

Did she even want such a thing? How long would she be in Inverley, with her siblings pestering her every other day about moving to London as fast as could be arranged?

It would be lovely to enjoy Arabella's company for however long she could keep it, though.

"Is it so different from friendship?" Grace sipped her tea.

Caroline hesitated. "I worry about hurting Arabella. What if she wants more than I can give?"

"Do you want to give it to her?"

Did she? She loved being with Arabella. She loved their intimate encounters, she loved talking with her, she loved being with her. But she wanted to prove that she was worthy of their relationship, that she was as put together as Arabella expected.

Even though she felt like she was falling apart at the seams, like her old chemises.

"I don't know what I want. I have leaned on her far too often. She deserves better than always having to help me with my family troubles. I want to protect her."

"A relationship means that you help each other. You support each other."

"I want to be *good* to her. And good *for* her." Arabella deserved everything. She was the one who deserved to be an heiress.

"My advice is to encourage her. Support her. Find what she loves, and do more of that."

Arabella certainly loved to be touched. Caroline's body tightened as she thought of lovemaking with Arabella. It could easily become her favorite pastime, and she thought Arabella would like more of it too. She resolved to take the very next opportunity to show her how much she meant to her. She might not be able to put how she felt into words, but she could put it in her touch.

CHAPTER FIFTEEN

Arabella's heart was full as she sat on the swing across from Caroline. If she ignored Caroline's new hairstyle and fine muslin dress, she could pretend that nothing had changed, and that this was life *before*.

Caroline slid her arm along the back of the swing, her fingertips resting on Arabella's shoulder, and she was reminded that life *after* had its charms.

"This is tempting fate," Arabella murmured, looking up at her. But she couldn't move away. Not when it felt so nice.

"There is no one out here, and we are well established to be old friends," Caroline said, smiling. "Who would take any notice?"

She moved her hand lower so that her gloved fingers dipped between the edge of Arabella's bodice and her fichu.

"I am certainly noticing." Her nipples felt tight beneath her chemise, and the deep pulse of desire started to throb inside. "We really shouldn't."

Caroline shifted closer. "We probably shouldn't be doing a lot of things this summer."

"I don't mean to protest all of them."

"Simply the public ones?" She lifted her arm from behind her and clasped Arabella's hand, moving their hands to rest in Arabella's lap. "Are you sure? I could find a way to pleasure you right here on this swing, without anyone being the wiser."

Arabella gasped. "*I* would be the wiser!" She could feel the flush starting to creep up her neck. "And you know that I am not able to keep quiet."

"This is true." She withdrew her hand from Arabella's grasp and inched up her thigh until the edge of her hand was gently pressed against her lower belly. "But who would hear? Matthew and Rachel are not home. You have no neighbors to the left of you anymore since that *dreadful* Reeve family left. The hedge around the garden is high enough to shield us from anyone's view. Are you sure you don't wish to indulge?"

Indulge.

Arabella was certain that she was ready to come apart at the merest brush of Caroline's hand. She craved to give in, to allow her legs to fall apart and to beg Caroline to press with urgent fingers against her center, to muffle her scream against her shoulder as she felt pleasure wrack her body like a shipwreck as the swing swayed beneath them, suspending them somewhere between heaven and earth.

She wanted it. The sunlight beating on her face, the sea air in her nose as she shattered, as natural and wild with abandon in the sexual act as any of God's creatures that roamed the countryside.

The naughtiness of it made her ache in all the right places, and even now she wanted to arch her hips to meet Caroline's hand, giving her unspoken permission to touch and stroke and press and caress.

But it wouldn't be enough.

She didn't want to give in to persuasion, and she wanted more than a furtive encounter. More than a kiss or a come on a bench, a hurried embrace, no time to even take off her dress.

"Come with me to the attic," Arabella said instead. "We can be private there."

Caroline stepped off the swing and offered her hand to help Arabella step down. "I would be delighted to take a tour of your studio."

Arabella harbored a hope that Caroline was watching her bottom as she ascended the stairs and was rewarded by her sly smile when she glanced behind her. She flung the shutters open to let the afternoon light stream in.

"I had forgotten how sparse it is up here," Caroline said.

The studio ran half the length of the attic, the other half being the servants' quarters. The desk with her painting supplies was pressed against the wall beneath the window. There were stacks of papers and canvases, and a chair with a deep cushion where she liked to sit when she wanted to escape from the rest of the household.

Furniture and wooden chests for household storage were stacked in the far end of the attic. Arabella grinned. She strode over and opened the chest nearest to her.

"Sparse, but we can make it comfortable," she said, holding up a thick winter quilt and a down-stuffed pillow. "These could use a good airing, but I daresay if we were game enough to roll around in the grass outside, we can make good use of this."

Caroline took one end of the quilt and they spread it on the floor together. "Very snug," she announced. "We shall want for nothing."

How could Arabella ever work in here again, with these new memories to clutch so close to her chest?

Arabella kissed Caroline, her hands roving over her hips as she traced her lips with her tongue. She fumbled with the laces at the back of her dress, unwilling to forgo the pleasure of her lips to undress her, and finally the frock was undone and slid from Caroline's lithe body to pool on the floor at their feet. Arabella removed her stays and shift, and then Caroline stood naked.

Sunlight highlighted the planes and slopes of her body, leaving shadows in her hollows and valleys that Arabella craved to explore with her mouth. She wanted to grab her pencil and commit every beautiful line to the page so she could marvel at perfection any time she wished.

Caroline was elegant in nudity and was made even more beautiful by the mole on her left shoulder, the scatter of freckles across her collarbone, and the charming asymmetry of her breasts, the left being slightly fuller and lower than the right. Her breasts were a perfect handful, her nipples a mouthful, and her hipbones had an angle to them that Arabella stroked with her thumbs as she held Caroline's hips against her own.

She sucked one of her nipples into her mouth and revelled at the feel of Caroline's body beneath her mouth, warm and responsive, the faint scent of her lemon soap now the most erotic thing that Arabella could imagine.

"You are rather too clothed," Caroline murmured, laughter glinting in her eyes.

The most surprising part of lovemaking was that not only was there the endless joy of discovering Caroline's body, but there was also Caroline's evident interest in how hers worked too. She had been so caught up in wondering how it would feel to have another woman in her arms that she hadn't given much thought to how the woman in question would handle *her*.

It turned out that Caroline handled her like expensive jewelry. Careful, but firm enough that she wouldn't slip and break apart— unless she wanted to.

She slipped Arabella's clothing off and then drew her down to the floor. Their legs tangled together as they kissed, and Arabella couldn't think of a better use for the winter quilts than as a makeshift summer bed.

She ran her hands down Caroline's body, learning her angles and how she fit against her like they had been made to cleave together. She slipped a hand between Caroline's thighs and found that she was ready for her, slick with need, encouraging her to slip her finger inside her. Arabella claimed her mouth again as she moved her hand against Caroline's center, rocking against her with the gentle force that she was learning that Caroline liked.

She stroked another finger inside her and was rewarded with a sweet sound of pleasure that sent a thrill through Arabella. She moved her lips to Caroline's breast and kissed her nipple as she pressed her fingers against her sensitive nub in a rhythm that soon had Caroline gasping and shuddering beneath her.

"How much do you know about kissing?" Caroline murmured after a moment.

Arabella felt a pulse of alarm. "I thought I was doing well with it."

She laughed. "I mean a different sort of kiss. I want to give you everything you want, even if you don't know what that is yet."

She blinked, unsure of her meaning, until Caroline moved her hand down her body to rest against her pelvis.

"I mean a kiss *here*."

Arabella had heard a bawdy limerick or two before and didn't have any more depth of knowledge than a rhyming couplet could provide, but she did have a vivid imagination. "I might not know much," she confessed, "but I am willing to learn."

Caroline grinned at her. "Good."

Caroline kissed her throat and left delicate kisses between her breasts and down her ribcage and over her belly, until she reached the curls between her legs. Arabella shivered with anticipation, and then promptly lost all capability of thought once Caroline's mouth covered her quim.

She had no words for what was happening except that it was the most intimate kiss she had ever experienced. Caroline's lips were hotter than a brand and her tongue stoked fires of unimaginable heat between her thighs. It was slow and sweeping, grand and majestic, fierce and tender and loving all at once, and before she knew it she was hurtling toward the highest of peaks. Caroline moved against her one last time and Arabella saw starbursts behind her eyes. She shuddered and gasped, the movement shaking the nearby bookcase that held her sketchbooks. One of them fell with a thud beside them.

She lay breathless on the quilt, trying to put her mind back together.

"That was beautiful," she breathed.

Caroline kissed her forehead. "You made many lovely sounds that told me as much. I have never had a lover as expressive as you."

Arabella cuddled up to her. "I do hope that isn't an encumbrance."

"Far from it. It's endearing."

It had felt like Caroline was brushing her with life, filling her up with color and passion and spreading it across her body and her mind.

And her heart.

Oh, her foolish heart.

Caroline laughed and sat up. "We are disrupting the earth as well as the heavens. Apologies, Bell— I didn't mean to throw your work into disarray."

She picked up the sketchbook that had fallen from the shelf and extended it to Arabella. Then she paused, blinking down at the page.

"What's the matter?" Arabella asked, drowsy from pleasure.

"I had no idea that you drew anything but landscapes."

Arabella shot upright and grabbed the book. "I don't."

"You clearly do. There was a truly wonderful pencil portrait in there. Could I see more?"

Arabella frowned. This was private. She had never shared her portrait work with anyone. "I don't think—no, I don't want to."

"Oh." Caroline was clearly surprised. "Well, as you wish. I'm sure they are wonderful, though."

Arabella fiddled with the edge of the book, a little stung. "That isn't the reason I wouldn't want to show them." She paused. "You know I have been drawing all of my life."

"Of course. How could I forget all those times we sat together on the bluffs while you filled book after book?"

"Mother and Father never valued it. I wasn't a boy, so they couldn't hire me a tutor for oil painting and make anything grand of my skills. All I could do was draw pretty pictures, and paint with watercolor. The same as any gentlewoman might."

She didn't like to speak of it. She had yearned so much for her parents' praise, and they had been so dismissive of her talent that it had been hard for her to admit that she even had any. It had taken a long time to build the courage to sell her seascapes.

"I remember," Caroline said softly, her hand on her knee. "You used to cry about it. You used to tell me you wish you had been born a boy."

God, if she had been born a boy, her life would have been much different. She gazed at Caroline, feeling the ache of secret love pressing on her. In more ways than one, it would have been easier.

"My parents might have been willing to help me pursue an artistic career if I had been a boy, or if they thought I had exceptional talent. But of course I wasn't as skilled then—I couldn't see as well. I have improved since I got my spectacles, but by then, they had already moved to be closer to my grandparents."

"Do you miss them?" Caroline missed hers every day.

"I was never as close to them as you were to your parents. I am content to see them twice a year, but I am much happier with Rachel and Matthew than I ever was in their house." Her stomach dipped. It was hard to reconcile her feelings of gratitude with the desire to have her own space. "I have been accustomed to people telling me my whole life that my art isn't valuable. Even the visitors consider it to be no more than a quaint reminder of their travels."

"The paintings represent memories. Ones they will wish to treasure, which they will always see when they look at them," Caroline said. "It means something important. Don't discount the joy you bring to people with your work."

"That may well be, and I appreciate it. But all I do is paint the same scenes over and over. What I am selling is almost nothing more than a copy of hundreds of paintings that I have done before. Many visitors could accomplish the same work, if they thought to bring their paint sets with them on holiday and spend an afternoon or two by the sea painting instead of being dipped or sipping on tonics."

"Is this different?" Caroline asked, nudging the closed sketchbook on Arabella's lap. Her eyes were sympathetic, and Arabella felt the tension ease out of her shoulders.

She pulled the quilt up and moved to sit closer to Caroline. "I love drawing people. I love sketching the expressions on their faces, and painting with all the different colors of hair and clothes and skin. I have drawn the grocer's wife, and the maid-of all-work." She smiled. "And Grace, and Maeve." She fiddled with the sketchbook again, and then decided to open it, flipping the pages to the one she wanted. "And you. Of course."

Caroline took the book from her, her face shining. "Bell! It's— why, it's *me!*"

She had drawn it the night that Caroline had her over for dinner with Mr. Taylor when he had arrived in Inverley. The night they had shared their first kiss. She hadn't painted it until the next day, but she had sat up in bed with her pencil and sketchbook, reliving the sweet press of their lips together. The portrait showed Caroline in her old patched evening dress, with a soapy dish in one hand and a cloth in the other. There was a look of yearning and wonder on her face.

"This is magnificent," Caroline whispered, her eyes wide. "Bell, I remember that moment so perfectly when I look at this."

A thrill went through her. "So do I. I love it."

"I don't understand. You are a brilliant portrait artist. Why don't you show people?"

She laughed. "Who would want a painting of the grocer's wife scowling when she told me there were no more potatoes to be had for love or money? Who would want to look at the expressions on the bored socialites' faces from that first assembly we went to?"

"I would! Please could I look through the rest of the book?"

Absurdly pleased, Arabella nodded, hugging herself as Caroline touched the pages as gently and reverently as if they meant something. As if they were worth something.

As if *she* were worth something.

"These are stunning. You have such a way with expressions— why, I can almost hear what they're thinking. Oh, you should consider selling these."

Happiness bloomed in her chest. "Maybe I should." She straightened her back. She had been trying to take more chances this summer, hadn't she? She made her decision. "In fact, I will."

❖

Caroline thought about Arabella's paintings on the walk back to the townhouse. Everything was changing around her. Even Arabella was changing, and she had always been as reliable as the north star. She was astonished to find how much she was learning this summer about a woman who she had thought she knew inside and out.

Arabella was flourishing these days. She seemed more confident when out in society, more comfortable. More settled. Caroline was delighted to watch Arabella realize just how wonderful she was.

Caroline had wanted to show Arabella by her touch how much she valued and cared for her. She had wanted to let her body express her emotions, when she wasn't certain how to put anything into words. All she had expected was an intimate and private side to one of the most important relationships in her life.

But *private* didn't feel like enough anymore. Caroline wanted to support her in everything she did. She wanted to knock on all the doors of all the houses of Inverley and shout how wonderful Arabella and her artwork were.

It felt so easy and natural between the two of them that sometimes Caroline forgot that no one would be happy to discover what was transpiring between them. Why could she not stand beside Arabella proudly and take her hand in public without fear?

It wasn't fair.

She sighed. In a way, perhaps it didn't matter whether or not it was fair. It was reality, and they were forced to accept it.

But no one would fault a woman for staunchly supporting her friend. Caroline resolved to cheer her on at every step of the way if she wished to pursue her portraiture. She would sharpen every pencil and refresh every pad of paint if it would help Arabella with her work.

She would do most anything she could, artistically or not, for more nights to hold her.

But she was starting to worry about what it meant for her heart when the summer drew to a close.

CHAPTER SIXTEEN

A rabella had always loved the seashore. On sunny days, it was filled with people and birds and donkeys and an air of holiday. On stormy days, it was a private sanctuary, a place perfect to wrap a shawl around one's shoulders and cry into the sound of the waves.

Always, it was a place she felt was home.

Today, however, she felt decidedly out of place.

"Why did I agree to this again?" she asked Caroline as she struggled to carry her paints and brushes in her canvas bag in one hand, and a pair of stools in the other.

"Because you're a brilliant painter, and you deserve to have clients say lovely things about your work. People will adore having their portraits taken on the beach. You'll see. Give that here," Caroline said, and made a grab for one of the stools.

"You shouldn't risk your new frock to carry my old furniture! What if there was a stray nail or wood splinter to catch in your muslin? Besides, I need to be able to do it by myself. You won't always be around when I set up on the beach."

"You needn't fret over my gowns. You never had a regard for them before." Her eyes danced and she hooked a hand under the stool leg, stealing it away.

She had a regard for them now. Caroline's new dresses were frothy and filmy and fanciful, like the whitecaps dancing on the waves.

"I appreciate you meeting me here," Arabella said.

"Where else would I be?" The easy sincerity in Caroline's voice tugged at Arabella's heart. "I want to be right here for you. I want to help you achieve your dreams, Bell. Now, where would be the best place for you to set up?"

Arabella scanned the beach. A pie seller strolled by, calling out his wares. A peaky-looking man was riding a donkey led by an attendant. Bathing machines in the distance were on their last round for dipping. The aroma of salted nuts, hot enough to scorch one's mouth, and the scent of sweet buns tangled together in her nose. A group of singers caroled down the beach, their voices indistinct beyond the crash of the waves and the general hubbub.

It was the very picture of summer in Inverley.

"Here is perfect."

She set her stool in the sand, digging the legs deep, and snapped open her easel. She withdrew her paints and a jug of water from her canvas bag. She sat down and settled the jug into the sand and the paintbox on her lap.

"You look wonderful. Exactly as a lady painter ought to look."

She laughed. "Flummery. A lady painter ought to look exactly as she pleases. And really, I think *painter* ought to do."

Now that she was set up, she felt excitement rushing through her. She was here, about to take an artistic leap of faith.

But no one approached.

A pit of anxiety opened in her belly, and she popped a ginger comfit into her mouth. Caroline put a hand on her shoulder. "People will come," she said. "There are vendors all up and down this beach. Someone will want their portrait done any minute now."

But the minutes ticked by.

"Perhaps they think I'm here to paint the ocean," Arabella said with a start. "Caroline, I should have brought a sign! How will anyone know that I am here for portrait work? This is all wrong—and I've wasted your afternoon on top of everything." She wanted to sink into the sand.

"Then we will make a sign for next time, but we are not giving up." Caroline looked fierce, her brows low and her jaw set. She set her hands on her hips and scanned the crowd. "Look, there's a young lady and her mama. I can charm them into a portrait."

Caroline strode over to speak to them. The tips of Arabella's ears felt hot as she saw the lukewarm reception of the mother, and then they walked away. This was unbearable.

She rose and joined Caroline, catching her hand. "You don't have to do this. No one wants a painting. It was a fool's dream, best tucked up in my sketchbooks in the attic. Come, let's go home."

"We are going nowhere!" Caroline cried. "You are too talented by far and I will not have your light under a bushel."

"There are many other things we could be doing," she cajoled her. She wanted the press of Caroline's lips against hers and to feel the crash of pleasure engulf her, forcing her to forget the embarrassment of the afternoon.

"We can do those things later," Caroline said. "We need to show people what they could have." She brightened and grabbed the stool, repositioning it so that her back wouldn't be against any onlookers. "I have it, Bell. Paint me!"

She sat with her chin up, her hands folded on her lap, and a defiant look on her face.

She was magnificent.

After a moment's hesitation, Arabella picked up her paintbrush and started to work. She poured her emotion into the portrait with the paint, every brushstroke like a caress. This hadn't been the purpose of the afternoon, but she couldn't deny what a pleasure it was to have a public opportunity to stare at Caroline with all the intensity and longing that she wished.

Arabella was aware of every breath that Caroline took, every slide of her eyes toward the visitors, and she knew that Caroline hoped to encourage them. A few wandered by, close enough to peer at her work, but they did no more than nod and tip their hat to her in passing.

After an hour, she put her brush down.

Caroline rose and stood beside her. "It's wonderful. You are such a talent."

She reached out to touch it, and Arabella laughed and stayed her hand. "It's still wet!"

Caroline frowned. "Oh. Right. But then how could the customers take their portraits home?"

Arabella's heart sank. She hadn't thought about it. "I suppose they would have to come by my house the next day to pick it up." It wasn't an ideal solution, but it would have to do.

If, that is, she ever had a customer.

Maybe she wasn't as talented as she thought. Or perhaps people didn't wish for portraits.

She didn't like this feeling of being wrong. Not when she had just convinced herself that she was good enough to try.

She packed up her belongings, feeling as out of place as she had when they had arrived.

Thank goodness Caroline had been with her. Being with Caroline always felt like home. She tucked that thought deep in her heart.

CHAPTER SEVENTEEN

Caroline was nervous as she welcomed her guests for dinner. Jacob, Betsy, and Susan had all been delighted at the prospect of introducing people to their new house and had therefore promised to be on their best behaviour. True to their word, she saw no evidence of poor manners or overt flirtations at the table.

She had fretted over the numbers until Lady Margaret reminded her that they were not in London, and wasn't it lovely to have friends everywhere one looked? But even with an extra leaf in the table, it was a shocking squeeze to fit the Reeves, the Setons, Grace, Lady Edith, Maeve, and several other new friends whom her siblings had insisted on inviting.

At least the conversation was lively and the dinner of lamb well received.

"It's going well," Arabella murmured, pressing herself close while most of the guests removed themselves to the parlor.

Caroline squeezed her hand, making sure their hands were hidden behind their skirts. It was a joy to be here with Arabella. Almost as if they were welcoming the party together. "Thank you for being by my side."

Arabella's answering smile was brilliant.

"Thank you for having us to dinner," Matthew said, grasping Caroline's hand in a handshake.

"Especially as I am in a rather delicate condition," Rachel added. "It was most kind. We have missed you and your brothers and sisters."

"You are always welcome to visit us," Caroline said. "I am happy to have you here in any condition—and I cannot wait to meet the baby." She kissed Rachel's cheek.

"We will be off for home now, and leave the dancing to the young people." Rachel hugged Arabella before she and Matthew left.

More guests had been invited for dancing than for dinner, and soon the house swelled with people. Except for the pianoforte, the furniture had been cleared from the parlor. Jacob and Betsy had been adamant that it was more than big enough if only people had enough spirit in them, and Caroline had to admit that they had been correct. Bows were issued and curtsies returned without a second glance for the narrow dimensions of the room, and a rousing country dance began.

Three or four couples were able to take their turn. The windows were thrown open for fresh air, and the room shook with movement and mirth and music. Those who were not twirling on the dance floor contributed their fair share of noise through clapping and foot tapping and conversation.

Caroline danced a set with Mr. Taylor, then went to join Arabella at the edge of the room. She plied her fan, out of breath. "I suppose this is a success, given the number of people who seem to be enjoying themselves."

Lady Margaret overheard her and said, "A crush is the very best compliment you could have in London."

"In Inverley, we are not so accustomed to hardly having air to breathe," Arabella said.

"Then take a turn in the garden and refresh yourselves! It is a sad sight to see young ladies denouncing the opportunity to dance. I have never seen such behavior in my life." Lady Margaret shook her head.

Before Caroline could make good on the offer and steal some time away with Arabella outside, Betsy tapped her on the shoulder. There was a crease in her brow, and she was worrying her lip with her teeth. "I have someone I would like you to meet."

She tugged them out of the warm parlor and into the hall, where a young man fidgeted with his cravat. He was tall and sandy haired, and his left coat sleeve was folded up and pinned to his shoulder.

"This is Mr. Graham, formerly Captain Graham."

"I am pleased to meet you," Mr. Graham said, bowing. "I sold my commission after my injury this past winter and thought to spend the summer by the seaside to speed my recovery."

Caroline's heartstrings tugged. "War is a terrible thing," she said. "You are brave, sir."

Betsy stood tall beside him. "He is a wonderful poet, Caroline."

"I blush to hear it," he said with a grin. "But I am not half the poet your sister is. Miss Betsy has an extraordinary way with words."

Caroline was so surprised she could have fallen over, had there been space enough in the hallway. Her sister, a poet? Though she supposed it shouldn't be a shock, given the volumes of verse that she consumed.

Betsy beamed at him. "Mr. Graham is ever so dashing. He fought a duel once, you know. I have invited him tonight for the dancing."

A duel? Caroline's heart sank. There went her hopes that her sister had found a decent man.

"Bonaparte took my arm but not my legs, and I am always happy for an opportunity to dance. Especially with a fine woman like your sister." He gazed at Betsy.

Lady Margaret clapped her hands. "A former army captain! What a wondrous thing. You are certainly welcome."

"I am pleased to meet you, Mr. Graham." Caroline studied him. He had a kind face, and there was no doubting the affection in his eyes when he stared at her sister. But Betsy had so many other opportunities waiting for her inside already, which would provide her with wealth and security. Most importantly, with men who hadn't fought duels. "However, I am sorry to say that the parlor is full."

His face fell, and Betsy looked outraged. "There is enough space for one more," she argued.

"I am sorry," Caroline repeated.

"There is always room for a fine military man and a young lady on any dance floor," Lady Margaret said, glaring at Caroline. She ushered the couple into the parlor, leaving Caroline and Arabella alone together in the hall.

"Caroline, that was not well done of you," Arabella said, pushing her spectacles up.

"Betsy needs no encouragement right now for unsuitable suitors."

"What's unsuitable about him?" Caroline could see the censure in her eyes. "The duel? I agree that it doesn't bode well, but we don't yet know the circumstances. You have grown too proud."

"Proud? I am not," she snapped. "I am not convinced, after one meeting where Betsy has ill-advisedly invited him to a party already far too crowded for propriety's sake, that he would be the right choice for my sister. You know she is all too willing to throw herself at a pretty face with a scoundrel's heart."

"He seems nice—and she seems *happy*. How many suitors has she had that have ended up in nothing? What is the harm in allowing her to dance with Mr. Graham for an evening?"

"This is the first serious suitor she has had since the inheritance. I was the one responsible for turning away her former beaux when Jacob was not yet of age. But would Jacob deny his favorite sister if Mr. Graham asked for her hand tomorrow? He would give her whatever she pleased. They are two halves of the same coin."

"Give them both some credit, darling. But don't worry for now. There is time to learn more about Mr. Graham, and time for you and Jacob and Betsy to speak of it. But not tonight."

Caroline didn't want to talk about it. She darted a look around, then leaned forward and kissed Arabella, pressing her against the wall. She trailed kisses from her mouth down her neck, and then pressed one against the swell of her breast. "Stay with me tonight?"

Her eyes were shining. "I would love to."

The front door opened and shut with a bang. Caroline sprang apart from Arabella as Jacob and a passel of exuberant young men with wild eyes and rumpled hair staggered into the house, laughing riotously.

"Jacob Reeve, what is this?" she asked. "We have no room for more guests."

He darted into the library and came out with a decanter of brandy and a brace of snifters. "Don't worry, Caro! We're all set up in the garden. I had the footmen set up a table and there are lanterns aplenty, so we shan't be a bother to you."

The reek of drink was unmistakeable as Jacob and the gentlemen filed past.

"We'll be as quiet as anything!" he called out over his shoulder.

Caroline sighed and leaned her forehead against Arabella's for a moment. So much for her guise that everything was running smoothly in the Reeve household. "I must find Mr. Taylor."

She located him in the parlor, speaking to Lady Margaret over a cup of tea. The bigger parlor was for dancing, and the one across the hallway had been set up with refreshments. The baker had proved generous whenever the Reeves placed an order, in great charity with them after having earned so much through George's indiscretion, so the tables were groaning under the sweets and savories laid out for a cold supper.

"I heard the cub come in," he said before she could speak, and she relaxed. "Don't worry—I'll keep an eye on him and his friends. I'll join their card party in a moment and make sure it doesn't get out of control."

"Thank you," she said, meaning it with every fiber of her being.

He grinned. "Anything for a Reeve," he said, and left for the garden.

Caroline didn't know how she survived to the end of the night. It passed in a blur of heat and exertion and laughter and trouble. She was sure that more people kept arriving who she hadn't invited, but it was difficult to keep track because her attention was pulled in a thousand different directions. There were indiscretions to interrupt in the sitting room between young people with less sense than discretion, there was a fight to break up between a couple of solicitors visiting from Kent, and Lady Margaret had dipped into the sherry and accidentally swung her fan into a slew of vases displayed in a cabinet, sending china shards flying.

But the depleted larder and tea caddy proved to Caroline that at least the evening had been well enjoyed.

Caroline went outside with a maid to extinguish the lanterns after the last of the guests had left. She found that the leg of the card table was broken, and at least one young man had cast up his accounts in the flower beds.

She would be hearing about this from the neighbors tomorrow.

Arabella put her hand on her shoulder. "This will go down in Inverley history."

"The Reeve family shall be infamous." Caroline tried to find the humor in it, but it was too depressing. "This party had been meant to show the town that we are ready for higher society, but once again it proved that our family chases chaos. The evening got rather out of control, didn't it?"

"It was spirited," Arabella said. "If people enjoyed themselves, then they will speak of the evening favorably." She took her hand in hers. "Now—let's go up to bed."

❖

Arabella had never thought of sunlight as *loud* before, but how else could she describe the pounding heat that poured in through the window the next morning? She flung her arm over her closed eyes, her head aching from an excess of last night's wine. She tried to calm the panic that threatened to overwhelm her.

After all, the situation shouldn't warrant panic. She was snuggled deep in a feather bed under a crisp linen sheet, while Caroline slept beside her. It should have felt idyllic.

Even in sleep, Caroline was elegant. She lay on her back, one hand resting beside her head, her glossy curls as pretty as if they had been purposefully arranged on the pillow. Her lips were barely parted as she breathed, and her lashes were dark against her skin. Arabella didn't know how she managed to look so lovely. She had seen her own reflection in the mirror enough times in the morning to know that her hair was always tangled mess when she woke, with her cheek creased from the pillow.

Last night had been a great deal of fun. Too much fun, judging from her headache. It had been chaotic—Caroline had been right about that—but everyone had been in perfect charity. For once, Arabella felt comfortable at a social event. Everywhere she had turned, she saw a friendly face. There were no Martins skulking in the corners with little witticisms. There had been no snobby ladies from London to put down everyone's dress.

And to be next to Caroline for the whole night had been wonderful.

But once again, none of this was hers. Just like her brother's house was for Matthew and Rachel and their yet unborn babe, this townhouse was for the Reeves. It was Caroline's house. Her dinner party. Her bedchamber.

Lovemaking was more than she had ever dreamed they could have together. It was the culmination of wild hope and good fortune, and she would be forever grateful that she had taken on the role of the suitress and won a place in Caroline's bed.

But it was all a good deal more...*real* than she could have imagined.

Loving Caroline was more than kisses and intimacies. It was more than burning looks in a drawing room with the promise of slaking their lust afterward. It was more than stolen moments where they pressed against each other a little too often, held hands a little too tightly, or lingered a little too long while exchanging fans or teacups.

It was the reality of their thoughts. Their dreams. Their hearts.

It was terrifying.

Her dreams of love had been safe and pretty. Soft words, sweet kisses, gentle touches. There had never been any misunderstanding or confrontation.

She was discovering that a relationship was difficult, messy, and complicated.

But it was also *real*. She hugged that fact close to her chest. Shouldn't that mean she should be happy?

It was simply that her dream of Caroline was altogether different from the real woman in her bed who had worries and problems.

Caroline had changed since the inheritance.

Arabella had thought that money would help ease her burdens, but in many ways it had increased them. Why didn't Caroline trust her enough to confide them in her? Arabella caught sight of her from time to time with a furrowed brow, and she always pushed it aside when Arabella asked her what was wrong.

Caroline seemed more determined than ever to do what was best for her siblings, but Arabella wondered if she was paying enough attention to their happiness.

In the realm of fantasy, there were no problems. But real life was full of them—how could they build a partnership together if they couldn't truly *talk* to each other?

Caroline stirred and opened her eyes. "Hello, beautiful."

Arabella banished all of her worries from her mind and kissed her cheek. "Good morning."

"Is it morning? I thought we would sleep until midafternoon at least."

She laughed. "We could while our time away in bed until then, couldn't we? The household must still be asleep after the goings-on last night."

A furry orange blur leapt between them.

"Oh, Shelley!" Delighted, Arabella grabbed him and stroked behind his ears. "I haven't seen him in ages. It looks like the Reeve household is treating him well."

"He does all right for himself," Caroline said, studying the cat. "Will and George take good care of him."

Yet here he was in Caroline's bedchamber, waiting until she awoke. Arabella hid her grin as she patted Shelley, who squirmed out of her hands to press his head against Caroline's forehead with a meow.

"Off the bed, Shell." She pushed him away, and he leapt back up.

"It appears that maybe you have a routine?"

"I certainly do not. Your cat is nothing but a fish-stealing miscreant."

Arabella looked around the room. In the corner was a large pillow with a well-kneaded towel on it. "Is that why he has his own bed in your own bedchamber?"

"I don't know what you're talking about," Caroline muttered as Shelley continued to paw at her, then she relented. She picked up the cat, buried her head into the fur of his neck, and crooned nonsense to him as he purred.

Arabella fell back against the mattress, wheezing with laughter. "Fish-stealing miscreant indeed. More like beloved lap cat to one who always said she would never have such a creature in the house."

Caroline poked her shoulder. "Fine, I admit it. He is beloved. Shelley is officially my favorite in the ongoing war in this family of which poet is best. But he's still a pain when he wants to be. Always demanding attention when I least have it to give."

"That reminds me. Where is my attention, I wonder?" She stretched on the bed and watched as Caroline's eyes turned sharp.

They made love, slow and quiet and peaceful, which Arabella discovered was every bit as satisfying as the frantic rush that had marked their previous encounters.

After her heartbeat slowed and her mind cleared, Arabella screwed up her courage. "What are we doing?"

"I thought we were seeing where things lead us. Isn't that what we agreed on? I don't recall being handed a map." Caroline pressed a kiss to her cheek.

Arabella shrank back. "I suppose I still don't really know what is and isn't possible between ladies. I only know—I want you."

Caroline frowned. "Are you sure there isn't something specific you want? I know how you dislike conflict." She took her hands in her own and gazed into her eyes. "You deserve to say what is on your mind, and have it given weight and respect. I always want to hear what you think."

"Then why aren't we talking about the important things?" Arabella asked.

"What type of important things?"

"Your family, for instance."

Caroline's face became as impassive as the cliffs. "There's nothing to talk about."

"Then why do you seem so much more worried these days than you used to?"

CHAPTER EIGHTEEN

Arabella was adorable as she leaned forward with the sheet pulled up to her chest, her eyes wide without the cover of her spectacles. She was earnest and sincere and so impossibly optimistic, as if all of Caroline's problems could be banished with the power of positive thought.

Caroline felt a wave of irritation wash over her, "You know why I worry. My siblings are a major responsibility and I take it seriously. You saw how they behaved last night."

"Then why don't you wish to talk about it?"

"Because not everything can be resolved through talking, Bell," she snapped. "I can't *talk* things into seeming better than they are. I don't have the luxury to dream my problems away."

"You think I don't know this?" Arabella cried. "I, who kept my secret for years about Mr. Worthington? I worried myself sick, dreading the repercussions to my name if he breathed a word of our indiscretion. I coped by dreaming away my problems because I didn't wish to live forever doing penance through memory. But nothing was more healing to me than opening myself to you about it. Talking about it *helped*." She was magnificent with her face shining, and her chest heaving, the strength of her conviction in every taut line of her body.

Caroline's heart ached. "I'm so sorry. I spoke out of turn. It was unkind of me."

"You wanted me to speak my mind. Well, we used to talk more every day when we were neighbors. I miss it. I miss—you." Arabella picked at a stray thread in the linen sheet.

"We still see each other all the time," Caroline said.

"It's not the same as it was."

Even though they were more intimate than ever as lovers, it had stripped away her ability to talk to Arabella as a friend. It wasn't fair to either of them. Caroline realized with a start that she had been so concerned about deserving Arabella's affection and hiding her fears that she had eroded the most important part of their relationship.

Caroline blew out a breath. "I'm having a hard time of it, Bell." The words felt stuck in her throat at first, but it was easier to continue once she started. "I have raised my family alone for so many years. It was hard enough before, when we had nothing but each other. I kept Betsy and Susan out of trouble as best I could. I helped Jacob to be hired at the shop. I taught Will and George to read and pushed them to accept extra tutoring from the vicar. And now that they have the world at their fingertips—what need do they have of me?" She could hear her voice rise higher and her breath caught.

Arabella wrapped her arms around Caroline's middle. She pulled her close and buried her head in her neck. "You did everything for them. You have been a wonderful sister."

Had she been? She wasn't sure. "They don't need me anymore. Not like they used to. I wanted so much to believe that they still do, but each day seems to bring more trouble from one of them. I'm not even sure if they *like* me anymore."

That confession was at the heart of her fears. She couldn't control herself anymore. She clutched Arabella as she cried, sobs robbing her of breath as she gasped for air. Her tears soaked Arabella's hair, but she didn't move away.

"Who am I?" Caroline cried. "Who am I, if I cannot hold this family together?"

Arabella murmured to her as she wept, the words soft and soothing, and finally Caroline drew in a deep breath. It felt like the worst was over, though tears continued to wet her face.

"Your family will always need you," Arabella said, rubbing her thumb over her cheek. "You will always be their big sister. They will always turn to you, and you have shown them time and again that you will help them through anything."

"If I have shown them, then they don't remember." Caroline huffed out a sigh. "Ever since we inherited, they have run wilder than ever. Nothing I do can control them. I have been trying so hard to hide the truth of it from everyone, but I am failing them at every turn."

"If they don't remember now, they will later. They are young, and impetuous, and a handful—but they are family." Arabella wiped another tear from her face. "They love you. And you love them."

"I do." Her voice trembled, but she felt more confident.

"Of course you do." Arabella drew back, and she tucked a tendril of Caroline's hair behind her ear. "But you have to listen to them, darling. Will and George are children, but the others aren't. They are grown, and they have their own wants, and you need to let them make their own mistakes and grow on their own."

"It would be easier if they weren't so keen to fall headlong into trouble."

"If they find trouble, then so be it. You can love them and protect them, but you can't live your life for them. You need to live your life for *you*. For what *you* want."

"It's hard to imagine," Caroline whispered. "I've wanted my whole life to provide for them."

"But you are so much more than the eldest Reeve. Love isn't contingent on what you can provide or how you can help someone. You are more than the sum of all of your best qualities."

For the first time since the inheritance, Caroline felt the weight on her shoulders ease. Arabella had been right. She had thought that she would be seen as weak if she revealed the depths of her worries. But sharing her thoughts about her family wasn't a bad thing. In fact, she felt stronger than ever with Arabella by her side.

"If I could preserve every minute of this summer through your art, I would ask you to do a thousand different paintings," Caroline said, filled with gratitude. "But I would settle for a seascape." She gazed into her eyes. "And maybe a painting of the two of us."

"I would love that," Arabella said. "Something intimate. Private. Just for you."

"Exactly."

Arabella sat upright. "That's it, isn't it?"

"What?"

"That's what I'm missing from my portraits. People want something intimate. Something that captures their emotion of that one day. Something that they can gift to another."

"Which would be what, exactly?"

"Miniatures! It solves everything, does it not?"

"Does it?" Caroline asked, frowning.

"Yes! The painting I did of you on the beach took over an hour, and it was still wet when I was done. People might not want to sit for so long—they want something immediately. That's the beauty of the seaside. They can buy a handful of nuts, or go up to their ankles into the water, or listen to the musicians, all at the drop of a hat. Life is a holiday for them, with everything offered up to them at the ready. I need to offer the same thing."

"And a miniature would accomplish this?"

"Yes. Something small is quick to dry, and it creates a keepsake that they can take out now or again. It's more personal than a landscape."

"And it's something that they could secretly gift a lover," Caroline said, grinning. "It's discreet."

Arabella laughed, her face shining. "I can't wait to get started."

❖

Although Arabella steadfastly continued to bring her novels every Wednesday, Caroline loved visiting the lending library now that she could afford the subscription. She had brought Susan and Betsy to meet Lady Edith and Grace.

Betsy had refused to speak to Caroline since the party, and instead huddled with Lady Edith and Susan and shot Caroline dark looks whenever she chanced to glance her way.

Caroline stood with Grace at the other end of the room.

Grace frowned at the books in front of them. "I enjoy a verse or two in the evening, but I confess to being sick unto death of Lord Byron. Some days, it's all the conversation I have from Lady Edith."

Betsy was sitting in an armchair, Susan was sitting on one of the arms, and Lady Edith was leaning over the back. She could hear them giggle amidst lines from *Childe Harold's Pilgrimage*.

"His verse makes me want to cover my ears," Grace confessed. "Would that be unfathomably rude in a library? I suppose one ought to encourage literacy, even if I don't care for the source."

"I advise you to encourage it in other ways," Caroline said. "Otherwise, you end up with young ladies who go so far as to naming the neighbor's cats after aggravating poets."

"Is that how Arabella's cats received their names?" Grace smiled. "That's dear of them."

"Susan found them when they were kittens, abandoned and half-starved, and brought them home. Arabella wanted them as soon as she saw them—she has a soft heart—and her brother relented, hoping that they would at least be good mousers. Which they are not," she said, laughing.

"How are things with Arabella?"

"She is working on a new artistic project—she is painting miniatures for the visitors on the beach." She was so proud of Arabella for taking the risk of painting in public. She knew how private Arabella was, and that it had taken a great amount of courage for her to do this.

"That's a splendid idea."

Caroline struggled to express the delight she felt when she looked at Arabella's portraits—the clever expressions, the wonderful attention to detail, the delicate touch she had with color—but words failed her. "They're the best," she said finally. "Simply the best."

She told Grace about her plan to help Arabella at her next portrait session and was happy to have her support.

Grace leaned closer. "And what of your relationship?"

"Perfect."

"Really? How wonderful!"

Caroline felt a warmth deep inside as she thought about confiding in Arabella last night. Nothing had felt so right.

"Really," she said firmly. "If you are tired of poets, might I suggest looking for something besides books?" she added. "The lending library has a good many other things to loan, if you have need of anything."

"Oh, yes. That reminds me—Lady Edith!" she called out.

Lady Edith straightened, looking self-conscious at having been caught leaning over the chair like a schoolgirl. Caroline wished Susan and Betsy had such concerns, but they kept giggling together.

"Betsy, Susan. That's enough," she said. "You own that copy at home and have no need of borrowing it."

They rose as if it was the most laborious chore in the world, and Susan plopped the volume of poetry back onto the shelf with a thunk.

"Lady Edith, did you not wish to check if the library has a flute in their musical instrument section?" Grace asked.

She brightened. "Oh yes! I would love the opportunity to play again. I was worried that bringing my own would damage it during the journey," she explained to Betsy, who nodded as if she knew anything at all about instruments, which Caroline knew she did not.

"There are ever so many in the music room," Susan chirped up. "Do let us go and see what is available!"

They moved to the music room, where Betsy slid onto a stool in front of a pianoforte that was used for evening performances, and began very prettily to ask one of the gentlemen perusing the room if he would be so good as to tutor her in all things musical.

Caroline pressed a hand to her head, then strode over. She wedged herself between Betsy and the gentleman, who was peering with great interest down Betsy's dress. Where on earth had her fichu gone? Had she no modesty?

"My sister needs no such help, thank you," she said, ignoring Betsy's pout.

"I thought you would wish me to encourage other suitors, as you seemed displeased with Mr. Graham." Fire snapped in her eyes.

Caroline didn't choose to respond to that. "Betsy, why don't you help Lady Edith choose some sheet music for her flute?"

Betsy sulked over to Lady Edith, where Susan was already flipping through ballads and singing off-key. Caroline went over to them as well and cupped Susan's elbow, leaning in close. "Susan dearest, perhaps we could employ a singing tutor if you have any interest in performing in public. Would you enjoy that?"

"I don't think so," she said after a moment of thought. "I rather like my voice. Edie says it's very energetic."

Lady Edith looked apologetic. Caroline couldn't blame her. It would be difficult to tell a friend that she was not in the best voice for company.

"Perhaps you could restrain yourself here and give us all a chance to focus on the tasks at hand."

Susan nodded and flipped another sheet of music.

Jacob strode in. "Caro, there you are! I was looking all over for you!"

His eyes were wild, and Caroline was shocked as he came closer and she smelled gin on his breath. It was but half past two in the afternoon. His chest was heaving as if he had run across town.

CHAPTER NINETEEN

Jacob was less than steady on his feet. Caroline gripped his arm and wrenched him out of the lending library. "Have you no decorum? Could this not wait until we were home?"

Susan and Betsy came after them, their heels clacking loudly on the stairs.

"I have things under control, Caro." He ran his hand through his hair and tugged at his dishevelled cravat.

"The devil you do!" Caroline snapped. "What is the meaning of this?"

The street wasn't empty, but thankfully it wasn't so crowded that they would be overheard. Of course, none of her family members would have cared if it was thronged with curious visitors with eager ears.

"I might be in a spot of trouble," he said, his voice low. "But don't worry. I will leave Inverley for a spell, and all this will blow over."

"Leave Inverley!" Betsy cried. "Oh, do take me with you!"

"And me!" Susan said.

"No one is going with him," Caroline said sharply. "Why are you so desperate to leave, Jacob?"

"I may have gambled a little too much last night at our party, and—and—dash it all, I had to leave my vowels." He rubbed his brow with his thumb and forefinger, and Caroline noticed that his hand was shaking. "I don't have the blunt to cover the debt. I must be off to London to visit our banker."

"How much did you lose, Jacob?"

She stared into his eyes, willing him to give the answer, but he looked away.

"I have enough to cover it," he muttered. "I think. I'm going to handle this. But I must away, and at once. I am off to fetch my curricle and then I shall kick the dust of Inverley from my heels." His bloodshot eyes were narrow and determined, his mouth in a harsh line.

"How much?" Caroline asked again.

"You haven't even packed a bag," Susan said.

"I am rushing home to pack before I leave."

"Where will you stay?"

"Mr. Taylor gave me leave to use his rented rooms at the Albany, and he said I could have the use of anything I needed."

"Oh, Jacob." Caroline felt weariness settle all the way to her bones.

He glared at her. "This is *nothing*, Caro! The merest trifle. Everyone understands that a man must sow his wild oats."

"Why can a man sow his oats, and a woman cannot?" Betsy cried. "Oh, how I wish I could gamble until dawn and drink myself silly!"

"Trust me, you do not," Jacob snapped. "You would do well to listen to Caroline and cease your nonsense before you get into as much trouble as I have."

He broke free of Caroline's grip, and his long stride soon had him out of view as he raced toward home.

They followed more slowly. Betsy and Susan were engrossed in family gossip that for once didn't center on themselves, whispering to themselves all the way home.

Arabella had told her that she should let her brothers and sisters make their own mistakes. But how could she, when those mistakes became disastrous? Her heart ached as the weight of responsibility pressed down on her. What was the correct course of action? How was she to know how to help her family?

Maybe this would be the last of it. Maybe they all had a hiccup or two that they needed to get through while they grew accustomed to their new life. Maybe Jacob's problem was the nasty shock that he needed before he learned to settle down. Maybe—just maybe—this was salvageable.

❖

Arabella pushed the cart that she had borrowed from a neighbor, which carried stools, her supplies, and a wooden sign that she had painted to promote her miniatures. It was far easier than carrying everything between herself and Caroline.

She puzzled over moving the cart into the soft sand, then decided that the best location for her painting would be close to the promenade, which opened onto the beach. She could settle her cart on the grass and work from the sand. There was a better chance of attracting paying clientele from that side of the beach, after all, and if people had already spent an afternoon strolling, then they might wish to sit for a spell and have their painting done before moving on to seek other shoreside pleasures.

Caroline helped unload the cart, and soon they were well established near both the promenade and the food vendors. She seemed quiet.

Arabella was disappointed. She had thought their conversation after the dinner party had been so meaningful. Hadn't it meant anything to Caroline? Why wasn't she talking about what was troubling her?

Then she frowned. She too had to share the responsibility in improving their communication. Her tendency was to keep silent, letting an unpleasant situation continue because she didn't wish to go against the grain.

If she wanted Caroline to confide in her, then she owed it to her to be direct. "Is something troubling you?" she asked, worried that Caroline would keep it from her.

Caroline dug the sign into the sand. "Yes," she admitted. "It's about Jacob." Arabella was alarmed at her somber tone, but Caroline held up a finger. "No, Bell. This moment is not to be overshadowed by Reeve problems. I promise I will tell you every single detail later. But I want today to be about you. This is about your talents and accomplishments. This is a special moment, and I want to make sure that you feel celebrated."

Oh. Arabella's heart clutched. This was a gift that she hadn't anticipated.

"Now we wait," Arabella declared, trying to feel positive. The memory of last week's failed portrait session weighed on her mind. *Confidence*, she reminded herself.

"I arranged reinforcements," Caroline said, her face brightening as she pointed to Maeve, Grace, and Lady Edith hurrying toward them.

"I do hope we aren't late," Grace said, looking at her with a crease in her brow.

Arabella's heart swelled as she glanced at Caroline. "Late?"

"I thought if you started with a line of people waiting for their portrait to be done, it would attract other people. From far off, they will see that something of interest is going on, and that should draw them close enough to read the sign."

She was too choked up to speak, but as she gazed at Caroline, she saw by the softening look in her eyes that she knew how much this meant to her.

"I want my miniature done first," Maeve declared. "May I sit, Arabella?"

"Of course."

For a moment, she took in the scene. Her friends were here, and Caroline was grinning as if she had been told that a crown prince had offered for Betsy. The sun was shining, and she was having...*fun*. It was less like work when friends were here. She wasn't thinking about the money that the portraits would provide, or her dreams of the cottage.

She dipped her brush into water and stroked it across the paints, choosing to lay down the skin tone first, then added hair and lips and eyes and clothes, stroking in a tiny seashore behind her, and adding little seashells to the corners of the page. To capture Maeve's air of fashion, she paid extra attention to the lace at her throat and the ribbons in her bonnet, dabbing a little paint away with her handkerchief to represent the shine of ribbon and the gleam of jewels on her earbobs.

She was working with finer brushes today and had cut her paper into little squares no larger than the palm of her hand. Her work was detailed but came together quickly due to the small size of the artwork, and she felt like she was finishing almost as soon as she had started.

Maeve leapt from the stool as soon as Arabella said it was done and peered at the page. "I love it!" she declared.

Warmth spread through Arabella. What a joy it was to bring such instant happiness to others.

"Would you like to choose your frame?" Arabella opened a wooden box to reveal the frames that she had purchased, hoping that one would suit Maeve. She had bought a variety of styles of oval frames, from fine filigreed silver to plain gold to carved mahogany. Some were meant to be worn as lockets, with a lock of hair kept tucked inside next to the painting, and others were designed to be hung on the wall or kept in a keepsake box.

Grace looked over her shoulder at the painting. "What a fine likeness, Arabella! It looks exactly like her. Well done!"

Maeve chose a locket frame and Arabella set it aside with her miniature. "If you would be so good as to wait for a quarter hour, the portrait will be ready to frame and you can tuck it into your reticule."

Lady Edith smiled. "You are wonderfully talented, Miss Seton. Please may I sit next?"

By the time Arabella had finished Lady Edith's miniature and had moved on to work on Grace's, a pair of ladies had approached, curiosity on their faces.

"Good afternoon. Pray tell, is anyone free to sit and have their likeness taken?" one of them asked.

Arabella was too surprised to speak. Were they truly interested?

"Anyone with a pair of crowns in their pocket for a portrait and a frame," Caroline said while Arabella struggled to find her words. "Miss Seton is very accomplished. She has already done portraits for these ladies, and you can see by her current progress how talented she is. All of Inverley has been proud of her artwork for many years."

Arabella cleared her throat. "I would be delighted to paint such fine ladies as yourselves."

They stepped behind Arabella, and she couldn't see their faces as she continued to lay in Grace's sweet smile and kind eyes on the paper, but she heard their delighted sounds.

"I would love to have a miniature. I've never had one done before," one of them said. "I am Miss Anderson of Dover, and there certainly are artists in residence in my hometown, but they mostly work with oil paints. They are ever so dear."

"It takes *so* long for an oil portrait," her friend said. "I had to sit for several sessions. It is a marvel to have one done so quickly. I have never seen an artist work out of doors before."

"Ladies, may I request you to give the artist a little space?" Caroline asked. "Perhaps you could stand over here while you wait, if you don't mind."

Arabella hadn't been aware of tensing up, but she felt her shoulders drop and her breath come a little easier and realized Caroline must have noticed and made sure that she was comfortable.

The sun was bright on her work as she finished up Grace's portrait and moved on to the ladies from Dover. She had chosen her widest-brimmed bonnet to shade her eyes but eschewed a pair of gloves. Her hands would tan by the end of the summer, but she didn't care. She was no fine lady, after all.

She was something much better in her opinion. A fine artist.

Mr. Worthington strolled up and greeted them. "Why, Miss Seton, I thought you a landscape artist. How charming it is to see that you do likenesses as well."

"Miss Seton's work is excellent," Caroline said coolly, staring at Mr. Worthington. "It is more than just a good likeness."

Without asking leave, he picked up one of the portraits that was drying in the sun. Arabella was annoyed at his presumption.

"These are superb." There was surprise in his voice.

"Thank you," Arabella said, and continued to paint.

Miss Anderson handed over her two crowns, and Mr. Worthington's eyes sharpened. "A most excellent business. I congratulate you." He tipped his hat to her before taking his leave, much to Arabella's relief.

A few more people wandered over to them, and their conversations washed over her as easily as her brush moved across the paper.

Arabella felt like she belonged here more than she did in a ballroom. She was now part of the long string of vendors and singers and people who worked near the sea to earn their bread, to bring pleasure and entertainment to the visitors who wanted a slice of escape.

While she worked and talked with them, she was able to escape too. Into a slice of *their* life.

For all that they sighed about how nice it was to be here by the seaside, what they really wanted to talk more about was where they were from. What they did at home. Whether they worked or were lucky enough to have no profession. What the conditions were with their local canals or the mines or the wool trade, depending on the circumstance of their towns.

She was learning more about England listening to them than she ever had by skimming the papers or discussing the news of the day with the neighbors over dinner.

Arabella hadn't realized how wonderful it would be to talk to the visitors and learn about them as she created their artwork. It was an exchange she didn't have when painting seascapes, and she was delighted to discover how much she enjoyed it.

Susan and Betsy flew across the beach as the line dwindled in the late afternoon, at the hour when visitors tended to seek out their lodgings to ready themselves for dinner. Grace and Lady Edith and Maeve had all long gone to other engagements.

"I am ever so sorry we're late!" Susan cried. She was carrying a basket piled high with tarts, which she lifted above her head as proud as if she had won it in a tourney. "I thought you might need sustenance after all this work."

Arabella beamed at her. "You're so thoughtful. I would love something sweet."

Betsy laughed. "We thought so. There's a chocolate bun for you, Bell—I remember you're more partial to them than the raspberry tarts. And there's a jug of lemonade."

"You are kind, girls."

She took a bite of her bun and was too hungry to savor it, happy to stretch out her cramped fingers and to taste sugar on her tongue.

"Are we too late to have our likenesses done?" Susan asked, biting her lip.

"For today, yes. But there will be other days. Today was good." She grinned at Caroline. "Your sister helped make it a success for me. Without her pushing people toward me, I never would have had such a line of customers."

Betsy heaved a sigh, then raised a shoulder. "She's good at fixing things like this," she said in a rush, as if the words were hard to say. "Was this one of her plans? She always has a plan. *And* a list."

"Yes. But it made everything perfect. I love Caroline's plans."

Caroline put her hand on Arabella's shoulder and gazed into her eyes. "Your success today happened because of *you*, Bell. Not because I had a few ideas to nudge things along. People were drawn to your talent, and your demeanor. You are so good with the visitors."

"Bell really sees people," Susan chirped up. "I like the way she paints, like her whole focus is on what is before her."

Arabella felt absurdly happy. "You are too kind, all of you. Now if you all help me pack up my cart, I have enough coins in my reticule to treat us all to a fine dinner at the eatery near the hotel."

Caroline frowned. "You should save what you earned today. I can take us all there—"

"No," she said. "I want to spend the coin that I have earned on a celebration with people I love."

She was part of more than the scene on the beach, and the group of vendors who sold their wares. She grinned at the Reeves. She was part of these people. And that was all she wanted.

CHAPTER TWENTY

Caroline told Arabella everything she knew about Jacob and his gambling debts after they left the eatery. After they had finished dinner, Betsy and Susan had gone in search of Lady Margaret, as they were to attend a soiree later in the evening.

"Jacob is in a predicament," Caroline said as they walked through town, arm in arm. "That much can be deduced. But the rest of the details are foggy indeed."

Arabella frowned. "Did he tell you to whom he lost the money?"

"Yes, but the name is unfamiliar to me. No one I've asked has ever heard of him."

"I suppose he was a visitor, wishing to impress. But oh, how awful for Jacob."

Caroline had to bite her tongue before saying much more, because she wanted to tell Arabella that this had proved her point. Her siblings still needed protection from the vagaries of life.

Two weeks passed, which stretched Caroline's nerves to the breaking point. The only pleasure in her days was when she accompanied Arabella to her painting sessions on the beach, each one more successful than the last. It brought her a deep joy to see how people reacted to Arabella and her art.

After all, how could anyone *not* react with joy around Arabella?

She certainly did, when they found a private hour or two to spend by themselves.

Caroline's evenings were strained. She spent them dancing at the assembly rooms or dining with new friends and acquaintances, all the while maintaining the facade that the Reeves were respectable. She pushed Betsy and Susan at every suitor who looked their way, despite her sisters' lukewarm reception.

Caroline found relief in an invitation from Rachel and Matthew to dine one night. Her return to Belvoir Lane felt like a balm to her soul. She needed no airs or pretensions at the Seton dinner table. The Setons were like family. And Arabella, smiling at her from across the table, was becoming so much more than family.

Matthew offered the service of Fred, the Setons' manservant, to escort Caroline home after the last sip of tea and the last crumb of cake had long since disappeared.

"I shall go with her," Arabella announced.

"Yes, do spend the night at the Reeves'," Rachel said. "I am sure you two miss having so many opportunities to talk in a day, as you once did!"

The evening turned to dusk as they left the house, pink and orange streaking across the sky from the setting run. The air was warm and lovely, but Caroline felt restless. She wanted to hold this moment in the palm of her hand, perfect and eternal, and at the same time she wished to speed their way through Inverley to tumble Arabella onto her feather bed.

She wanted it all. The past and the future. Why could not time hold still? She spent so little of the present enjoying it, always worried about what would come next. Why were the minutes so fleeting, forever changing her life into something else?   .

There was the faint strain of music in the air, and Caroline slowed as they walked past the grocer's.

"You need something to distract yourself from your troubles," Arabella said. "Shall we? For old time's sake?"

Caroline grinned. "Yes."

Fred was more than happy to accompany them to the second floor of the grocer's shop for the evening. The monthly dance was welcome to all in the neighborhood.

They made their way upstairs, and a crowd of familiar faces awaited them. The grocer and his wife, Mr. and Mrs. Elmaleh, were busy handing around refreshments. There was the butcher, the blacksmith, and the candlestick maker, and their sons and daughters.

Caroline had moved but half a mile from her old home, and yet she hadn't seen these people in ages. The realization humbled her. Was it possible that Arabella had been right? Was she growing too proud of her new station, for her to have forgotten where she came from? These were friends and neighbors who had always treated her well and never had anything but a kind word for her and her family. She would have to do better by them. She wanted to be Caroline of Inverley, not treated like a visitor in her own village.

There were no grand musicians trained in London here tonight—there was simply old Mr. Brown playing rousing music on his fiddle, his rheumatic wrist slipping up a note here and there.

"Why, Miss Reeve! Thought you might be too grand for us these days." Mr. Elmaleh grinned at her. "I used to see you all the time in the shop, and now you've a manservant to do the shopping for you. Thought you forgot all about us."

"Never, sir!" She dug into her reticule and dropped a guinea in his palm.

He tried to press it back into her hand. "You know better than anyone that this is no fancy place, with subscription fees and whatnot. Townsfolk having fun, that's all we want here."

"Keep it," she said softly. "For the shop. I used to owe you every week for groceries and you were always so good about it."

"Bah, we don't need charity. Shop's doing all right for itself."

But she closed his fist over the coin and he gave her a gruff thank you.

"There aren't enough partners for dancing right now," Mrs. Elmaleh said apologetically. "There are six couples tonight, but they are paired up already."

Caroline looked at Arabella. "Perhaps—well—could we not dance together?"

Mrs. Elmaleh laughed. "Why yes, you might as well! Not enough men for dancing now that war has taken so many away from us, so why not take your turn where you may. Off with you now."

Caroline had always enjoyed dancing but hadn't realized what fun it would be to swing Arabella around the room. It took a moment for them to establish who would lead and who would dip, but after a few minutes of laughter, they found a rhythm. It was satisfying beyond all measure to stomp and twirl and clap their hands together in the country dances that either of them had only danced before with men. It was wonderful to laugh and shout on each other's arms, almost as comfortable as they were in their own home.

Mrs. Rivendell was cutting generous slices of her famous peach pie, and Caroline's mouth watered. A helping of pie baked by a dear neighbor was heaven in comparison to the fancy jelly that graced her dessert table too often these days. There were shouts and cries of delight when Mr. Brown tucked away his fiddle and slyly pulled a bottle of French brandy from his satchel. Caroline found herself sharing a dram from a chipped teacup with Arabella, as there weren't enough cups to go around for everyone.

Caroline grabbed the teacup and took a sip. "Jacob thinks he's clever by hiding an extra bottle of brandy in the back garden. I have been enjoying a lovely drink now and again when Betsy gets too out of hand."

Arabella laughed. "Your brothers and sisters are never dull," she said, and snagged the cup to take another drink of her own.

Once upon a time, an evening like this had been the highlight of her life. She drank from the teacup again. Caroline didn't want it to end. She wanted to engrave each step and smile and laugh in her memory so she could carry it with her forever.

"Do you miss it?" Arabella asked softly.

She blinked, having lost her train of thought. "Miss what?"

"Do you miss your life before wealth changed everything?"

"Yes," she said, and the enormity of it hit her. How was Arabella so insightful? She hadn't admitted it even to herself. "It was easier before. We might have riches now, but in so many ways this inheritance is nothing more than a wealth of inconvenience." She blinked back tears that threatened to spill. "Shall we go back to dancing? If Mr. Brown tires not with his fiddle—and he must be seventy if he's a day—then how should we be too tired to dance again?"

If Caroline never stopped dancing, then she wouldn't have to think, and if she didn't think, then she couldn't worry.

The result was that she ended up dancing with Arabella for three sets in a row.

"If I were a man, we would be considered engaged right now," Arabella said with a laugh. "Shall I ask your brother for your hand tomorrow?"

Caroline's breath caught. Perhaps it was the warmth of the brandy running through her veins, but oh, how she wished it were possible! It was agony knowing that it was something they could never have. Such a simple thing to arrange between two people—if those two people were one man and one woman.

Caroline laughed, though it hurt. "All of this between us is a dream, isn't it?"

"It's not a dream," Arabella said, her face set. "It's simply that it's private. Just for us."

"I want more than that."

"So do I," she said softly. "But that isn't what is given to us to have."

❖

Near the end of the night, Arabella followed Caroline downstairs past the stockroom and through the back door. Arabella sat down on the wooden stair, tipping her head back and gulping in the cool night air to soothe her throat, raw from brandy and aching from shouting her conversations above the din of the fiddle. Her dress was damp with sweat, and she was giddy from drink.

Even from downstairs, she could hear the thumping of shoes and boots as the fiddle played on and the dancing continued. She was relieved to have a break from the pell-mell party to focus on the crash of the waves and the stillness of the night around them.

Caroline slid down beside her, and Arabella leaned her head against her shoulder. "The stars are beautiful tonight."

They were twinkling sharp and brilliant in the deep black night. But tonight when Arabella looked up into the starlight, she felt overwhelmed by their terrifying beauty. It made her feel afraid. Small and alone. She shifted closer to Caroline and received a kiss to the top of her head.

"I'm right here."

Of course she was. Caroline knew all her fears, great and small. She knew every trivial like and dislike. And she was always a shoulder to lean on.

Those three dances weighed on her. A token of her involvement, a sign meant for the two of them.

But did Caroline see it the same way?

Her heart was thudding, and it wasn't from the dancing.

"We aren't meant for this life anymore, are we?" Arabella asked.

Caroline stiffened and pulled away. "I am *not* too proud, despite what you said before—I assure you—"

"No, no. I mean that *we* aren't the same anymore. We aren't the same girls we once were, or the women who used to come out here on the last Thursday of every month for dancing."

"No one stays the same forever."

They didn't, but somehow the events of this summer felt like the sands shifting during the tides in triple time.

"I suppose they don't," was all she said, and she summoned a smile. "Shall we see if Fred is ready to escort us home? Shall we go back to your rooms for the night?"

Caroline's smile was sweet, and it filled her heart up enough to get her through the walk home and to slip between Caroline's linen sheets and make love to her with every emotion she had.

But she felt sad and lost and unsure as she lay awake long after Caroline had fallen asleep, looking up through the window at the fathomless night sky and the patch of winking stars.

CHAPTER TWENTY-ONE

Jacob's face was drawn and ashy, as haggard as if he hadn't slept a wink of the two weeks that he had stayed in London. He sank into the armchair, slouching down as if he could hide behind the starched points of his collar.

Caroline felt a flutter of anxiety in her chest. "How bad is it, Jacob?"

He slumped even further. "It isn't good." He scowled. "You don't have to say it. I know I'm a damned fool."

"You are," she agreed, and touched his knee. "But you're still my brother. And I shall stand with you."

"I don't deserve it."

"Well, out with it," she said briskly. "Tell me everything, and we shall put our heads together."

He took out a cheroot and twisted it in his hands, frowning down at it. "I was deep in my cups at the housewarming party. I oughtn't have had so much brandy—but I've never had a problem to hold my own at the end of a night's carousing with the lads. These fellows at the party not only drank deep, though, but they played deep. I wanted to show that I could too, especially as a man in my own house. I hardly knew what I was doing, but I spent everything in my pockets—and I had already taken out more from the bank than I should have."

"How much?"

"The most that the Inverley bank would allow me to withdraw was three hundred pounds." He swallowed. "I lost it all."

Before the inheritance, that would have gone a long way to support the Reeves. Caroline felt sick at the thought of wasting it on the flick of a wrist at cards, but she held her tongue. There was no use heaping blame when he was already so miserable.

"But I kept playing. I should have known better, but I thought I could win it back. I was too drunk, too befuddled to pay attention."

"How much did you lose?"

"Forty thousand."

Caroline reeled in shock. *"Forty thousand pounds?"*

"I talked to the bankers, and to a solicitor, and they agree that I am honor bound to pay my debts. I am of age, after all. I must take my responsibility."

"But that's almost everything you have."

Caroline could hardly believe what she was hearing. She gripped the arm of her chair to steady herself. They had already sold the house on Belvoir Lane, and although she had set aside funds to pay the rents on the townhouse, that money would run out by the end of the summer.

All of their hard work to improve their situation in life, all of their plans for the future, were gone in the snap of a finger.

What was to become of them?

"Maybe I can woo a young heiress with more money than sense."

"Don't speak that way," Caroline said sharply. "Those young ladies deserve your respect."

"Will you marry one, then?" he asked, almost with disinterest.

Her heart skipped a beat. "An heiress?"

He laughed. "Of course not, you goose. A fortune hunter."

"Maybe I shall have to."

"Though you haven't much fortune left, truth be told. I wasn't a complete cad. I did work out a way to save some of the investments that protect your dowries, though they are worth less than a quarter of what they were initially."

Her heart railed against it. How much more did she need to sacrifice for her family?

But this mistake was far more serious than the spilled ink bottles or broken windows from Jacob's youthful high spirits. Poor Jacob. His life had changed more than any of theirs—how could anyone avoid mistakes when one transformed from a shopkeeper's assistant to a young baronet overnight?

If she married, at least she would be able to provide a home for George and Will. And if she married the right man, she might salvage the reputation of the Reeve name for Betsy and Susan, as it surely would be tainted by Jacob's reckless gambling.

She should make sure that Betsy and Susan married well and fast, or they would be living in penury by the time there was snow on the ground. After the wild excess of the summer, it was hard to think of living like they used to.

She felt the hot flush of shame on her cheeks. Just this past week, she had laughed and danced with Arabella at the grocer's, reminiscing about the way things had been. Faced now with going back to that life, she felt devastated. She had indeed become proud of her station and hadn't known the depths of it until now.

It wasn't well done of her.

Her heart felt like it was twisting in a vise. If they were to survive, then all of her attention must be focused on her family.

Not on herself.

Not on Arabella.

What would Arabella think of her?

But Arabella had her own future to plan now. Caroline had never seen her happier than when she had been painting the miniatures on the beach. She deserved better than catering to the Reeves and their messes.

Her stomach churned again as she thought of all those years she had taken Arabella for granted. How many times had she expected Arabella to stop by after she had finished painting for the day, or to coax her for a walk on the bluffs, or to pour her a glass of elderberry wine for a long coze before they both went their separate ways to bed?

No more. Arabella deserved a full and complete life, not a half life lived for her brother, and certainly not lived for her.

❖

Caroline marched her sisters and Lady Margaret to the assembly rooms the next evening. She was explicit before they left—their goal was to find wealthy men to marry.

"No officers," she said, glaring at Betsy as they drew on their gloves. "Sensible men with wealth shall do, now that we have lost our own."

Lady Margaret sighed. "It is a shame how fast one's fortunes can fall. I have heard of it being the ruin of many a debutante, you know."

Susan blanched, and Caroline shot a warning glance at Lady Margaret. "There is no ruin here," she said, trying to sound calm. "All we need to do is act quicker than the rumor mill."

"You will need to be fleet of foot," Lady Margaret said. "But I will do my best to help you girls."

The room was warm tonight, despite the open windows. It was the swell of the summer season, with dozens of gentlemen that she didn't recognize fetching lemonade for swan-necked ladies who were as pretty as any of Arabella's paintings.

Thankfully, she soon spotted Arabella as well.

She left her sisters with Lady Margaret and strode over to her.

Arabella squeezed her hand. "How is Jacob?"

"Sulking in his rooms. But I cannot blame him. He has lost everything."

"He must be devastated. Is there anything he can do?"

Caroline squared her shoulders. Though she was dressed in a muslin frock, with pins in her hair and dance slippers on her feet, she felt like a general about to go to war. "There is not much that Jacob can do. We have nothing, Bell. I need to refocus all my attention on making sure Betsy and Susan are provided for. There's only one way left that I can try to provide for them."

Arabella went very still. "You would—marry?"

Despair clawed at her throat, but she swallowed the words that she wanted to say. "If I must."

She felt brittle, as if she could blow away in the breeze coming in through the windows.

"You're not alone in this," Arabella said, reaching for her hand. "You have *me*."

That glow on her face pained Caroline to the core. "My dear, it's not enough," she said, and moved her hand away. Arabella's face dropped and her shoulder slumped. "If my brothers and sisters cannot settle themselves because they fall into one scrape after another, then it is up to me to see us all respectably arranged again. I must set it all to rights."

"But—"

"There is no but. Our name depends on my success."

"You don't have to sacrifice yourself for your family! You would be miserable married to a man."

Arabella wasn't looking at her anymore. Caroline knew from long habit that it was because she couldn't conceal her emotions, so she was staring into the sea of dancers, her bosom rising and falling with shallow breaths.

Caroline reached out and tipped her chin to turn it toward her. "Bell, it's what I must do. I must endure unhappiness for their sake."

Arabella's eyes were luminous and her face was splotched with red.

A gentleman approached them, and Caroline steeled herself to admit that she was free for whichever set he wished to dance.

To her surprise—he was here for Arabella.

"Miss Seton, the portraitist!" He bowed and then kissed her hand. "I so admired your work when I saw you on the beach last week."

"Oh yes, Mr. Williams. I do remember you stopping by to chat." Arabella shot a look at Caroline, who knew perfectly well what she meant by it.

As per the spinsters' agreement, Caroline should dissuade him from asking Arabella to dance. But she hesitated.

"Dare I hope that you are free for a dance, Miss Seton?"

Arabella fidgeted with her fan. She took her time before replying, but was forced to when Caroline said nothing. "I suppose I am."

This was different from thwarting unwanted advances. Arabella had a business to run. This gentleman could become a customer and could recommend her artwork to his friends. Arabella deserved the chance to grow her success where she could.

Arabella and Mr. Williams joined the dancers, but it was Caroline's mind that whirled round and round.

It was wonderful to see Arabella being appreciated. But a spark of jealousy flared inside her. After all, she had always appreciated Arabella. Everything about her, in fact, from her talents, to her warmth, to her sweet nature.

In fact, she more than appreciated Arabella.

She loved her.

Love was the name of this half-sick agony that had her clenching her hands as she watched Arabella in a man's arms.

Love had been growing on her all summer, as slow, tenacious, and unnoticeable as a barnacle beneath a ship's prow.

Now she was deep in its throes, and it was too late to do anything about it.

She watched Arabella dance, the candlelight shining on her face and glinting off her spectacles, and wanted to weep for the loss of what she had just learned that she had.

How was it that all these weeks had been wasted in flirtation and lovemaking, and not enough time spent in putting the truth of her heart to words? Arabella had been right. They hadn't spent enough time talking about things that mattered most.

She wanted to pour her heart out now.

She wanted to rage against the future of money and marriage and misery.

She wanted to throw herself between Arabella and Mr. Williams and declare herself to be Arabella's lover, to claim her for her own.

She wanted to tell her family to find their own solution to their troubles.

But she couldn't.

Why had she jettisoned her chances for success during all these weeks? Why had she turned away from respectable gentlemen who would have leapt at the chance at her dowry? Where were those men now?

She hated the idea of wedding a man for his name and position and for what he could provide for her family, and more than anything, she hated the idea that it was because she had failed so spectacularly at providing for them herself.

She didn't want her circumstances to change, and to be whisked off to some town house in London or an estate in another county. She had never traveled so much as fifteen miles beyond these shores. The idea of settling in another part of England felt as strange as the idea of relocating to France.

At least in France, she wouldn't be in any danger of ever seeing Arabella again after her marriage.

How would she endure the touch of a man, when all she wanted were Arabella's hands and lips upon her?

Standing there with no dance partner and no friend in sight, Caroline felt her stomach twist as she realized that while Arabella was being pursued because of her own merit and talents, Caroline had only been pursued because of a fluke, a happenstance of fortune. And now it was gone.

Caroline felt flustered. At every event she had attended, she had been courted. Tonight, everyone was polite, but distant.

Had she shown herself to be too proud this summer, declining so many dances and opportunities to talk with gentlemen?

Or had news of their faded fortunes already made its way through the assembly?

She tried to flush her worries away with her fan, plying it so fast that her wrist would ache later. A drink would do her good. She made her way to the refreshment table to select a glass of the least-warm looking lemonade that she could discern, when a shadow loomed over her.

James Martin.

CHAPTER TWENTY-TWO

James smiled at Caroline and offered her a glass of wine. "A woman who looks like you should never appear in such dire need of sustenance. Gentlemen should be lining up to offer you refreshments."

He wasn't her first choice of companionship, but the wine was more than welcome. She thanked him and took a healthy sip.

"Why is there trouble on that pretty face of yours?"

She shook her head. "No need to concern yourself."

"It's Jacob, isn't it?" He shook his head. "I've played a hand or two with him this summer. The lad has no skill at cards, I am sad to say."

"Of course he doesn't," she snapped. "Where on earth would he have learned any? Playing for ha'penny stakes at the tavern?"

"Well, I was sorry to hear the news." His face was uncharacteristically serious. "I had thought it high time that you were living the life you deserved this summer. I always thought well of you, you know."

She took another gulp of wine but didn't say anything as she couldn't return the compliment.

"It pains me to say it, but there are not so many challengers for your hand these days, are there?" He scanned the room. "I see no champion emerging."

James would be surprised if one did, as any challenger for her hand or heart would have been Arabella.

"You are correct. I am not so in demand anymore. And yet, my position on matrimony has changed from what it once was."

His gaze sharpened. "Indeed?"

Oh, how wretched this was.

The idea filled her with no pleasure, but it was well known that the Martins had the largest estate in Inverley, with a sizeable fortune. His family was very well regarded. He knew her family from when they were all children together. If he was serious in his pursuit, then it would go a long way toward improving the situation for Betsy and Susan to find respectable matches.

"Very interesting. Perhaps you may finally look kindly on a suit from an old friend, in that case." He raised a brow.

She nodded and finished her wine. "I think I might."

He bowed and took his leave of her.

Arabella marched back to her after the set ended. Her chest was heaving, and her eyes were bright with anger. Caroline stared. This was most unlike her.

"You should have saved me," she said. "I didn't want to dance."

"It's for the best. You should be taking the opportunity to talk up your business, especially to people who have already expressed interest." It was the sensible approach. Why wasn't Arabella agreeing with her?

"I didn't wish to. Not here. Caroline, I was counting on you."

She blinked. "You can always count on me. I was only thinking of you, Bell."

"You don't always know what's best for everyone, Caroline Reeve."

Arabella stalked off.

Nothing was going right anymore.

❖

Maybe Caroline was right.

Maybe Arabella should have been thrilled at the opportunity to dance with any gentlemen who asked, and to ask them about their desires for a painting or two. After all, that was why they had asked her to dance—odd Arabella Seton had finally found herself to be fashionable.

People now wanted to talk to the quaint local miniaturist. Arabella felt as overlooked as ever, as if the painter was a persona that she was struggling to embody.

She didn't like it above half.

She had spent so long this summer convincing herself to be brave, and now when faced with warmth and appreciation, she found herself quaking in her dance slippers. It hardly made any sense. She might feel like she fit in on the beach, but in the assembly rooms, she felt like the biggest fraud in Inverley.

Mr. Worthington approached her with a glass of wine in hand. "May I offer you refreshment, Miss Seton? The evening is fine, and I thought perhaps we could stroll on the terrace."

She was annoyed enough with Caroline to agree. If this is what Caroline wished to see, then let her watch as she left with Mr. Worthington.

The night was warm, and the terrace was full of couples staring up at the stars or strolling closer together than was quite proper.

Arabella realized too late that this was not going to be a casual walk.

"I am so pleased that you accepted, Miss Seton." Mr Worthington brought her hand to his lips in a show of gallantry that she didn't remember from their previous courting days. "I thought my attentions too marked to be unnoticed by a shrewd woman."

Oh dear. She ought to have been clearer with him from the beginning.

"Miss Seton, I talked with your brother yesterday. I do not mean to flatter myself, but he was very pleased by my visit."

"You spoke to Matthew?"

This was a disaster. She was sure Matthew had been thrilled. Now she needed to disappoint not only Mr. Worthington, but also her brother. Being shy had helped get her into this mess, so she swallowed and told herself to be direct. "Mr. Worthington, what is your meaning?"

"Miss Seton, would you do me the honor of marrying me?"

Arabella stared at him. "Marry you?"

He must have seen the distress on her face, for he took a step back. "I apologize for asking in such a public space, but I was carried away by seeing you in the setting that you paint so charmingly."

She had never painted the assembly rooms or the terrace that surrounded it. It wasn't important, but she was cross that he hadn't paid too much attention to her *fine* landscapes after all.

He led her down the steps into the garden, and they sat down on a marble bench.

He leaned forward. "Are my attentions so unwelcome, Miss Seton? I thought we had put the past behind us and had struck up a new friendship. This time, instead of youthful exuberance and emotion, our friendship is encouraged by business."

She was surprised into silence.

"Although I am a man in need of a wife, and a mother for my daughters, you know that I am a painter first and foremost. I was married to a woman with no artistic sensibilities, and it proved difficult for me. I want a partner who can understand my art."

Arabella felt a blossom of pleasure as he spoke. Her parents had been dismissive of her painting, discarding it as no more or no less what any lady could accomplish. "You appreciate my art?"

He leaned forward. "There is value in it, Arabella! You would have a great career in Bath if we stayed there. But if we moved to London, you would be in even greater demand."

"Would there be such an audience for my work?" London seemed a huge remove from Inverley.

"Not simply an audience—a *clientele*. Why, you could be booked for months in advance by women wishing for a quick portrait. Under my guidance, you shall be a success. We could get much more than a crown for a portrait there. There could be nothing easier."

Arabella narrowed her eyes. "Is that all you think of my art? That it is easy?"

He looked surprised. "Is it not? That was my first thought when I saw you painting on the seaside. You are able to work up a painting as quick as a wink. There's no telling how many you could do in a day when you are in a proper studio. It is all very well and good to paint visitors, but this is inconsistent income. Visitors only come for a few short months, and the local townsfolk have no frequent need of portraiture. I have connections in London, and a name that is well-known in the artistic community. I could guarantee work for you. Women who are looking to gift a small keepsake to a lover, perhaps. London never runs out of such ladies."

"Are you looking for a partner who shares your artistic sensibility? Or one to increase your finances?" she asked.

He frowned. "It's part and parcel of the same thing. Few of us are in the happy position of working without any thought of money. There is enormous potential for us to help each other. You know you would have an easier time of it with a husband. After all, how many of the most successful female artists are the wives or daughters of painters?"

Arabella saw it all too clearly. "You think I would be a financial success, and the money would help fund your own artistic career."

"My first wife was a lady and didn't understand such things as trade and finance. But with a practical woman by my side, I can accomplish so much. You must agree that my paintings deserve a place in history, don't they? You always admired them so."

A practical woman. Was that all she was?

Did he see her as a pitiful spinster, scraping her earnings together without any sense of what she was worth?

She wanted to be so much more than *practical*.

She thought of Caroline's eyes, hungry and watchful as she toppled her onto the bed.

She thought of the warm press of her hand against Caroline's back as they whirled around the grocer's second floor storeroom, giddy with excitement and flush with love.

Love.

That was what was missing from Mr. Worthington's proposal.

She gazed up at the stars, blazing bright in the heavens, and wanted nothing more than endless nights staring up at them by Caroline's side.

"Thank you for your kind attention," Arabella said finally. "But I am more than a business asset."

She didn't want to paint in a London studio, choking on the smoke of the city with people pressed all around her, trying to fit as many clients into her day as she could manage in order to pay for Mr. Worthington's oil paints and canvases and fees for artist's models.

She wanted to work with the breeze in her hair, chatting with visitors about their lives as she gave them a keepsake of both of their time on the beach.

But most of all, she didn't want to marry without love.
Her path to happiness was clear as day in front of her.
Her future was here.
With any luck, it would be with Caroline.

❖

Arabella stormed into Matthew's office at the docks. She didn't come to his workplace often anymore. It was a bustling operation in a building with rooms for storing hemp and flax fibers as well as the ropes and nets that they made. The ground floor was designated for laying the rope, with rooms for tarring and twisting the yarns, and the second floor was for spinning and finishing the ropes.

"You accepted an offer of marriage on my behalf?"

Matthew looked up as she barged in, surprise on his face. "I accepted nothing," he said. "I did tell Mr. Worthington that if he thought his suit would be welcome to you, then he would have my blessing. He has a secure enough position, and I know how much you love painting. I thought it would be a welcome opportunity for you."

"Well, it wasn't," she said, and slumped into the chair by the door so she could watch the ropemakers ply their trade.

"I'm sorry to hear it, Bell." His tone was gentle. "But you have been so unhappy. I thought maybe this was the right move for you. A change of scenery might do you good. Inverley isn't for everyone."

"Inverley is for me," she said. Then she bit her lip. "You thought I have been unhappy?"

He smiled at her. "You never could hide a feeling, however fleeting, on that face of yours. It's been the same since we were children."

"It's not that I am unhappy." She struggled to find the right words. This was hard. It was a conversation that she had always been afraid of starting. "I love living with you and Rachel. But I have felt for a while that I am an extra in your life." His face turned stormy and he opened his mouth, but she put up her hand. "No, Matthew—you have never made me feel that way. And Rachel has treated me like a beloved sister since you married. But this is your life. And with the baby on the way, I have been giving a lot of thought to *my* life, and what I want."

He nodded. "And that would be marrying and establishing your own home. It's grand news, Arabella—and if it's a local Inverley man you want instead of Mr. Worthington, then I know we can find one for you."

"No," she said with as much dignity as she could muster. "I do not wish to wed."

Matthew sat back, a puzzled look on his face. "Then I don't know what you want then. You have but two options. You can marry, or you can stay with myself and Rachel."

"I want a house of my own, but no man to run it. I want my independence, Matthew. The freedom of setting up my space as I wish and doing as I wish."

His eyes narrowed and he crossed his arms over his chest.

Arabella took a deep breath. "Everything you have done has been above and beyond what I ever could have asked for. You gave me a room where I could live, the attic studio where I could work, the front parlor in which to sell, and then you even built the swing in the garden so I could dream. It's been a wonderful ten years, Matthew, and I have appreciated it from the depths of my soul. But it is time for me to establish who I am, and I need my own space to do it in."

He took a few minutes to digest this. "Rachel will take it powerful hard."

"The last thing I ever want to do is to hurt her. And I know I promised I would help with the baby. But Inverley is not big. I will still be here to help," she said. "I promise."

"How will you make your living?"

"I have been saving my coins for years with this plan in mind. I should have enough put away now for a few months in a cottage. If I am careful, I could make ends meet until next summer when the visitors come again." Arabella tried to put as much dignity as she could in the words.

Matthew sighed. "I have taken so much of your profit since you started selling."

Arabella's heart started to pound. This was the conversation that she could never bring herself to have with her brother. "It was fair of me to contribute to the household," she said as evenly as she could manage. "But it was too much, in my opinion."

He shook his head. "I took it so I could invest it for you. I didn't want you to squirrel away your savings when you could be doubling or tripling your earnings on the 'Change. Didn't think it was right."

"You invested it?" she repeated.

"I wanted to help give you a good dowry when the time came. And if you never did marry, then the money would provide for you if I was no longer living. The money was always yours, Bell. If you've decided that now is the time you have need of it, then you shall have it. It should be enough to buy a cottage outright, with enough to spare for your comforts for a good long time."

For once, she couldn't speak because she was struck speechless from happiness, instead of her tongue being glued to the roof of her mouth in fear. She wrapped her arms around Matthew. "You are the best of brothers," she whispered, and kissed his bearded cheek.

She knew what she had to do next. She had to tell Caroline that she loved her.

CHAPTER TWENTY-THREE

Arabella rushed into the parlor. Caroline looked up from the list in front of her on the escritoire. "Is something the matter?"

Arabella's chest was rising in shallow breaths and her eyes were shiny. She was struggling to untie the bow in her bonnet. "That all rather depends."

Her voice was higher than usual.

Caroline twisted the corner of the page, which held the long-ago list of potential suitors she had written up for Betsy. She didn't think any of them would ask for her hand now.

"Depends on what?"

"I received a marriage proposal today." Arabella fought the knot apart and snatched the bonnet from her head, clutching it so tight that she ruined the straw brim.

"Congratulations." Caroline felt the words like arrows to the heart and refused to show the mortal wounds they left.

Arabella's eyes narrowed. "*Congratulations?* What is this, Caroline? What are we?"

"Friends," she said as crisply as she could muster. "The very best of friends, Bell."

Caroline scratched out a name on the list. This was what she needed to focus on. Her family.

She couldn't give Arabella what she deserved. She should be feted and applauded by everyone who saw her work. What could Caroline offer her instead? Infrequent lovemaking whenever she chanced to be back in Inverley? If she married, she would have to go wherever her husband dictated. Her stomach churned. Even if she married James, he only spent the summer in Inverley, and the rest of his time in London.

"Which is why you should marry Mr. Worthington." Caroline supposed she ought to work on adding some enthusiasm in her voice, but what was the use? Arabella would know that it was false.

She gaped at her and dropped her bonnet. "However did you know?"

"I went looking for you after you ran away at the assembly. I found you on the terrace with Mr. Worthington and heard him ask for your hand."

Caroline had felt like she turned to jelly when she heard the words. She had mustered enough energy to wobble back to her sisters and tell them that she was unwell before stumbling home to bed.

The proposal was the best outcome that Arabella could have for her artistic prospects. But Caroline hated the thought of it.

Arabella's eyes were round and large behind her spectacles. "Yes, Mr. Worthington asked for my hand. But I don't want to marry him."

Caroline sat back and gazed at Arabella, awash in a lifetime of memories.

The girl who had cried on her shoulder when her parents dismissed her artwork.

The adolescent who dreamed atop the bluffs of the big world that awaited them as soon as they were older.

The young woman who was so excited to go to Bath, and so withdrawn when she came back.

The spinster who had settled in with her brother after her parents moved away, and established a career for herself with her seascapes.

That woman was made of grit and determination.

She had worked hard for every success that had come her way, and now she was finding her path to fame through her portraiture work.

Arabella deserved this opportunity.

"Think of what Mr. Worthington can offer you, Bell. You should say yes." The words tasted worse than sea tonic on Caroline's lips.

"You're as dictatorial as Betsy ever accused you of being," Arabella shot at her, and the words hit home.

She wasn't dictatorial. She was in love. Caroline wanted to tell her that this was the biggest sacrifice that she had ever made, more so than taking responsibility for her siblings, more than finding a man to take her hand in marriage.

It was the loss of Arabella that was sure to cause her sleepless nights ahead.

But it didn't matter how much it hurt. What mattered was that Arabella was going to have a good life, even if Caroline had to force her to the altar to accept it.

Every tear that gathered in Arabella's eyes felt like a fresh dagger to her foolish heart.

Why couldn't logic rule her heart like it ruled her mind?

"You will be better off with Mr. Worthington," Caroline said, trying to stay calm. "You told me when I inherited that you could not imagine someone unexpectedly giving you everything you wanted. Now you have exactly that. You would have independence and artistic fame. How can you turn away from it?"

Arabella drew in a breath. "You weren't so pleased about it when *you* inherited."

"I would suggest that you do not make a hash out of your dreams coming true, the way my family has made a hash of ours."

"I don't want Mr. Worthington," Arabella said with quiet dignity.

Don't say it, Caroline pleaded with her silently. *My heart can't bear it.*

"I want *you.* I love *you.*"

The knowledge of her love flooded her with warmth for an instant, until cold reality washed back over her.

This was the moment Caroline had been dreading. She had hoped to reason Arabella into accepting her dreams.

"I don't want the same thing," Caroline lied, as gently as she could. She knew she had a better face for falsehoods than Arabella did, but it was the struggle of a lifetime to keep the agony from her face.

Especially as she watched Arabella's crumple.

Along with Caroline's heart.

Arabella took a shaky breath, her face wet with tears. "Then we are friends no longer. You are as overbearing as Mr. Worthington is, telling me how my life should be! However you define 'friendship,' I want no more part of it."

After Arabella fled, Caroline sat with her list for a long time. She stared down at the pen and paper and wished more than anything to turn back time to when she had first written it months ago.

But she was used to denying herself for the greater good of her family, and although she had told Arabella that they were no more than friends, she knew the truth. Arabella was far more than a friend, and more even than family. She was in a category all her own, encompassing all the best parts of Caroline's past and present.

Her future yawned ahead of her, bleak and boring, without Arabella's sunny face and Wednesday novels and ginger comfits.

❖

Arabella pushed her way out of Caroline's townhouse, tears blurring her vision. She didn't notice if anyone saw her rushing down the street, but she didn't much care. She had left her bonnet in Caroline's parlor, she realized as the sun hit her eyes. She must have dropped it—though she couldn't remember anything she had done while her heart was breaking. Whether she had been sitting or standing. Whether she had been at the far end of the room or near the window.

None of those details had mattered when it felt like a cannonball was ripping through her chest.

Even now, she didn't feel like she had control over her limbs. She had no sense of where she was going, just that she had to get away from the row of townhouses that had always been a good seller in her paintings.

She was never going to paint them again. Not after today.

In a daze, she passed through town and up the cliff and stood at the top of the bluffs. The sea sparkled, glittering and majestic, heaving and churning like it was a living being itself. Like herself. She must have raced up the hill because she was gasping for breath, her chest aching. Her brow was sweaty without her bonnet to protect her face.

There was a group of visitors traversing a narrow path nearby, and she was close enough that she could hear their laughter before they wandered out of view. Oh, how she envied them. They were happy and carefree, enjoying their holiday away from all their everyday troubles.

Not that a broken heart was an everyday trouble. If this was what if felt like for everyone, then she fervently wished it to be uncommon indeed.

Arabella sank to the ground, exhausted. The grass was warm against her back, and the sun was hot on her skin. It was a relief to grieve in private. There was no one here to ask questions or pass judgment, or to force her down a path that she didn't want.

Her chest tightened. She hadn't thought that Caroline would ever be adamant to see her marry, let alone to someone that she must know would take her away from Inverley.

There was only so much crying one could do in one bout, and her chest finally eased and her tears stopped flowing. She was sure that she looked a fright in her grass-stained dress with her hair mussed, puffy-eyed from sobbing, and was grateful that she met no one as she walked back down the bluffs to Belvoir Lane.

Arabella spent the rest of the day in bed. She was miserable enough that sleep evaded her. Time passed in a hazy blur with Byron purring against her chest and a novel from the lending library in her hand with the pages unturned. Lethargic, she spent the next day in her shift with her hair unbrushed. Although she was still too upset to come down for a meal, Rachel brought her tea and blancmange at luncheon. Matthew, knowing her rather better, dropped a basket of iced buns on her dresser after he came home from work.

By the third day, Arabella felt a good deal improved.

She had the energy now to be angry.

How dared Caroline decide for her what she should do?

Long before she and Caroline had ever kissed, her worst nightmare was that she would be rebuffed if ever she told Caroline that she loved her. After a summer spent in courtship and lovemaking and a thousand intimate details, the reality was far worse than the nightmares.

And yet, there was relief in the pain.

If the nightmare had come true, then it also meant that it was over and could hold no more fear for her. Whether or not she agreed that it was right or fair, Caroline had ended things between them. For the first time since she had tumbled into love at thirteen, she felt a sense of detachment that felt…healthy.

She hadn't wasted her life away while pining for Caroline, after all. She had friends and neighbors and family and her art and her cats. All of those things filled her life with blessings.

The absence of one person had the ability to wound.

But she would mend.

She was her own person, capable of making her own decisions, and now she had the freedom of choice before her.

CHAPTER TWENTY-FOUR

The next week was the worst that Caroline could remember in years.

It was awful knowing that she had hurt the dearest person in the world to her. She had sobbed after Arabella had left, but she felt a bone-deep certainty that it was the right choice. More than anything, she wanted to make sure that Arabella had the very best chance for happiness

Even if it was at the expense of her own.

It would be worth it to know that Arabella finally had found the freedom that she was looking for. Whether she married Mr. Worthington or whether she made her own success with her miniatures, there was no one in Inverley who deserved success more than her sweet, kind Arabella. It was better that she didn't have to worry about the Reeves any longer.

After all, she had already done so much for the family.

Arabella had been by Caroline's side for every headache as she tried to raise her siblings. She had helped the boys learn to walk with cheers of enthusiasm. She had read aloud to the girls on lazy summer evenings after spending the afternoon looking for seashells with them. She scolded Jacob as much as Caroline had when he had tried to climb the vicar's tree on the front lawn of the rectory during the sermon.

Arabella had been there that dreadful summer when her parents had died. Her throat closed up as she remembered. Time had helped her manage the pain of their loss, but it could never close the hole that their absence left in her heart. Arabella and her family had stepped in and taken care of them, making meals and doing chores and doing all they could to ease their grief. Rachel had even kept the youngest children at the Seton household for a few weeks while Arabella had helped Caroline meet with solicitors and bankers to try to understand what was left of the Reeves' finances.

The only memories that Caroline *didn't* have of Arabella were from the year that she had spent in Bath when she turned nineteen. It had been the year after Caroline's parents had died, and she had felt lost without Arabella next door. It hadn't been entirely unexpected. Plenty of young people left Inverley when they were grown, finding a spouse or a career in a bigger town. Someone was bound to see what a prize Arabella was and snatch her up into holy matrimony.

Caroline had coped by writing Arabella letters every week and guiltily expecting her to pay the postage upon receipt. It had felt like a luxury to cross a page with all of her thoughts and feelings and the news about town, much as she had wished Arabella was right there. With each return letter, she held her breath as she opened the seal. She was shocked each time that there was no announcement of an engagement.

It wasn't a surprise now to find out that there *had* been a suitor, and there *had* been an opportunity. But Arabella had always been so shy. She might not have felt capable of taking the chance at nineteen. At twenty-seven, however, she had proven that she had confidence in spades. Marriage was a risk worth taking when there was so much to gain.

That's what people said of it, anyhow.

Caroline endured the week with stoicism, forcing herself to attend the assembly rooms with her family. She listened with half an ear to her sisters' complaints about the decided lack of attention that they received now that word of Jacob's fall from financial grace was making its rounds.

It seemed as if none of the Reeves were happy with Caroline.

Betsy was angry because Caroline still hadn't approved of Mr. Graham as a suitor, and she spent her days mooning about love lost.

George and Will were sulking because they had been looking forward to attending Eton after hearing stories from Lady Margaret about the mischief one could get up to at school.

She caught sight of Jacob scowling to himself in the library from time to time, swigging more brandy than was good for him, but she couldn't bring herself to say anything. He was enduring his own private hell, after all, still struggling to understand what was left after he had drained most of his investments and sold off the land that wasn't entailed.

Mild-mannered Susan was in poor spirits, pacing her room filled with beautiful clothes and nowhere to wear them.

Even Shelley was cross with her. He had found a hatpin from the bonnet that Arabella had dropped on her last visit, and it had become a cherished toy that he pawed under the dresser and dragged out every time she entered her bedchamber. It pained her to see anything that reminded her of Arabella, though her battered bonnet was kept safe in the lowest drawer of her dresser. Her refusal to toe the hatpin across the room for Shelley to scamper after meant that he now stayed in Will and George's room in the evenings.

Jacob spent his evenings with her and Lady Margaret, as he had decided to try to pay court to the young ladies who fluttered and fawned over him. There were plenty of women willing to exchange money for a title, as minor as Jacob's was. He would have been buried under competition in London, as thick on the ground as penniless baronets were there, but in Inverley Jacob was still considered a good prospect.

The sole comfort to the family was Mr. Taylor.

He brought flowers when it was rainy to coax a smile from her sisters when it was too wet to go visiting, he listened to Jacob with sympathy when he railed against his situation, and he purchased a set of tin soldiers for George and Will to brighten their spirits.

At the assemblies, Caroline could always count on him for a dance and a chat, and she realized how much she had misjudged him.

He sat across from her now in the parlor as she went through her meagre invitations for the coming week. There was an invitation from the Martin family for a private ball, and, written in a different hand from the rest of the card, was a note—*I look forward to your presence. J.*

It must mean what she thought it did. James was going to come up to scratch.

"It is nice to know that we are still invited out," she said, tucking the card behind the others. "Shall we see you at the Martins' on Tuesday?"

He nodded. "You shall indeed. It must be pleasing to see a bevy of cards in your salver, after so many years without proper socializing."

She frowned. "I had plenty of socializing before." She thought of the evening she and Arabella had spent dancing at the grocer's, staring up at the stars, sweaty and happy.

How she wished to turn back time.

"I suppose that must be true. But, Miss Reeve, you must appreciate your new social circle? It has brought you such opportunities."

"Yes, it has been an entertaining summer." It was wretched now, but though she appreciated his kindnesses, she didn't intend to pour her heart out to him.

"I wonder if you would perhaps be amenable to the idea of widening your circle still further?"

Caroline stared at him.

He cleared his throat. "That is, if you wished to—you could join mine."

Oh dear.

Caroline stared at Mr. Taylor, dread creeping into her heart.

This couldn't be happening. Not when she had James where she needed him to be. Mr. Taylor wore fine suits and had elegant manners, but he was also now somewhat of a poor relation. He would never do.

She looked down at the cards again. "Nothing but the urgency of my current situation could compel me to marry, Mr. Taylor. You must understand why I must decline."

"We would be a good match, Miss Reeve. Consider the benefits. I know your family, and we rub along together well enough. We can remove to London. Please reconsider."

"We would not suit, sir. As you are aware, we are in need of funds." It was blunt speaking, but Jacob had confided in him enough for him to know the depths of their situation.

She rose, and in some confusion, he followed suit. "I must bid you a good afternoon, Mr. Taylor. I shall see you on Tuesday."

He left Caroline alone with her thoughts.

Two proposals within the past week. She told herself to be grateful for the opportunity to help her family, but instead she felt exhausted.

She was caught between memories of the past, and worries for the future, and neither of them brought her happiness. If she stopped and thought about her desires for the present moment, if she was free from any obligation or responsibility, it was clear what she wanted.

Arabella.

It was cruel that they had found romantic love so late. They could have had years together already. Instead, it was over almost before they had a chance to begin.

But it was proof enough that one should always take what was offered, and to enjoy it. No one knew the future. She couldn't have predicted the loss of her parents and how it would change everything. The inheritance had been the stuff of wildest fantasy.

If she had kissed Arabella at sixteen in the cherry orchard, the entirety of their lives would have been different. But she hadn't trusted enough that it wouldn't be a disaster.

If she could do it again and secure her happiness, she would.

But because she couldn't, she needed to do the next best thing so someone else could have that opportunity.

Caroline found Betsy in her bedchamber, scribbling in a slender tome. She snapped it closed and shoved it aside when Caroline entered.

"We haven't spoken in some time," Caroline said, and sat on the corner of the bed.

Betsy frowned at her. "That is because all that falls from your lips is censure or a scold."

It stung, but she took a moment and thought about their recent interactions. "I deserved that," she said. She took a deep breath. "But ever since you had that fever, when Mama and Papa died, I have been so terrified of not doing right by you. You were spared. It felt like a miracle to me, and so I always wanted the very best for you. But I'm realizing now that what I think is right might not be the same as what you would choose for yourself."

"I always knew you were looking out for me," Betsy muttered, her eyes averted. "But I want a different life than you do, Caro. I don't care about money and reputation." She rose from the chair and flopped on her back on the bed beside Caroline. "I want late nights and *romance*. I want to laugh with my friends and do interesting things. Most importantly, I need a life filled with art."

"You believe you could have that with Mr. Graham?"

"Yes." She sighed out the word, her voice full of longing. Her face shone like a martyr. "He writes the most incredible verse I have ever read."

"Better than Byron?" Caroline teased with a smile.

"Much! He is a marvel. To share my life with that kind of brilliance would be…oh, it would be magic."

"He said some impressive things about you as well," Caroline said.

Betsy smiled and ducked her head. "I have some talent for poetry. No one has ever read it but him, but he tells me it's very good."

Caroline smiled at her. "Then why should you not have your heart's desire? Mr. Graham would be a fine husband for you."

"Truly, Caro? You are the best of sisters!" Betsy tackled her into a hug.

At least she had brought happiness to someone. Caroline took comfort from the thought.

❖

Matthew came in the front door with a handful of letters. "I was just at the post office, and here's a letter from my business acquaintance in Somerset."

Arabella blinked. She had forgotten about the inquiries regarding Mr. Taylor. For all that she told herself that the Reeve family's business no longer mattered to her, she couldn't help but be curious.

"What news does he have of Mr. Taylor?" Rachel asked.

Matthew took up his penknife and slid it through the envelope. "Let's see." He unfolded the letter and frowned. "Well. This is unexpected."

"What it is?" Arabella blurted out, unable to stop herself.

"Hmmm. It seems Mr. Taylor is not well liked in his home county."

"That *is* unexpected," Rachel said. "I found him charming."

"Why is he not liked?"

"Mr. Richardson is not a man to spread gossip," Matthew said, folding up the letter and shoving it back into the envelope. "All he says is that Mr. Taylor owes some debts."

"That is no surprise," Arabella said slowly. "He lost his inheritance before he came to Inverley."

"This seems to be a long-standing issue, going back some years."

"Years?" Arabella frowned. This didn't make sense.

After Matthew and Rachel departed to pay a visit on a neighbor, Arabella took up the letter and read it through. It was altogether odd. Mr. Taylor's debts stemmed from gambling.

Like Jacob's had.

Hadn't Mr. Taylor been playing cards with Jacob the night of the Reeve's dinner party?

Jacob had lost the money to another young man of fashion, but it had been a gentleman that no one had heard of before that night, and who had left Inverley the next morning.

The coincidence was most unusual.

She snatched a piece of paper and a pen and started a letter in return to Mr. Richardson. She knew Matthew would disapprove of her prying, but she had to know more. If she rushed, she could make it to the post office before the mail coach departed Inverley, and then she might even have an answer the very next week.

She dashed a series of questions across the page and sealed it closed while the ink was still damp, but there was no time to lose.

The post office wasn't far, but even still, she sprinted down the street, ignoring the stares from passersby. It didn't matter that Caroline had broken her heart. It didn't matter that she might never see her again.

What mattered was that the Reeve family may have been grievously wronged by someone they trusted, and they deserved to know the truth. Her love for them as a family would never waver, despite the romantic love for Caroline that had been torn to shreds.

The post office was busier than usual, and Arabella stood some distance behind the counter as another customer settled his account with the postmaster. She worried the corner of the letter with her thumb, straining her ears for any sound of the mail coach. She didn't want to delay sending the letter by even one day.

Instead of the coach wheels rolling over the gravel, Arabella heard something unexpected.

Mr. Taylor's voice.

CHAPTER TWENTY-FIVE

Arabella's blood ran cold. Mr. Taylor's voice was too low for her to hear the words, but she was sure it was him. She rose on her toes and saw him speaking with his secretary at a table in the corner of the post office. He was writing something, most likely to post it for today's mail coach, as she herself was planning.

She slipped out of her place in line and moved closer to a shelf stacked with letters and parcels, which she hoped would shield her from view as she crept close enough to hear his conversation.

"Everything is all set," Mr. Taylor told his secretary, signing his name with a flourish. "This letter should ease the creditors at the bank at last."

"Finally," the secretary said, slouching in his seat. "Then we can leave this godforsaken tiny village behind us."

"Ah, but Inverley has been a blessing. Nowhere else would it have been so easy to fleece a fortune from a stripling. Smith played his hand well the night of the party and should be happy enough to get his cut of it. It will be even easier to wed one of those foolish Reeve sisters. A trio of more unsuspecting ladies there never was in London, after all."

The secretary laughed. "Yes, there is that. After the wedding, then, are we to return to London?"

"It will be quick, never fear. Lady Margaret will turn a blind eye to any shenanigans I may need to conjure up as a reason for a wedding. She will be none the wiser. The eldest Reeve was my choice, as her dowry is still the largest—but she's also a bit too sour for my tastes and the chit already turned down my suit. Their dowries may only be a pittance now, but I want to wrest all the pennies I can from the estate. I would be happy to settle for one of the others. They would be easier to manage anyway." He laughed and pushed the chair away, letter in hand.

Arabella shrank away in horror. The Reeves were in danger. Her mind was whirling. Her letter forgotten in her hand, she sped away from the post office as fast as she had arrived.

She must warn Caroline.

At once.

❖

At the Martins' ball, Caroline caught sight of her and her family in the mirror that lined the back wall of the ballroom. It was hard to reconcile the fashionable, glittering reflection with the siblings that she had raised. They looked every inch the wealthy family that they no longer were.

Though there wasn't a smile to be had among them.

"To look at us, one would presume we were each waiting to have a tooth pulled," Caroline said. "Yet instead here we are at a fine ball surrounded by fine people."

"Because our fortune has brought us nothing but misfortune," Betsy said. "If I had never had a dowry, you would have dropped your objection to Mr. Graham's suit much sooner."

Jacob nodded. "I would never have wagered more than a guinea at cards if my head hadn't been turned by talk of thousands in the bank."

Susan shrugged. "I am not discontented with our new lot in life, but it's duller than I had anticipated. These London visitors are too full of themselves."

Caroline had to laugh. "Not three months ago, you were all complaining about one thing or another. Jacob was dissatisfied with his work. Susan and Betsy were forever looking for adventure."

"It's not like that," Jacob said. "Not really. You're not *listening*, Caro."

"I am listening," she said. "This is why I will accept James Martin's hand tonight in marriage, if he is so generous to extend it."

She was wearing Mama's amethyst necklace tonight, and she rubbed her thumb over the stone at the base of her throat.

"He never said anything to me about it," he said, glowering at her. "I'm not so sure I would approve the match."

She put a hand on his shoulder. "This is my sacrifice. My choice. To give you all a chance at having what you want. My marriage would give us security. It gives Betsy the opportunity to marry for love. I would stipulate that Susan and the boys would come live with me until they married."

"It isn't right," Jacob declared. "This isn't what you wanted for yourself."

"You don't even like James," Susan said, wrinkling her nose. "Neither do I."

"It's not a matter of like. It's what I must do."

Betsy grabbed her hand. "No, Caro. You should follow your heart. You don't need to do this for us."

"We don't need it," Susan insisted. "I don't even wish to marry!"

"No one needs to marry," Jacob said. He squared his shoulders. "It's our turn to come up with solutions, Caro. It doesn't always have to be you. We're adults. We are in this together."

"I could never ask it of you—"

"You aren't asking," Betsy said. "But we're giving."

"Jacob is right," Susan said. "We Reeves stick together. And when we put our heads together, we can do anything."

For the first time in years, Caroline felt free.

If she were truly free, she wouldn't choose marriage.

She would choose Arabella. A thousand times over.

All she had to do was find her. And then apologize for the rest of her life, if she were lucky enough to be loved in return.

❖

Arabella didn't have an invitation to the Martins' soiree. It was likely a snub, as the Martins knew how close she and Caroline were.

Or rather, how close they *had* been.

She took Fred with her and they set off for the Martins at a pace that she was sure would leave her heels blistered for days, but there was no time to lose.

When she got to the estate, she gave Fred a note. "Please find Miss Linfield at once," she said, and waited outside the servants' entrance in the dusk. It wasn't long before a maid appeared and ushered her inside the narrow staircase up to the second floor of the manor house, guiding her to Grace's bedchamber.

"What on earth are you doing?" Grace asked as soon as she saw her, concern in her eyes. She was ready for the evening, down to the reticule on her wrist and her fan in her hand. "Are you quite all right?"

"I need to speak with Caroline," she said, breathless from the stairs. She felt more determined than she ever had in her life.

"I would imagine that she's in the ballroom."

"I have no invitation and couldn't come in the main door. I thought you could help me to get to the ball unnoticed."

Grace frowned. "In your current state, Arabella, you would not only be noticed but you would be thrown out of the room. You are not ready for a ball. We must remedy that immediately."

She poked her head out the doorway and called for the maid again.

"I need a dress to suit Miss Seton," she said, her face as calm as if she asked for such favors every day. "Would any of mine do for her?"

"Please do not trouble yourself," Arabella said, her face burning. Nothing of Grace's was going to fit her.

"Forgive me, Arabella, but you have mud three inches deep round your hem, and you look like you've been running. You need a quick rinse in the washstand and a change of clothes before you can enter that ballroom."

"Could we not summon Caroline to join us here?" Changing gowns would take time that she didn't know they had.

"I don't think Caroline would come," Grace said gently. "She was devastated, you know, at"—she glanced at the maid, who was riffling through her wardrobe—"at what happened."

"This one should do, ma'am." The maid held up a pink muslin.

"Fine." Arabella snatched it from her. "Let's get on with it."

She made quick work of the water in the basin and was tearing off her day dress before she even towelled her face dry. The maid helped her into Grace's dress, but she frowned at the reflection in the mirror.

"I look rather different in this dress than I am sure you do," Arabella said.

Her bosom strained the thin material, and so did her hips. The buttons wouldn't do up in the back. Grace had a coltish elegance that Arabella decidedly did not have. Sighing, she took the shawl that Grace offered her and wrapped it around her shoulders to cover the worst of it. "I'm ready."

They left the bedchamber and slipped down the stairs. Arabella was relieved to discover that she had been right in her assumption that as a houseguest, Grace could access another entrance to the ballroom, without going through the main door where the butler announced everyone's name.

Arabella saw Caroline at once. Even in a room of a hundred people, she could pick out the tinkle of her laugh.

"Good luck," Grace said, and squeezed her hand.

"Thank you." She straightened her shoulders and set out for the Reeves.

"Arabella! I didn't expect to see you." Caroline's face brightened when she saw her, and Arabella felt a pulse of gratification when her eyes strayed down to where Grace's dress pulled tight against her body. She looked at Arabella as if she was the most beautiful woman in the room, despite her too-small dress and her barely presentable hair, and Arabella's heart finally settled back into place from where it had tumbled out of her chest when they last saw each other.

"I need to speak with you at once." Arabella nodded to Jacob. "Alone, if you will."

Jacob looked taken aback, no doubt at her tone. She had never spoken to any of the Reeves so crisply.

"Of course." He left them.

"Bell—"

Arabella cut her short. "I don't know how much time we have. Where are your sisters?"

"Susan is there with Lady Margaret. Betsy was here with me a few minutes ago, but I'm not sure where she is now. Why?"

"I overheard Mr. Taylor today at the post office. He was saying... well, I am worried that he might take advantage of one of your sisters to force her hand in marriage."

"No!" Caroline gasped.

"I'm afraid so. You were right from the beginning not to trust him, Caroline. You were right about everything." She explained how Mr. Taylor had fleeced Jacob and was planning to take the biggest dowry he could from the Reeves.

"We need to find Betsy," Caroline said, looking around wildly.

They drew Jacob and Susan to the side of the room first and Arabella told them what she suspected. Jacob was in a towering rage, and Susan paled.

Arabella took Susan's hand. "It's going to work out and we will find your sister, but we need your help."

Caroline drew in a deep breath. It was past time that she trusted her family in a crisis, and they needed all the help they could get. "Arabella and I will search the house, and you two should look around the terrace and the garden. You know the estate well enough from visiting over the years."

"I will find the wretch and tear him limb from limb," Jacob vowed, his voice seething with rage.

He strode outside with Susan beside him.

"You take this side of the ballroom and I'll take the other," Arabella said, "and we shall meet in the middle."

Caroline nodded, and they fanned out.

Arabella scanned dozens of guests and peeped behind curtains and into alcoves but didn't see Betsy. She met up with Caroline in the center of the ballroom. Caroline shook her head.

"Where could she have gone?" Arabella asked.

"You know her as well as I do," Caroline said. "Betsy could be anywhere."

The despair in her voice clutched at Arabella's heart, and she grasped her hand. "We will find her. I promise. I won't rest until we do."

"Thank you," she whispered.

"Miss Seton, I don't recall your name on our guest list?" James stood behind them, a smirk on his face. "A quiet card party with my father is one thing, but locals in poorly fitted dresses in my mother's ballroom is quite another."

Anger welled up inside of her. Why had she ever felt intimidated by his shabby behavior? "You are nothing but a small-minded and ill-mannered boor, James. Your opinion of me is baseless but ought to be best kept to yourself. I have no interest in hearing your comments about my person ever again."

He turned to Caroline. "You should tell your friend to keep a civil tongue in her mouth if she ever wants to visit you as Mrs. Martin."

Arabella laughed. "You think Caroline Reeve would deign to marry you? Not in a thousand years."

Caroline's gaze slid away, and Arabella's blood ran cold for a moment. Then Caroline shook her head and swung her gaze to lock eyes with James. "I thought I could go through with it for my family's sake. But not even for them can I affiliate myself with you. Arabella is right—you are small-minded."

"*And* ill-mannered," Arabella repeated for the sheer pleasure of it. She had never spoken so boldly to anyone before.

He looked incredulous.

"We shall remove ourselves from your presence if you find it too onerous to bear." Arabella took Caroline's elbow and guided her out of the ballroom. "Betsy *definitely* wasn't there," she said to Caroline once they were alone. "She would never have stayed hidden during a confrontation like that. She would have been drawn to the drama."

Caroline stopped her and grasped her face in her hands. "Bell." She gazed into her eyes. "Bell, you were magnificent."

She kissed her, and it warmed Arabella after a week of cold misery. For a moment she leaned into the kiss, lost in the expression of love and wonder and beauty, but there was no time to savor the moment.

Caroline pressed her forehead against her own. "She could be anywhere."

Arabella frowned. "If Mr. Taylor intends to ruin her and draw attention to the fact, then she must still be here somewhere."

"This is distasteful in the extreme." Caroline's face was shadowed.

"It is. But it's far better for us to find them, and not a stranger," Arabella said firmly. "Together, we can protect Betsy."

❖

Arabella's help meant more than Caroline could ever say.

Having her here meant the world to her. Arabella was her comfort, her support.

Her love.

She loved her. And for her to come charging into the ballroom tonight as magnificent as any knight errant could only mean that Arabella loved her too.

But there would be time for words later. Now, she needed to find Betsy.

They searched the library and the drawing room, careful to evade servants and other guests who seemed to be looking for their own privacy. Caroline marveled at how well she and Arabella worked together, hardly needing more than a word or a gesture to convey what they were thinking. Side by side, they made quick work of the downstairs, but there was no sign of Betsy.

Caroline spotted Mr. Graham outside the ballroom as they circled back toward the main staircase to the second floor.

He bowed. "Have you seen Miss Betsy tonight?"

He was reserved, and Caroline felt embarrassed at her treatment of him after her dinner party. She had indeed been too proud. "I am looking for her, sir. Unfortunately, I am worried for her safety from a villain."

His face turned thunderous as she explained. "Where is he?" he asked, his eyes sharp. "If one hair on her head is harmed, I will destroy him."

"We have searched the downstairs already."

"Then let us go upstairs," he said grimly, and took the steps two at a time. "I fought a duel with a blackguard for my sister's honor, and I wouldn't hesitate to do the same for Miss Betsy."

A duel for his sister! Arabella had been right. Caroline had been too quick to judge his past.

Arabella and Caroline followed him up the stairs. Their pursuit so far had been thorough but quiet, but it appeared Mr. Graham had no intention of being discreet.

"Betsy!" he called down the hallway, thronged with doorways leading into bedchambers and sitting rooms. "Betsy, are you here?"

They strained their ears.

"There! Did you hear that?" Caroline grabbed Arabella's arm. "Did you?"

There was a muffled sound coming from one of the bedchambers.

"Either we find them, or we embarrass someone else on our quest, but it's worth it." Arabella nodded sharply.

Mr. Graham pounded on the door, then threw his shoulder against it to force it open.

What was inside was not what Caroline expected.

Betsy and Lady Edith stood together over the prone body of Mr. Taylor.

Chapter Twenty-six

B etsy!" Caroline rushed into the room and hugged her.
"Are you all right?" Mr. Graham was only a step behind
Caroline.

"I am more than all right," she announced. "Edie and I have this
under control."

Lady Edith nodded. "Can you believe the audacity of this man?
He wrote Betsy a note and had a footman deliver it to her in the
ballroom, saying it was from *me!*"

"Of course I came upstairs straightaway. I barely even registered
that the handwriting wasn't what it should be." Betsy paced around
the room. "When I got to Edie's bedchamber, I was so surprised to
see Mr. Taylor."

Arabella urged a ginger comfit on her, and she happily accepted.

"It must have been an awful shock," Mr. Graham said, grasping
her hand.

"I was never so surprised in all my life. He asked me to marry
him, and when I refused, he said he would ruin me!" She looked
outraged. "Ruin *me!* As if anyone in Inverley would believe that he
was the first."

Caroline gasped. "Betsy Reeve!"

She tossed her curls. "Well, it's true! Mr. Graham knows all
about it, and I have no shame here among friends. I told Mr. Taylor
I would make a laughingstock of him if he dared to try such a thing.
Then his face got all mottled and he lunged at me, so I bashed him
over the head with the candlestick."

Mr. Graham peered at his prone body. "He's not dead. You've a strong arm though. Good on you." His voice was filled with pride, and Betsy's chest puffed out.

"I found Edie right away and we've been arguing how to go about things, and then you lot arrived. But however did you find me?"

"I am so grateful that you are unharmed," Caroline said, and drew her into her arms again. It felt like a miracle. "Arabella overheard Mr. Taylor's plans and rushed here to put a stop to things."

"Bell!" Betsy cried, and threw her arms around her neck. "You have always been the best of neighbors. No one could ask for better."

"I would have been devastated if anything were to happen to you." Arabella hugged her close. "I should have known that you are as strong as you are capable. I have never met the man who could get the better of you."

"And you never shall," she declared.

"But what are we to do know?" Lady Edith asked, her brow furrowed. "I've never had an unconscious man in my bedchamber before. It's not at all the thing."

Mr. Graham nudged Mr. Taylor's ribs with his booted foot, and was none too gentle about it from what Caroline could see. Mr. Taylor moaned, then stirred, his eyes opening blearily.

"What have you got to say for yourself?" Mr. Graham snapped.

Caroline was impressed at how fast he resumed the role of the military captain. Gone was the concerned suitor, and in his place was a steely-eyed man, thirsty for vengeance.

He struggled to sit up. "I can explain." Then he looked around at everyone in the room and fell silent.

"Is it true, then?" Caroline asked. "You deliberately set out to ruin my brother?"

"That money was rightfully mine," Mr. Taylor snarled, getting to his feet. "I did nothing wrong by winning it back."

"But you were the one who came to tell us of the inheritance. Why did you bother?" Caroline couldn't make sense of it.

"My mother knew about your branch of the family years ago. The older she gets, the more she talks about claiming the connection. I had to stop her multiple times from writing to you over the years. I had to wait until Jacob was past twenty-one, and legally able to give up his fortune on a turn of cards."

"You are reprehensible," Caroline snapped.

He glowered at her. "Sir Francis thought nothing of your father or what became of him after he moved here and started your woeful branch of the family. It should have stayed mine! All of it. The money. The estate. The funds for your dowries. I wanted to regain the estate and the fortune, and to grab as much of what was left as I could by marrying one of you. I deserve it."

Betsy scowled at him. "You don't mess with a Reeve," she snapped. "We fight back."

He sneered at her. "I still have the fortune. Your brother remains in possession of an empty shell of an estate with no funds to keep it running. Your dowries are a pittance compared to what I have won."

"But you have lost your good name," Caroline said. "And that to us is worth more than any hoard of gold ever could."

"Tales of your exploits will soon circulate Inverley, then London," Mr. Graham said. "We will make sure of that. Then how much will you enjoy your ill-begotten funds when no good society will welcome you?"

"Who will good society believe?" Mr. Taylor laughed. "The former baronet, who has behaved impeccably for years? Or this unknown branch of the family, with its ill manners and odd airs and vulgarity?"

The door swung open to reveal Mr. and Mrs. Martin, with James and Grace in tow. Grace peered into the room, her mouth dropping open at the sight of the crowd in Lady Edith's bedchamber.

"What do we have here?" Mr. Martin boomed.

Grace hurried in and stood beside Lady Edith. "Are you all right? I heard noises, and couldn't access your room through my own, so I thought it best to alert our hosts."

"We are fine," Lady Edith said, hugging her. "But Mr. Taylor is the worst villain to ever walk these halls! He tried to take advantage of Betsy."

"What?" Mr. Martin staggered back. "In our house? This is unconscionable!"

Mr. Taylor slinked out of the room with his tail between his legs.

"We ought to stop him." Mr. Graham made a move toward the door, but Betsy put up a hand.

"Where would he go?" she asked. "He got mostly what he wanted. He has Jacob's money, so he wasn't in need of a dowry—which means the other ladies here are safe. He just wanted my dowry because he resented the family."

"It doesn't matter. He ought to be held accountable." He glowered at the door. "He should be held in contempt for what he did to you."

"He did nothing," Betsy said briskly. "I took care of myself and am no worse off than I was an hour ago."

"He cannot show his face here again without facing condemnation," said Mr. Martin. "We will make sure of that."

"You brave girls!" Mrs. Martin commended Betsy and Lady Edith. "These young ladies have intrepid hearts."

James looked at Caroline in a daze. "I daresay, I do not think I am up to the challenge of marrying into the Reeve family after all."

Caroline grinned. "We are a handful—every last one of us."

Arabella and Caroline exchanged looks. Caroline's heart was full, knowing they had more to talk about, and feeling hopeful for what that conversation would bring.

❖

It was late when Arabella and the Reeves arrived at the townhouse. Arabella sent Fred home with a message to Matthew and Rachel that she would stay the night with the Reeves. She knew that she and Caroline had much to discuss.

She hated confrontation. Tonight had been no different, but she had *felt* different about it. It didn't fill her with the heart-stopping dread that it always had before. She felt stronger. Something felt like it had shaken loose inside of her, and she knew she would never be ruled by that fear again.

She could stand alone. She had always had the power but had never realized it before. The power of choice. The power of saying what was necessary, instead of bowing her head and going along with what someone else wanted.

Arabella watched as Caroline shook out her curls from the pearl-studded web that her maid had arranged on her head. It was like seeing a fairy creature, so elegant and so lovely, and yet she was also still her very best friend.

Even after everything, she loved her.

"I don't have words to express how grateful I am that you came to Betsy's rescue today," Caroline said, perching a hip against the dressing table as she removed her earbobs and her bracelets. She shuddered. "Tonight was my worst nightmare, and you saved us. Thank you from the bottom of my heart. You were brave, strong, and simply wonderful. It means the world to me that when I needed you most, you were right there."

"There was nowhere else I would rather be than by your side. We work well together, don't we? All our lives, we have fit together like puzzle pieces." Arabella sat on the edge of the bed and started to undo the laces of the dancing slippers that she had borrowed from Grace, and which pinched her feet. "I would do anything for your family." She held her gaze for a moment. "Anything."

They had always been comfortable like this, even before they had become intimate. The easiness between them could never be erased, no matter what happened.

"I would do anything for yours," Caroline said. "I hate to think what might have happened if Mr. Taylor had his way."

Arabella shook her head. "When we first opened the door, I thought he had expired. I thought we were going to be called upon to help dispose of the body."

"I did too. I was so shocked, I didn't know what was going on at first."

"You raised Betsy well," Arabella said. "She is brave and resourceful, and she learned so much of that from you."

"From me?"

"Where else did your brothers and sisters learn their values? You have raised them as much as any parent. They love you."

"I love them." Caroline pushed away from the dresser and strode over to where Arabella sat on the bed. She took her hands in her own. "But what I should have told you a long time ago is that I love *you*, Bell. I am so sorry for how I acted and what I said when I told you to accept Mr. Worthington's proposal. I wanted to make sure you had the best life possible. But I hurt you, and I am so sorry."

Arabella felt a ray of sunshine where her heart should be. "I love you too, Caroline." *At last.* The words tasted sweet on her lips, as if they had been coated with the sugar that enveloped her ginger comfits. It was wonderful to say it out loud.

Caroline's smile dazzled her. "I am so happy to hear it."

Arabella bit her lip. "It did hurt me when you tried to push me toward something that I told you I didn't want. I didn't want Mr. Worthington, or marriage to any man."

Caroline sank to the bed beside her. "I am sorry that I didn't listen to you. You should always be free to make your own choices. I should have supported you in what you wanted for yourself, instead of thinking I knew best." She shook her head. "I have a lot of humility to learn. I thought it was the fortune that swelled my head and encouraged me to think too highly of myself, but after all the heartache I caused you and Betsy, I can see it was my own pride in my capabilities. I need to listen better. I want to be a better person—worthy of your love."

"You are always worthy," Arabella said. "I will always love you." She took a deep breath. "But I need more than words."

"More?"

"I know we love each other. It's the deepest, purest love that I could ever feel for another person. I've loved you since we were thirteen, you know. The year that you cut your hair and climbed the tallest tree in the orchard. You were a veritable hoyden, and I couldn't help but love you." She smiled at the memory.

"Then what more could we ask for?"

"I wish to be courted."

❖

"Courted?" Caroline tried to make sense of it. "Are we not past the courtship phase?"

Arabella sniffed. "*I* courted *you.*"

"I thought we both had a hand in it."

"You're talking about seduction," Arabella declared. "I mean *wooing.* Pursuing. Courting."

She was puzzled. "Even though we are already in each other's beds?"

Arabella nodded. "In fact, I shall not share any further intimacies with you until I have been thoroughly wooed, Caroline Reeve."

"I don't think that's the usual way of things."

"We are in an unusual relationship in the eyes of society, so why not have unusual rules?"

Caroline laughed. "I can't argue with that. If it's wooing you want, then it's wooing you shall get."

"You won't do better than I did, though," Arabella said. "You would have been proud of me. I made a list and everything."

"Did you?"

Arabella explained her suitress plan as they finished disrobing.

"You went to such trouble," Caroline said, touched. "All you had to do was be your sweet self, you know. I would have woken up eventually to see what was in front of me all along."

Arabella curled up beside her in bed. "It was no trouble at all. It was simply love."

CHAPTER TWENTY-SEVEN

Caroline gathered her brothers and sisters into the drawing room the next afternoon.

They were the same family they had always been. Through thick and thin, they were as strong as ever. She felt closer to them since their tumultuous summer had begun.

She poured tea and dispensed of petit fours and biscuits. When everyone was served, she cleared her throat.

"I owe you all an apology."

George dropped his teacup. There were looks of astonishment on every face.

"Ever since Mama and Papa passed away, I have taken my responsibilities toward you very seriously. I promised to raise you the best that I could and to see each of you as well settled as could be in your adulthood. But ever since the start of this summer, I failed to take into consideration what you might want for yourselves, instead of what I thought was best."

George brightened. "Does this mean I can order from the bakery again?"

She fixed him with a glare. "That was still wrong of you, George."

He scowled and bit into another petit four.

"I pushed hard for Jacob, Susan, and Betsy to conform to what I thought was the best situation I could imagine for them—to join society and to marry as high as we could reach. But I put us in harm's way by encouraging Mr. Taylor to accompany us everywhere, to guide us when we didn't know the way, and to ultimately take advantage of us at every turn. I should have tried to find out more about him instead of trusting my instincts."

Jacob shifted. "You couldn't have known," he said gruffly. "And I don't know if I would have listened if you had cautioned me away from his friendship. I thought the world of him until last night when we discovered his true nature."

"He's gone now," Betsy said. "We are none the worse for wear, for all of last night's excitement."

"Jacob is still living with the harm that Mr. Taylor did to him." Caroline shook her head. "I am sorrier for this than you can know, Jacob."

He took a deep breath. "I have been in the doldrums for the past few weeks, cursing my own stupidity. But that's what it was, Caro—I saw no evidence of foul play. None of my friends saw anything amiss either. The fact of the matter is that I had too much to drink and risked more than I had to lose. I hate that it was lost to *him*. But it was lost squarely, and I must accept my own foolishness as the reason."

"Are you still considering to marry an heiress?" Susan piped up.

He reddened. "That was not a plan thought up in my finest hour. I have nothing to offer a bride and cannot in good conscience take it upon myself to marry. No, I plan to travel to Somerset and see what can be done with the land and the holding. I am hoping I can make an honest living from the estate, as impoverished as it may be. It might not be much, but it is mine. I owe it to the tenants of my land to be as good a landlord as I can be to them."

"I have never been prouder of you," Caroline said, her heart full to bursting. "That is a commendable idea."

"I learned from your example," he said. "You were younger than I am now when you took on the responsibility of raising us. You weren't prepared, but you did everything you could for us. You did the right thing, even though it was hard. Now it's my turn. I have decided to mortgage the estate, and the money should be enough to keep us all afloat for now."

Susan looked enthralled. "Please, could I come with you, Jacob? I hope that the town near your estate has need of a milliner or a draper. It has been a dream of mine to have my own shop, but for a small town Inverley has ever so many already because it's so popular with visitors. I would love to see if I could have a better opportunity somewhere else, but I wouldn't like it above half if I didn't know anyone there. I could bring the fine outfits that Betsy and I never even wore and sell them until I had money enough to buy my own inventory. It would be fun to discover somewhere new together, don't you think?"

"Of course you can come with me, Susan." He grinned. "We Reeves shall have the area looking dapper in no time."

"I shall miss you, but you must make your own path in life," Caroline said, humbled that it had taken her so long to realize it. "I should have asked you what you wanted sooner, Susan. I had no idea you harbored such dreams."

"I would have told you eventually, I'm sure. I wasn't very interested in any of the suitors here. I shouldn't have liked a London Season. Perhaps someday I shall settle down with a respectable farmer." Her tone turned dreamy.

"You would do any farmer proud," Betsy said. "Though no one shall top me for being the happiest of us all with my Mr. Graham." She was radiant with delight. "We are planning on staying in Inverley, you know. Mr. Graham has the lease of a little house in town. Not far from here."

"I would love it if you stayed in the area," Caroline said. She felt a deep happiness welling inside of her. Finally, she and Betsy had mended their relationship, and she was looking forward to a future where her sister could truly become a friend. "I plan on spoiling any nieces and nephews rotten, and it shall be much easier if they are in arm's reach."

"What about you?" Jacob asked, leaning forward and propping his elbows on his knees. "What about your happiness, Caro?"

"Yes! After all this is said and done, what shall become of you?"

"I still have Will and George to look after."

Susan frowned. "Perhaps I oughtn't go with Jacob."

"You should follow your heart and your desires," Caroline said. She thought of what Arabella had said to her. "I raised you all to be strong, and independent. You will do fine in a new town, and I will be fine here in Inverley."

"I could have a long engagement," Betsy said, "if you would like some company for a while."

Caroline took a deep breath. She hadn't planned on saying anything to her family. Not now, and maybe not ever. But it felt disingenuous to have meddled so deeply in their affairs, and to have never revealed one iota of her own. She had good reason for her secrets. It was risky to reveal anything—but she wanted to tell them. She wanted her family to know *her*.

"I don't plan to be without company," Caroline said, then paused, searching for the right words. "I thought of asking Arabella to move in with me."

"We love Bell!" George said, bouncing up and down with excitement.

"She always has sweets," Will chimed in. "Do invite her!"

"That would be perfect!" Betsy cried. "She was forever at our old house anyway, so why should she not move in?"

"I don't know if she will be amenable. I may have to convince her." Caroline thought of Arabella asking to be wooed. "I feel very strongly for Arabella."

Jacob nodded. "We all love Bell."

"Well, I love her very much. Not…not exactly as a friend."

She wasn't sure if George or Will would catch her meaning, but the others would.

Jacob blinked and sank back into his chair. "You can't possibly mean…no. You aren't—*are* you?"

Caroline felt her pulse quicken at the base of her throat, but she refused to deny it. She didn't want to lose her brothers and sisters to prejudice, but Arabella had been right. It was time for her to live her own life and pursue her own desires. "I am indeed saying that. I love Arabella."

He shook his head slowly, but there was a thoughtful look on his face and Caroline relaxed. "Well, this is a good deal more shocking than being made an overnight baronet!"

"*What* is happening?" Susan looked perplexed.

Betsy tossed her curls, a mischievous look on her face. "I found a translation of Sappho in our lending library this summer now that we have a subscription. You don't read enough poetry, Susan. Our saintly eldest sister is professing to be a lover of other women."

Susan pressed a hand to her open mouth. "Caro!" She leapt up and threw her arms around Caroline. "I *knew* you were as scandalous as the rest of us, deep down!"

Betsy beamed at her. "This is *very* Caro Lamb of you. Totally outrageous. Risking everything you have for love. I am proud of you."

Caroline laughed. Finally, she was worthy of Betsy's highest praise. "Now that I have your blessings, I need your help to convince Arabella to stay with me."

"You *never* ask for help!" Jacob exclaimed. "This is a day of surprises."

"People change," she said with a shrug. "Maybe it's taken me longer than most to figure out what would make me happiest. Part of my happiness would be for more communication with you all, as adults and equals. I will always welcome it. I promise."

"Well. What does Bell love most? If we can figure that out, then you have a fair shot of using it to your advantage." Betsy nodded.

"Her cats. Her paintings." She smiled at them. "And the Reeve clan, if I am not very much mistaken."

"Mr. Graham wrote me poetry when courting me," Betsy said dreamily.

"The girls I've danced with always complimented my cravats and made me feel ten feet tall," Jacob said with a smile.

Susan shrugged. "I don't pay much attention to men, but I like it when people are kind. It makes me feel all warm."

Caroline had tears in her eyes by the end of tea. This had been a step in the right direction. Not just for her efforts to win over Arabella, but in healing her family.

Her heart felt full to bursting.

❖

Arabella packed up the last of her belongings and looked around the bedchamber that had been hers since she moved in with Matthew and Rachel. She would miss living here, but her heart felt light as she thought of the little cottage by the sea that she had purchased last week.

It was a dream come true.

Rachel peered in through the doorway. "Matthew has gone to borrow a wagon and a donkey to bring everything to your new home."

Arabella felt a pang. "You truly don't mind me leaving?"

"You shall be a scant five-minute walk away," Rachel said, and drew her in for a hug. "We shall be frequent visitors, and you are always welcome for Sunday dinner."

Rachel was looking less peaky these days now that she was further than half-way through her pregnancy.

"I loved having you live with us. But I understand the need for independence. I left my parents' house to marry Matthew and set up my own life, and I never thought that you could have the same opportunity if you didn't marry. Of course you may wish to have a home of your own. It's perfectly natural."

Natural.

After so many years of fearing that she was anything but, the word felt like a healing balm.

"Thank you, Rachel. You've always been the best of sisters. I could not love you more if you were my sister by blood instead of marriage."

She felt tears welling, and Rachel poked her gently in the arm.

"There's no need for tears. This is a happy occasion. Come now, I hear the wagon outside—let's get you settled."

CHAPTER TWENTY-EIGHT

The cottage was everything Arabella had hoped it would be. After Matthew and Rachel left, Arabella wandered through each room. All of them were hers. It was more than large enough for one person. There was an extra bedroom that she would use as a studio, and a parlor where she would entertain as she pleased. There was a thriving kitchen garden in the back of the house before the grass tapered off into sand.

She could set out a dinner or tea of her choosing for her own guests and welcome them to her own space. There was nothing that felt more freeing.

She spent the rest of the day unpacking the few cartons of her belongings. Matthew had already arranged all the furniture for her, some of which came from his attic, and some of which she had purchased new from her savings.

Tomorrow she would set about finding servants to live with her, but tonight, the house was her own. She latched the door, changed her chemise, and pulled the sheet to her chin when she got into the bed.

Byron leapt onto the bed, unconcerned about his change in surroundings, and she pulled him close to her chest for comfort. She sank her fingers into his thick fur and listened to him purr. It made her feel like everything could be all right.

It was an unfamiliar view of the night sky through her window, and the sounds were different here. The waves were louder, the crickets quieter.

There was one sound that she hadn't heard in years, and she sat up like a shot when she heard it.

Pebbles. Thrown at a glass window.

Her heart stuttered in her chest.

But the odds of it being miscreants were low.

The odds of it being a Reeve—well, she would put her money on that in a second.

She scrambled around the unfamiliar room in the dark for her housecoat, and then for the flint and tinder to light a candle. She flung the window open and squinted at a pale figure in the garden.

"Caroline!"

"Bell." She grinned. "Fancy a late-night walk?"

Arabella's heart gave her the right answer. "Of course."

Without hesitation, she would go where Caroline led.

Caroline waited for her at the back door, a lantern in one hand and a wicker basket in the other. A flickering fire beckoned to them from the beach. "Jacob and I set up a bonfire for us to enjoy. Look, Jacob and the footmen have a separate one over there. I thought you would like a quiet moment or two under the stars with me."

The stars were sparkling above like a thousand bonfires, magnificent and distant and no longer frightening, and she shivered in delight. Caroline sat her down on the sand, then wrapped her in a warm wool shawl. "I have wine, unless you would prefer brandy? That's what Jacob brought."

She drew a pair of glasses and a wine bottle from the basket.

The light danced across Caroline's face, warm and wonderful, and Arabella felt like they were in their own private world encompassed within the circle of firelight. It was beautiful out here in the darkness. Elemental.

Natural.

Arabella was wide awake now and was grinning so hard that her face hurt. "You thought of everything."

"I wanted to bring you pleasure," she said, and handed her a filled glass. "I thought about what you said. Of course I want to court you. I want to show you how much you are desired, how much you are wanted. How much you are *beloved*."

The words meant more than poetry.

"This is wonderful."

"I may have more than a farthing to my name now, but I don't have nearly as much as I did in the height of the summer. I can't buy you what you deserve. Jewels. Silks. Champagne."

"I don't need those things." Everything she needed was right here.

"What I can give you is love."

Caroline slid her hand into Arabella's hair and pulled her close for a kiss. Arabella melted against her, the heat from her lips rivaling the warmth from the flames. She parted her lips and tasted wine on her tongue, tart and sweet. The waves crashed on the sand and matched the roar of her heartbeat as she gripped Caroline's shoulders like she was the rope that would pull her to shore. She didn't ever want to let go. She would be drawn to Caroline forever.

"That was an *I-love-you* sort of kiss," Caroline told her as they pulled apart. "But really, they were all *I-love-you* kisses, ever since that very first one that changed my life forever. I just hadn't known it yet."

Arabella slid her feet from her shoes deep into the cool sand as she breathed in the smoky firewood and the lemon scent from Caroline's hair. "I love you."

"I love you. And I plan to show you. Every day of our lives."

❖

The next day, Caroline arrived with two more baskets. From one, she produced a fish for Byron (and assured her that Shelley had enjoyed the same). She set the other basket by the door.

"I assume you would like to be courted quite thoroughly before we discuss anything further about our arrangement?"

Arabella nodded. "No bedchamber visits, either," she reminded her, though it was killing her to say it. She missed Caroline's touch.

Caroline leaned forward and kissed her. "We could make do without a bed," she said. "Name the place, and I can accommodate it."

Arabella laughed. "I'm sure we could, but I am insistent."

She loved this. Every moment of Caroline's attention was on her. Courting. Wooing. However she wanted to call it.

She felt whole.

She felt *loved*.

The second basket contained a luncheon picnic, and Caroline led her to the top of the bluffs. Lady Edith waited for them with her flute, Susan standing beside her with sheet music clutched in her hand.

Caroline waved at them and guided Arabella to a large stone.

Susan began to sing, cheerful, loud, and off-key. Lady Edith's flute playing was charming.

"I wanted to serenade you myself, but my voice is even worse than Susan's." Caroline grinned at her, then fussed with bringing food out of the basket. She arranged cold chicken, fresh bread, cheese, and a cherry tartlet on a porcelain plate, and handed it to Arabella.

"Cherry pie." She stared down at it.

"From our very first almost-kiss in the orchard."

"You are so thoughtful."

"You may have second thoughts when Susan starts her second song. She fancied trying an opera piece."

Sure enough, Susan's warbling hit a much higher key.

Caroline fidgeted with the edge of her cloth napkin. "I confess, I brought them here for a reason."

Arabella took a bite of cheese. "To make sure we behaved ourselves and didn't tumble our way toward the first flat surface available?"

Caroline gazed into her eyes. "To remind you that not only do I love you, but so does every Reeve in Inverley. I would give you my life and my home and my heart without question—but I also want to give you family. I told Jacob, Betsy, and Susan that I wanted you to move in with me, and that we are not exactly friends anymore."

Arabella was shocked. She looked at Susan, who winked at her and sang even louder. "They *know*?"

"Yes. They know. And they love us. I want you to know that my love has no conditions, and no boundaries. My brothers and sisters will be there for us. We won't have to hide when we are at home."

Arabella took a deep breath. This was a gift more priceless than she could imagine. She had not dared to dream that anyone beside she and Caroline, and Grace and Maeve, would know of her love affair. She hadn't realized how wonderful it would feel to know that they had the Reeve family's acceptance.

"You are so brave," she whispered.

"You inspire me to be brave, Bell. You courted me and risked your heart in the process. You took a chance on your art and started a new portrait business. And when you overheard Mr. Taylor's plan, you leapt into action to save Betsy. You are courageous."

Arabella laughed. "When I made my suitress plans, I had thought about writing feats of bravery on my list, but I thought I would never ever be able to accomplish any such thing."

"But you did. And you succeeded marvelously."

Lady Edith and Susan finished their serenade, then came over to join them for luncheon. The conversation turned to Susan's impending journey with Jacob to Somerset.

Arabella lost herself in thought as Susan and Lady Edith chattered. This was all better than she could have imagined.

She caught Caroline's eye and smiled as she bit into the cherry tart.

She felt well and truly wooed.

❖

Caroline had one last gift for Arabella as part of the wooing. She spent the next afternoon at Arabella's cottage, a cup of tea in hand as they talked together as if it were the old days. At half past two, there was a knock on the door, and a man delivered a polished rosewood chair to the cottage.

Arabella stared at it after the man left. "What on earth is it?"

Caroline was overjoyed to see the piece of furniture in reality. She had tried to describe what she wanted as best she could to the wood carver, but the finished piece exceeded her expectation. "It's a drawing chair."

"A drawing chair?"

"For your portrait work. See, it folds up so that you can carry it in one hand when you are bringing it to the beach." She demonstrated, closing and opening the chair with a snap of its hinge. "When you unfold it, there's a cubby beneath the seat for your supplies, and there's an arm that you can swing up to rest your paints on. There's even space on the side to hang your reticule, so you will always have your ginger confits handy."

"This is far too dear," Arabella said, but Caroline saw the longing in her eyes as she gazed at the chair.

"I purchased it before we lost everything," Caroline said cheerfully. "It gave me pleasure to order it, and it gives me more pleasure now to see it in your own little cottage. What use was money if not to gift happiness?"

Byron inspected it, then jumped on the seat and curled up to sleep.

"It has the cat's approval already, so yours can't be far behind."

"It's perfect. I love it," she said. "I love *you*. And since I have had you in my heart, you have opened me up and expanded my horizons beyond what I could have imagined. You are the shore upon which I wish to rest my head. You are the tide pulling me closer and closer until I don't know how we could ever be drawn apart again."

Caroline felt tears well up. "I never thought I would have this kind of love for myself," she said. "I had never given a thought to what I wanted beyond providing for my family, until you showed me the wonder that we could share together. You are the music that I want to fall asleep to every night, along with the waves and the crickets and the owls. Your soft sighs as you turn in your sleep. The sound of you moving beneath my sheets. If I could listen to the symphony of you for the rest of my life, I would be a happy woman."

Arabella drew her into her arms and rested her head on her shoulder. "I thought my only chance to be with you was in dreams. Even in dreams, I didn't dare wish for too much. A look. A touch. The merest brush of your lips. I yearned for those things, but was too timid to reach out my hand for my deepest desires. You taught me that I could be confident. That my dreams are worth it. That it's better to try and learn and fail, and maybe reach higher heights than the bluffs."

"Together, we can reach anything we set our sights on," Caroline declared. "There isn't anything in Inverley or beyond that could stop us."

Epilogue

Two years later

"Remember when we lived on Belvoir Lane?" Caroline asked. "I caught sight of the sunset a thousand times through the tiny square of my kitchen window. I used to yearn for the luxury of time so I could enjoy it, instead of rushing to get the boys to bed. It's been a long time since I was out here at this hour."

"It's magic, isn't it?" Arabella breathed.

They watched the sun sinking into the cliffs, the sky stained with yellow and pink and purple, as vibrant as if the colors came undiluted from Arabella's paintbox. They strolled down the bluff through the dusky air, the night so warm that neither of them needed a shawl. Even with the sun setting, it was light enough that they could make their way home without a lantern through the familiar streets of Inverley.

After a year of living together in Arabella's cottage, Caroline and Arabella had decided that life was too quiet with only Will and George running around. Arabella's miniature portraits did well enough for them to enjoy a decent living together, but Caroline decided she needed something to busy herself and which would also bring in additional income.

They had arranged to build a boarding house near the seashore for young ladies recovering from a less-than-sterling London Season. Caroline, Arabella, George, and Will lived in a suite at the back of the first floor, and the rooms of the second floor were bursting at the seams with ladies who had an abundance of exuberance and high spirits.

Colloquially, the boarding house became known as the Destination for Disreputable Debutantes. The townsfolk of Inverley looked kindly on the bevy of women whose exploits made for entertaining stories around a card table, but whose trespasses were forgivable.

The tranquility of Inverley was most welcome after the stresses of London. It was the perfect place for the ladies to lick their wounds and remember that one season of one's life did not define one forever.

"Everyone makes mistakes," Lady Margaret told them kindly over cups of tea. "No one is ever *really* ruined in their heart. No one is beyond happiness."

She had been delighted to move to Inverley permanently and doted on the girls who stayed with them, who all adored her in return.

Arabella and Caroline entered the main parlor of the boarding house. Betsy and Rachel were there with their sons.

"Look, Bell! You're in this year's guidebook." Betsy waved the book, balancing her baby on her hip.

"We couldn't wait until you came home to show you." Rachel took the book from Betsy and flipped it open. "Look there—it's you!"

Arabella picked it up. Sure enough, there was a paragraph about her business on the seashore, proclaiming it to be the fashionable trend to be painted in a miniature watercolor by Miss Arabella Seton.

"Fashionable," she repeated. "Me. I still cannot get used to it."

Caroline slung her arm over Arabella's shoulder and peered down at the guidebook. "This is wonderful," she declared. "You deserve every accolade."

"This is exciting indeed," Arabella said. "But not as exciting as *your* news, Betsy."

Betsy preened and then laughed. "My newest book is doing quite well, isn't it?"

"You are our star," Caroline said fondly.

Betsy and Mr. Graham both had soaring poetry careers. They traveled to London once a quarter to meet with other authors, as well as give readings and attend lectures and literary soirees. Betsy had confessed with great sadness that meeting Lord Byron had been the disappointment of her life, citing a certain mean-spiritedness about him, but that she would still cherish his verse forever in her heart.

Betsy also kept up to date with great satisfaction regarding Mr. Taylor whenever she was in London. No one had a good word to say about him there. She was happy to report back to Inverley that Mr. Taylor may have taken a great deal of their money and remained very rich, but he couldn't possibly have anything that mattered. No friends. No family. No community. Wealth was certainly not worth the price.

Arabella sat down on the sofa, dislodging Shelley and Byron. The cats crowded onto her lap and pushed their heads into her hand for petting. It was lovely to be surrounded by family, she thought. They had a letter from Jacob this morning to report that life in Somerset continued to go well, and that he would be coming to Inverley with Susan for a visit later in the summer.

Their wealth was all around them. It was in the love that shone like a beacon between herself and Caroline. It was in the laughter of Rachel's son, Matthew Junior, and it was in the purring of the cats. It was in the happy shrieks of laughter from the Disreputable Debutantes as they discovered that although society considered them to be flawed, they were young and full of vibrancy —and that was a gift worth more than a thousand vouchers to Almack's.

Arabella had been wrong to think that nothing ever changed in Inverley. If one was open to it, change and good fortune were waiting all around them.

Caroline sat beside her and squeezed her hand. "We have everything and more, don't we?" she murmured.

"Everything beyond my wildest dreams."

About the Author

Jane Walsh is a queer historical romance novelist who loves everything Regency. She is delighted to have the opportunity to put her studies in history and costume design to good use by writing love stories. She owes a great debt of gratitude to the local coffee shop for fueling her novel writing endeavors. Jane's happily ever after is centered on her wife and their cat and their cozy home together in Canada.

Books Available from Bold Strokes Books

Cherry on Top by Georgia Beers. A chance meeting leaves Cherry and Ellis longing for a different life, but when Ellis's search for truth crashes into Cherry's insta-filter world, do they have any hope at all of a happily ever after? (978-1-63679-158-6)

Love and Other Rare Birds by Angie Williams. Ornithologist Dr. Jamie Martin and park ranger Rowan Fleming are searching the Alaskan wilderness for a bird thought to be extinct and they're about to discover opposites really do attract. (978-1-63679-108-1)

Parallel Paradise by Mayapee Chowdhury. When their love affair is put to the test by the homophobia of their family, community, and culture, Bindi and Rimli will need to fight for a chance at love. (978-1-63679-204-0)

Perfectly Matched by Toni Logan. A beautiful Cupid named Hannah, a runaway arrow, and just seventy-two hours to fix a mishap that could be the best mistake she has ever made. (978-1-63679-120-3)

Royal Exposé by Jenny Frame. When they're grouped together for a class assignment, Poppy's enthusiasm for life and love may just save Casey's soul, but will she ever forgive Casey for using her to expose royal secrets? (978-1-63679-165-4)

Slow Burn by Missouri Vaun. A wounded wildland firefighter from California and a struggling artist find solace and love in a small southern town. (978-1-63679-098-5)

The Artist by Sheri Lewis Wohl. Detective Casey Wilson and reclusive artist Tula Crane are drawn together in a web of passion, intrigue, and art that might just hold the key to stopping a killer. (978-1-63679-150-0)

The Inconvenient Heiress by Jane Walsh. An unlikely heiress and a spinster evade the Marriage Mart only to discover true love together. (978-1-63679-173-9)

A Champion for Tinker Creek by D.C. Robeline. Lyle James has rescued his dad's auto repair business, but when city hall condemns his neighborhood, Lyle learns only trusting will save his life and help him find love. (978-1-63679-213-2)

Closed-Door Policy by Erin Zak. Going back to college is never easy, but Caroline Stevens is prepared to work hard and change her life for the better. What she's not prepared for is Dr. Atlanta Morris, her gorgeous new professor. (978-1-63679-181-4)

Homeworld by Gun Brooke. Headed by Captain Holly Crowe, the spaceship Velocity's crew journeys toward their alien ancestors' homeworld, and what they find is completely unexpected—and they're not safe. (978-1-63679-177-7)

Outland by Kristin Keppler & Allisa Bahney. Danielle Clark and Katelyn Turner can't seem to stay away from one another even as the war for the wastelands tests their loyalty to each other and to their people. (978-1-63679-154-8)

Secret Sanctuary by Nance Sparks. US Deputy Marshal Alex Trenton specializes in protecting those awaiting trial, but when danger threatens the woman she's falling for, Alex is in for the fight of her life. (978-1-63679-148-7)

Stranded Hearts by Kris Bryant, Amanda Radley, Emily Smith. In these novellas from award winning authors, fate intervenes on behalf of love when characters are unexpectedly stuck together. With too much time and an irresistible attraction, anything could happen. (978-1-63679-182-1)

The Last Lavender Sister by Melissa Brayden. Aster Lavender sells her gourmet doughnuts and keeps a low profile; she never plans on the town's temporary veterinarian swooping in and making her feel like anything but a wallflower. (978-1-63679-130-2)

The Probability of Love by Dena Blake. As Blair and Rachel keep ending up in the same place despite the odds, can a one-night stand turn into forever? Or will the bet Blair never intended to make ruin their happily ever after? (978-1-63679-188-3)

Worth a Fortune by Sam Ledel. After placing a want ad for a personal secretary, a New York heiress is surprised when the woman who got away is the one interested in the position. (978-1-63679-175-3)

A Fox in Shadow by Jane Fletcher. Cassie's mission is to add new territory to the Kavillian empire—murder, betrayal, war, and the clash of cultures ensue. (978-1-63679-142-5)

Embracing the Moon by Jeannie Levig. Just as Gwen and Taylor are exploring the new love they've found, the present and past collide, threatening the future they long to share. (978-1-63555-462-5)

Forever Comes in Threes by D. Jackson Leigh. Efficiency expert Perry Chandler's ordered life is upended when she inherits three busy terriers, and the woman she's referred to for help turns out to be her bitter podcast rival, the very sexy Dr. Ming Lee. (978-1-63679-169-2)

Heckin' Lewd: Trans and Nonbinary Erotica by Mx. Nillin Lore. If you want smutty, fearless, gender diverse erotica written by affirming own-voices folks who get it, then this is the book you've been looking for! (978-1-63679-240-8)

Missed Conception by Joy Argento. Maggie Walsh wants a relationship with Cassidy, the daughter she's only just discovered she has due to an in vitro mix-up. Heat kindles between Maggie and Cassidy's mother in a way neither expects. (978-1-63679-146-3)

Private Equity by Elle Spencer. Cassidy Bennett spends an unexpected evening at a lesbian nightclub with her notoriously reserved and demanding boss, Julia. After seeing a different side of Julia, Cassidy can't seem to shake her desire to know more. (978-1-63679-180-7)

Racing the Dawn by Sandra Barrett. After narrowly escaping a house fire, vampire Jade Murphy is unexpectedly intrigued by gorgeous firefighter Beth Jenssen, and her undead existence might just be perking up a bit. (978-1-63679-271-2)

Reclaiming Love by Amanda Radley. Sarah's tiny white lie means somehow convincing Pippa to pretend to be her girlfriend. Only the more time they spend faking it, the more real it feels. (978-1-63679-144-9)

Sol Cycle by Kimberly Cooper Griffin. An encounter in a park brings Ang and Krista together, but when Ang's attempts to help Krista go spectacularly wrong, their passion for each other might not be enough. (978-1-63679-137-1)

Trial and Error by Carsen Taite. Attorney Franco Rossi and Judge Nina Aguilar's reunion is fraught with courtroom conflict, undeniable chemistry, and danger. (978-1-63555-863-0)

A Long Way to Fall by Elle Spencer. A ski lodge, two strong-willed women, and a family feud that brings them together, but will it also tear them apart? (978-1-63679-005-3)

Barnabas Bopwright Saves the City by J. Marshall Freeman. When he uncovers a terror plot to destroy the city he loves, 15-year-old Barnabas Bopwright realizes it's up to him to save his home and bring deadly secrets into the light before it's too late. (978-1-63679-152-4)

Forever by Kris Bryant. When Savannah Edwards is invited to be the next bachelorette on the dating show When Sparks Fly, she'll show the world that finding true love on television can happen. (978-1-63679-029-9)

Ice on Wheels by Aurora Rey. All's fair in love and roller derby. That's Riley Fauchet's motto, until a new job lands her at the same company—and on the same team—as her rival Brooke Landry, the frosty jammer for the Big Easy Bruisers. (978-1-63679-179-1)

Inherit the Lightning by Bud Gundy. Darcy O'Brien and his sisters learn they are about to inherit an immense fortune, but a family mystery about to unravel after seventy years threatens to destroy everything. (978-1-63679-199-9)

Perfect Rivalry by Radclyffe. Two women set out to win the same career-making goal, but it's love that may turn out to be the final prize. (978-1-63679-216-3)

Something to Talk About by Ronica Black. Can quiet ranch owner Corey Durand give up her peaceful life and allow her feisty new neighbor into her heart? Or will past loss, present suitors, and town gossip ruin a long awaited chance at love? (978-1-63679-114-2)

With a Minor in Murder by Karis Walsh. In the world of academia, police officer Clare Sawyer and professor Libby Hart team up to solve a murder. (978-1-63679-186-9)

Writer's Block by Ali Vali. Wyatt and Hayley might be made for each other if only they can get through nosy neighbors, the historic society, at-odds future plans, and all the secrets hidden in Wyatt's walls. (978-1-63679-021-3)

Cold Blood by Genevieve McCluer. Maybe together, Kalila and Dorenia have a chance of taking down the vampires who have eluded them all these years. And maybe, in each other, they can find a love worth living for. (978-1-63679-195-1)

Greener Pastures by Aurora Rey. When city girl and CPA Audrey Adams finds herself tending her aunt's farm, will Rowan Marshall—the charming cider maker next door—turn out to be her saving grace or the bane of her existence? (978-1-63679-116-6)

...unded by Amanda Radley. For a second chance, Olivia and Emily will need to accept their mistakes, learn to communicate properly, and with a little help from five-year-old Henry, fall madly in love all over again. Sequel to Flight SQA016. (978-1-63679-241-5)

Journey's End by Amanda Radley. In this heartwarming conclusion to the Flight series, Olivia and Emily must finally decide what they want, what they need, and how to follow the dreams of their hearts. (978-1-63679-233-0)

Pursued: Lillian's Story by Felice Picano. Fleeing a disastrous marriage to the Lord Exchequer of England, Lillian of Ravenglass reveals an incident-filled, often bizarre, tale of great wealth and power, perfidy, and betrayal. (978-1-63679-197-5)

Secret Agent by Michelle Larkin. CIA agent Peyton North embarks on a global chase to apprehend rogue agent Zoey Blackwood, but her commitment to the mission is tested as the sparks between them ignite and their sizzling attraction approaches a point of no return. (978-1-63555-753-4)

Something Between Us by Krystina Rivers. A decade after her heart was broken under Don't Ask, Don't Tell, Kirby runs into her first love and has to decide if what's still between them is enough to heal her broken heart. (978-1-63679-135-7)

Sugar Girl by Emma L McGeown. Having traded in traditional romance for the perks of Sugar Dating, Ciara Reilly not only enjoys the no-strings-attached arrangement, she's also a hit with her clients. That is until she meets the beautiful entrepreneur Charlie Keller who makes her want to go sugar-free. (978-1-63679-156-2)

The Business of Pleasure by Ronica Black. Editor in chief Valerie Raffield is quickly becoming smitten by Lennox, the graphic artist she's hired to work remotely. But when Lennox doesn't show for their first face-to-face meeting, Valerie's heart and her business may be in jeopardy. (978-1-63679-134-0)

The Hummingbird Sanctuary by Erin Zak. The Hummingb Sanctuary, Colorado's hottest resort destination: Come for the mountains, stay for the charm, and enjoy the drama as Olive, Eleanor, and Harriet figure out the meaning of true friendship. (978-1-63679-163-0)

The Witch Queen's Mate by Jennifer Karter. Barra and Silvi must overcome their ingrained hatred and prejudice to use Barra's magic and save both their peoples, not just from slavery, but destruction. (978-1-63679-202-6)

With a Twist by Georgia Beers. Starting over isn't easy for Amelia Martini. When the irritatingly cheerful Kirby Dupress comes into her life will Amelia be brave enough to go after the love she really wants? (978-1-63555-987-3)

p.

BOLDSTROKESBOOKS.COM

Looking for your next great read?

Visit BOLDSTROKESBOOKS.COM
to browse our entire catalog of paperbacks, ebooks,
and audiobooks.

Want the first word on what's new?
Visit our website for event info,
author interviews, and blogs.

Subscribe to our free newsletter for sneak peeks,
new releases, plus first notice of promos
and daily bargains.

SIGN UP AT
BOLDSTROKESBOOKS.COM/signup

Quality and Diversity in LGBTQ Literature

*Bold Strokes Books is an award-winning publisher
committed to quality and diversity in LGBTQ fiction.*